Praise for the work

Can I Trust Her?

I found this to be a thrill ride! I love the background of Katie and Virginia and the awkwardness of their past relationship! I enjoyed the twists and turns and the dynamics of their relationship! I also liked the backstory for Katie, sometimes I think it can take away from the mystery, but Frances Lucas intertwined them well! I also love that there is going to be more books, I can't wait to read what Virginia and Katie get up to next! And there has to be more Matty, he was absolutely fabulous! I highly recommend this if you like mysteries, especially ones with LGBTQ+ characters!

-Brady R., *NetGalley*

Can I Trust Her? is Frances Lucas's debut novel, and I must say it's a wonderful read. I enjoyed the writing in this book. I did feel like the pacing was perfectly executed. Virginia and Katie, plus the "side" characters were so fun and realistic! I really enjoy YA mysteries like this one here. It kept me guessing. Kept me glued to my Kindle. And me not wanting this story to end so soon.

-Rubie C., *NetGalley*

Can I Trust Her? is a well written and engaging story. The second-chance romance works in seamlessly with the mystery while both keep the reader on their toes. Lucas has a deep understanding of high school teens and life in Alaska which shines through in the storytelling. I was thoroughly entertained by this novel and highly recommend it.

-Della B., *NetGalley*

Perfectly paced, written, executed. Characters are well crafted with a background that's layered. This story was impossible to put down.

-Heather D., NetGalley

TEXT ME WHEN YOU GET THIS

FRANCES LUCAS

Other Bella Books by Frances Lucas

Can I Trust Her?
Is She Lying?

About the Author

Frances Lucas spent seven years in Alaska teaching. A full-time writer now, she lives in Colorado with her wife and two small dogs. She enjoys listening to true crime podcasts and catching up on old Law & Order episodes. In 2023, Frances was the recipient of the Golden Crown Literary Society award for young adult fiction with her first Bella novel, CAN I TRUST HER?

TEXT ME WHEN YOU GET THIS

FRANCES LUCAS

BELLA
BOOKS

2024

Bella Books, Inc.
P.O. Box 10543
Tallahassee, FL 32302

First Edition - 2024

Editor: Ann Roberts
Cover Designer: Kayla Mancuso

ISBN: 978-1-64247-522-7

Acknowledgments

This is my third published novel with Bella Books. I'm grateful to the Bella team and their support. I'd also like to say a big thank you to my wonderful editor Ann Roberts who has a lovely way with words and a keen eye for finding my mistakes and plot flaws. My books are better because of Ann. I'd also like to thank Barb, Kathy, Cil, and Susan. My friends—you know how much your encouragement means to me. And you, my readers, your kind words expressed in person and on social media keep me going. By the way, if you love books like I do and want to show your appreciation for an author, leave reviews. Everywhere. Reviews sell books.

And finally, thank you to my wife, Cheryl, for putting up with my bouts of OCD and weird moods. Because, yes, I'm a little like Nora.

I've got to get back to writing now. Happy reading to you all.

For all the girls who think they aren't good enough

PART ONE

CHAPTER ONE

Nora

Seventeen years ago, I killed my brother. Not on purpose. I didn't smother him with a pillow or crack him over the head with a lamp. Nevertheless, the thought of what he might have been if not for me is like a smudge in the corner of my glasses. No matter how many times I spit and wipe, it won't go away.

Here are the facts: we were twins, not identical as people sometimes ask because that's impossible when one of you is a girl, the other a boy. Fraternal is the word you're looking for. Dizygotic, if you want to get scientific. Two separate eggs fertilized by two separate sperm, sharing the same fifty percent of DNA as other siblings. For nine full months we grew together in our mother's womb. I, however, was the strong one.

I, Nora Thomas, emerged at the stroke of midnight, no doubt bawling my eyes out and demanding Mom's attention. Eight minutes later, Nick arrived—his single, solitary heartbeat faint, then forever stilled.

Nick and Nora are characters from an old detective novel my father's father read to him. My parents liked the sound of our names together. They fit like a pair of comfortable wool socks. Once, when I sat with my mother in a wide upholstered chair with my velcroed sneakers swinging high above the floor, I asked her if she wished Nick had been the one to live. I imagined his ghost on her other side, his tiny hand resting in her lap.

"Oh, sweetheart!" she replied. "Don't ever say that. Don't even think it. Yes, we loved your brother. But we will always, always love you." An unbearable look of anguish crossed her face as she pressed her lips to the top of my head. It made me wonder how often she thought of him. Had she bought him clothes, a blue outfit to match my pink one? Had she planned on teaching him to play piano? Would we have had a sibling Mitzvah?

These are questions I still have but can no longer ask. My parents, avid outdoor adventurers, vanished in a crystal blue crevasse three years ago on a Denali expedition. Their bodies were never found. In my darker moments I've wondered if they could have escaped but saw Nick waving in the distance and chose to stay with him.

That's in the past. I've had to move on.

Like now, as I prepare for my big day at the Alaska State Legislature in Juneau. I let out a carefully controlled breath, leave the safe spot in my mind, and turn my focus to the list of twice rolled items in my suitcase. Underwear, check. Nightshirt, check. Extra wool socks, check. A simple black dress and low heels for the semiformal dinner with legislators tonight, check. (In case you're wondering, I'm not a dress-wearing kind of girl, but Gran says it's required.) Hairbrush, shampoo, conditioner, deodorant, lotion, toothbrush—check. A clean shirt for tomorrow's plane ride back, check. Check. Check. Check. Everything's present and accounted for. I'm all about a good checklist as my second-grade teacher used to say.

I zip my grandmother's nylon carry-on as she pokes her head inside my bedroom, the room she used to call her den.

"Toothpaste, Nora? An extra pair of glasses in case the ones you're wearing break?"

My self-diagnosed OCD kicks in. I know I've got them, but I've got to look. Unzip. "All good." Re-zip.

"You sure you don't want me to drive you to the airport?"

"Thanks, Gran. Amber's parents are picking me up."

"Amber," she grumbles at my ex-girlfriend's name. "All right then, if you're sure. Have a good time, and be careful."

"I will."

Gran's a worrier like me, sometimes worse. Will the plane experience engine failure and crash into the Gulf of Alaska? Will some sketchy guy across the aisle slip a roofie in my drink? I get it, really I do, but you can't prepare for every contingency. We both know that. How can a sixty-seven-year-old widow battling breast cancer take on the responsibility of caring for a fourteen-year-old girl?

I was an ungrateful mess when I first arrived at her little bungalow on the southeast side of Anchorage. Gran lives on a budget, and I missed the things I had before.

One day, when I was being particularly insufferable, she sat me down and said, "Get used to it, Nora. You can't replace your family with stuff. All you can do is be your best and be proud of who you are."

I wanted to argue. "But a lot of kids my age—"

"Have even less than you do. Just listen to yourself. You're better than that."

Naturally, she was right. So, now I focus on being at the top of my class and one of only two North Anchorage High School students invited to spend a day at the state capitol. Gran still has that effect on me, encouraging me to work my hardest and not feel sorry for myself. I'd call myself a work in progress.

Three, two, one…

"Tell Mr. Abbott to watch his speed on Minnesota," she mutters, turning toward her tiny kitchen, big enough for only one small dining table and a couple of straight-back chairs. "There was a story about a horrible accident on the news last night. Cyclist versus truck."

And there it is. Her ever-present fear that tragedy lurks around every corner. I kiss her wrinkled cheek. "See you tomorrow afternoon."

"I'm counting on it."

I step outside the house with its peeling yellow paint and rusty, banged-up gutters into a yard surrounded by a twelve-inch picket fence and newly emerging daffodils. Green leaves poke through the rich black soil like a baby's little fingers. A spring chill fills the air, and the acrid smell of burning firewood from our neighbors' chimney drifts over.

Amber and her folks pull up to the curb a minute later. Her father pops the trunk so I can drop my scuffed-up bag alongside their nicer ones, then I hop into the back seat next to the first love of my life.

Amber Abbott has sleek, auburn hair cut in a stylish bob and a round, unblemished face. She's impossibly pretty, like a picture in a magazine. But what I really, truly hate is how smart she is. Together, we're always first and second in our class. We trade back and forth on a regular basis. One month it's me, the next her. This month's totally her.

I buckle my seat belt, and she barely glances up.

"Hey." Her thumbs tap the keyboard on her phone. It's a safe bet she's messaging her new girlfriend, a senior taking first-year algebra, *again*. I'd say she lacks good taste in girlfriends, but that would be dissing myself.

I give her a noncommittal chin lift that she likely doesn't see. We've spoken less than a dozen words to one another in the last few weeks, which is going to make it super awkward sharing a hotel room tonight.

Mr. Abbott gives a friendly wave to Gran watching from a window and sets the car in motion. Mrs. Abbott fills the conversation void with all the great things to see and do in Juneau. The Macaulay Salmon Hatchery. The Last Chance Mining Museum. The Alaska State Museum.

Amber rolls her eyes. "Seriously, Mother? It's friggin' Juneau, not D.C."

Mrs. Abbott looks embarrassed. She offers me a quick, over-the-shoulder smile and says, "I'm looking forward to the trip, that's all."

"Like I said, Juneau. And you do understand you're chaperones, not high school students, right?"

Mrs. Abbott opens her mouth.

"Let her be, Sue. Amber's nervous about the session." Mr. Abbott pats his wife's plump knee. She snaps her jaw with an audible click and takes to studying a colorful trifold pamphlet in her lap. Anything to keep Amber happy, I suppose.

It bugs me the way they cater to her. More so now that we're not together anymore, but it's always been this way. What does Amber have to be nervous about? Neither of us will have to speak. We'll probably shake a couple of legislators' hands, maybe say a few words to thank them for representing our interests. They're voting on increased student funding this afternoon, something every Alaska teacher and student alive has got to be on board with. We'll write our reports when we get back to school. Today is about soaking up the political experience.

As usual, the Abbotts are dressed to the nines. Amber's rocking tight, mustard-colored Chinos and a purple blazer over a short-sleeved cotton shirt. She's dressed the outfit up with a multicolored, cashmere scarf that pulls the outfit together in a way I wish I could but can't. Mr. Abbott wears a fancy three-piece suit and tie. Mrs. Abbott has on a shimmering red blouse, silk pants, and shiny shoes with just the right amount of heel for walking around Juneau, a pedestrian-friendly town, I've read. Me? I've got on a pair of J.C. Penney's khakis and an off-white button-down Oxford with a mysterious blue stain on the collar. Fifty percent off—thank you, little round stain.

The rest of the way to the airport, Mr. Abbott fills the time by quizzing me about Gran's ongoing health issues. She's two years into remission and upbeat about the future because that's just the way she is, content about important things. I'd love to be more like her instead of the messy headspace that I am. When we board the plane, I'm actually relieved to discover my seat is in the last row before the restroom between a woman with a crying baby and a skinny old guy who's already fast asleep and snoring. When the heck did he board? At least this way I won't have to talk to Amber and go on pretending that she didn't hurt my feelings when, the day after spring break, she told me she was in love with someone else. Said math whiz senior.

No surprise, the Abbotts have upgraded to first class. Amber gives me a sympathetic look as she heads to the front. "Oooh, Nora. Back row." Then she has to go and spoil it by adding, "Sucks to be you."

Did I say a dozen words? Now we're up to twenty.

CHAPTER TWO

Claire

Juneau International Airport has five gates, three jetways, a restaurant, a coffee bar, a gift shop, and multiple flights coming in and going out every day. The "international" part is a bit of a joke, considering our little city is home to approximately thirty thousand residents most of the year. More in the summer, when seasonal employees flock to town to work the cruise ship trade. We sit on the shoreline of the Gastineau Channel. Our landmass is larger than Rhode Island. It rains more than two hundred days a year. A good percentage of the flights come from Anchorage, especially when the Alaska State Legislature is in session, like now.

I've got all these facts memorized because this is my fifth time giving tours. And believe it or not, some people want to know these things. I wouldn't, but that's because I've lived here my whole life. I'm itching to see bigger cities and different landscapes.

I wave a hand in greeting to a guy I met last week at one of the ticket stations and make my way to Gate Two.

Nora Thomas and Amber Abbott will be arriving in ten minutes, according to the itinerary my civics teacher handed me yesterday. I've been selected to be their student guide, earning me extra credit for the one class I don't have an A in. My father, king of the Juneau new-build housing world, would say a B+ is good enough. But he never much cared for school, not like I do. He likes to say that no amount of formal education will teach you how to get along with people. Easy for him, when he doesn't have to listen to my older stepsister brag about the straight A's she earned in her four years at Douglas Bay Charter.

Last year, my parents got divorced. Dad should have seen it coming. For a man who prides himself on his communication skills, it's a marvel he never noticed how exasperated Mom got with him working six, sometimes seven, days a week. He'd often leave the house before the sun was up and return long after dinner. I might have thought he was cheating on her if he hadn't been so driven to be the best in his line of work.

Six weeks after their divorce was finalized, my mother married an orthodontist with two teenage daughters of his own. They live in a three-bedroom house that, ironically, my father built. Mom's new husband offered to put another bed in his oldest daughter's room for me. The room was crowded anyway with pillows on the floor and kitschy wicker furniture in every corner, and his daughter made it pretty clear she didn't want me there, so I passed, leaving me shut out of my mother's new life. Yeah, I know, kind of my own fault, but I've always gotten along better with my dad.

He's talking about moving to Anchorage in a few months, so I have a dual purpose for the tour today. I want to get to know Amber and Nora so if we do, I'll at least have a couple of friends in Alaska's biggest city.

My official job is to sit with them in session and escort them to the fancy dinner afterward. We've had blackened halibut, asparagus, and a loaded baked potato, with chocolate cake for dessert the last four times. I'm expecting the same tonight and I'm already plotting ways to skip it. Fish? Come on. I believe they have it in Anchorage too. There's a new Italian restaurant on the wharf I'd like to try if I can talk them into ditching another "Welcome to the Alaska Political Arena" speech and coming with me instead.

I check the time on my phone and scan the horizon for a plane coming in. Amber and I have been texting for the last two weeks. She sent a photo of her and Nora a few days ago. Cool, but I'd already looked them up on social media. Did she think I wouldn't? They're both cute, but Nora appears awfully serious in her old lady glasses and her hair pulled back from her angular face in a severe French twist. She's got big ears, but she'd have an interesting look if she'd crack a smile.

Amber, on the other hand, is vivacious. I can tell from her texts that she'll be a ton of fun. She dresses like a TikTok star and uses a lot of exclamation points and emojis in her texts, saying that she's super excited to meet me and she thinks we'll have a lot in common. Together, they started an LGBTQ club after school last fall. From early photos of them with their arms around each other's waists, I think they must have been girlfriends at the time. Amber's latest posts have her pictured with a different girl, which is too bad because I wouldn't mind spending time alone with her.

I say hi to a couple of other airport people I've met. It never hurts to have friends wherever you are, Dad tells me. The guy from the Alaska Airlines ticket counter sets a cup of coffee on the window ledge in front of me and says he's glad to see me.

"Good to see you too. How's your husband?"

"Bossy. Manipulative. A royal pain in the ass."

"In other words, you still want to spend the rest of your life with him?"

He laughs. "How can you tell? I probably shouldn't complain. He makes more money than I do."

"And don't forget he cooks you fancy dinners."

"Damn. Why did I tell you that?"

"Beats me."

"See ya next time, Claire."

"You got it."

He moves on and I turn my attention back to the window. When the plane lands, Amber and her parents are the first ones off. Her father grills me for a couple of minutes about humpback whale sightings and the Taku Glacier which is one of just a few glaciers in the world that is actually advancing. He wants to know the size of it and when it last calved. I've got the info at my fingertips, but it's hard to keep a straight face with Amber rolling her eyes and making faces behind his back. Her mother barely acknowledges my presence. She's busy looking at a leaflet about museums.

The crowd of passengers coming off the plane drizzles out. A couple of seconds later the cleaning crew starts to board.

"Did Nora change her mind and decide to stay home?" I ask, thinking I wouldn't blame her if she did. The first time I visited the Capitol, it was crazy impressive. Politicians greeting you by name can make you feel important. It was only later I realized they probably do it because they want your parents' votes. So, now, it's crazy boring. Well, most of the time. I still appreciate the process, but they meet each day in a stuffy room with their desks all facing the same direction. It takes them forever to accomplish anything because, apparently, it's part of their job description to talk each and every bill to death.

"Nora. Yeah, I wish." Amber sneers, glancing up from her phone. "Oh, there she is. Hooray."

I follow her gaze to a girl who's got a baby carrier suspended across one arm and the elbow of a shaky old man in the other. A frazzled-looking woman with the actual baby trails along behind her. There's something about Nora that looks familiar, but I'll be darned if I know what.

"You must be Claire." She gives me the once-over. Before I can answer, she's asking the old man if he needs anything else.

There's a patch of something blue on her collar, which must be vomit from the kid despite the color. A couple of strands of dark hair have escaped her twist. She steals a peek at Amber who's gone back to texting and ignoring her and releases an abject sigh.

So. Definitely not girlfriends anymore. If I had to guess I'd say they can barely stand each other. Great. It's going to be a long day.

CHAPTER THREE

Nora

Worst flight in my life. Well, that's not true since I don't have anything to compare it to. The farthest I've ever been from Anchorage is Valdez on another school field trip. For that, we took the ferry, a major part of the Alaska highway system, if you care. Let me just say that a woman with a baby ought to have sense enough to carry extra diapers with her. The poor thing smelled like, well, you know, what stinky babies smell like.

My elderly seat companion on the other side woke up midway through the flight and started telling me about a restaurant on Juneau's wharf called Marco's Pizzeria. They have more than pizza, he said several times.

He was sweet, but like I have time to go out for a meal? He kept talking about it even after I said I was having dinner in the state's legislature's lounge, a special treat I've been looking forward to because normally it's only open to lawmakers. When the plane landed and we got up, he stumbled, so I helped him into the airport and offered to hail him a cab.

"No, thank you. But I hope you don't mind my saying you're a delightful young lady. I really enjoyed talking to you. You'll make some lucky young man very happy one day," he tells me, when I hand him off to a waiting, grownup grandson.

"Thank you. I enjoyed talking to you, too," I reply politely. I pass the baby carrier to the woman and look back in time to see Amber snickering at me. Claire tries to hide her smile, but I can tell she finds it pretty funny, too. Give me a break.

When I heard Claire Tucker was going to be our tour guide, I looked her up online. She was easy to find on social media with not enough sense to make her Facebook and Instagram accounts private. She's queer, like us, and admittedly very pretty with curly blond hair, an upturned nose, and eyes like polished emeralds. She's got lots of friends. I'm talking tons. Like, she must have had her picture taken with every person she's ever met.

Today, she's wearing smart black ankle pants, a gray boho shirt with a frilly front, and jeweled leather sandals. Between Claire and Amber, I feel downright dowdy, especially as I note Claire taking in the blue spot on my collar.

So what? I tell·myself. Why should I care? I'm not here to impress Claire Tucker. I want to learn everything I can about the way our government works. One day it'll be me sitting in the hallowed chamber of the legislature.

Amber looks up from her phone long enough to ask me how I liked the flight. "Nora's never been outside of Anchorage," she confides to Claire. "She's a bit of a homebody when she's not at school. Doesn't get out much. She lives in an adorable tiny house with her aging grandma."

She tries to make it sound funny, but I cringe at a description that makes me sound like a loner with nothing better to do than stay home and bake cupcakes with my "aging grandma." It's not far from the truth, but she doesn't have to say it to a stranger.

It won't do any good to reference my trip to Valdez, so I say in an equally snarky voice, "The flight was lovely. Gran says to tell you hi."

Which, of course, she didn't. Gran thinks Amber's a poser. Her exact word was insincere. Gran's good at reading people. I should have listened to her last fall when she told me Amber would break my heart. But when Amber agreed to start the LGBTQ club with me at NHS sponsor Mrs. Hicks's suggestion, you could have told me she was a serial killer and I wouldn't have listened. I knew from the start that we weren't good together, but I enjoyed being the center of her universe, if only for a while.

Mr. and Mrs. Abbott tell us they'll meet up with us at the hotel later tonight. They take our bags and give us the address. Claire waves to people she knows and leads us to the short-term parking lot, chatting up Amber while I trot along behind them like a stray cat.

When we reach her car, she turns around. "You know, Nora, I've just been thinking. You look like a friend of mine, a guy named Ethan St. James."

"A guy?" Amber blurts, ready to make a joke.

"Ethan's been my best friend since freshman year." Claire unlocks the door with a key fob she carries on a plastic carabiner on a belt loop.

Amber gets in the front seat, leaving me to scoot in back. I push aside a plaid wool blanket and a pair of rainbow running shoes with dirty socks. A couple of sacks of crumpled fast food trash litter the floor. I shove them away with the side of my foot, carefully avoiding a shriveled french fry that's escaped through a hole at the bottom of a greasy sack. You'd never see that in my car. As old as my Suzuki is (twenty years), I still like to keep it washed and vacuumed. Probably something else I learned from Gran.

Claire starts the engine, then drags her phone out of the black messenger bag she's had slung over a shoulder. She unlocks it, turns around, and shows me a picture. "This is Ethan. See? Dark hair. Dark eyes."

"Right." I shrug. "He looks nice."

"Well, he is. Very. But what I mean is, check out the shape of his nose and chin. His cheekbones, and how far apart his eyes are. Don't you think he looks like you?"

I take a second look at the picture. "If you say so."

Amber holds out a hand. "Let me see." I pass her the phone. "Yeah, I guess. He's dark, like Italian or Jewish. Nora's Jewish.

He could have been your brother, Nora. No wait. He looks happy, so I guess not."

My chest tightens at her joke. I don't care that she thinks I'm dreary. But I'm furious with myself for confiding in her about Nick and at her for mentioning him to Claire. Before I know it, she'll be spilling all my secrets simply for a laugh.

"Jewish?" Claire backs out of a narrow parking space.

"Is that a problem?" I say brightly.

"No, of course not. Ethan isn't Jewish. I guess he isn't anything."

Wrangling an effort to retort, I keep my snide thoughts to myself. Alaska has a small but vibrant Jewish population that began with Russian fur traders and continued through the Gold Rush with fortune-seeking miners and savvy businessmen. Our mayor is a Jew. So is my favorite state senator, the stately, yet undeniably sensual, Senator Barbara Mills Roth.

I have to wonder if I'm being overly sensitive because I feel uncomfortable with these two. Amber's new girlfriend better watch her back. Claire oozes self-confidence like a spendy French perfume. She's stunning when she smiles, meaning she could be competition for the senior math whiz whose name I refuse to say.

Once we leave the airport parking lot, Claire detours slightly to point out cruise terminals and her favorite shops. They talk about clothes, classes, funny things that happened to Amber. Amber is a great storyteller, and she loves an audience. It's stuff I've heard before. I feel left out, but what am I supposed to say? *Hey guys, a funny thing happened to me the other day. I was chased by a bear around our high school parking lot.* It would be a total lie, but that's how desperate I am to be a part of the conversation. I keep my mouth shut, and they seem to forget I'm here.

"Oooh!" Amber yelps suddenly, causing me to nearly jump right out of my seat. "Look. Is that one of those Bilbo Sushi Shacks? A girl at school posted that they get their seafood from Japan." She rolls down her window and motions to a wagon in front of a T-shirt shop with a red and white striped awning. "Let's stop. I'm hungry."

Seafood from Japan? When we have it in abundance right here? I don't see the point.

"We'll be late," Claire warns.

"Please, Claire. Pretty please." Amber brushes her fingers over Claire's forearm and offers her the sexy smile she used to give me. "You want to, don't you? Who cares if we're five minutes late? You don't, do you, Nora?"

Of course I care. We only have so much time to spend at the Capitol. We're here for barely twenty-four hours, as it is. "I ate on the plane." I can hear the sulkiness in my tone.

"What, lemonade and pretzels? It'll only take a minute. Come on, Claire. Nora doesn't really mind. She's just being difficult."

Claire glances in the rearview mirror at me and hesitates, but when she sees a parking space half a block ahead, she signals and pulls in. "Let's get it to go, okay? It's considered bad form to enter chambers after the day's events have started." She unbuckles her seat belt and climbs out.

"You're adorable." Amber giggles flirtatiously.

"You both are," I grumble, not really caring if they hear me. I consider staying in the car, thinking they won't notice my absence anyway. I don't want to seem childish though, so I get out and follow them up an old-fashioned weathered boardwalk.

This must be the historic merchants wharf I've read about. The shops beyond are packed together and brightly colored. Charming hand-painted signs advertise their wares. The street resembles the kind of old west town you'd see in a movie. Nevertheless, it doesn't take long to see they sell the same kinds of touristy mug and keychain stuff you can buy on Fourth in downtown Anchorage. Pedestrians with plastic shopping bags clunk noisily along beside us. The salty scent of seawater envelops us like a cloud.

There's a huge red Tracy's King Crab Shack on the corner ahead of us. Amber, though, is determined to have Bilbo's Japanese sushi. She pumps her fists and marches forward, threading her way between groups of tourists like she's on some kind of war mission. Claire veers off when a girl selling candy from a doorway calls her name.

I'm caught halfway between them and have to leap out of the way when a little girl who isn't watching where she's going shoves another little girl who's licking an enormous soft serve vanilla ice cream cone. The first girl accidentally stomps my foot. The second drops her cone on the boardwalk with a splat. She lets out a tremendous wail like a distressed sea otter.

All at once, I wish I'd followed my first inclination and stayed in the car. Crowds have a tendency to make me nervous. Too many people. Too many noisy conversations. Too many unexpected and unpleasant smells. The howl of a siren sounds nearby, and it's all I can do to take a few more steps to a bench before a wave of nausea sweeps over me.

"Breathe, Nora. Breathe," I whisper to myself. I drop my head between my legs and lay my elbows across my knees as an old memory washes over me.

CHAPTER FOUR

Claire

I quickly explain to Dina, the daughter of one of my dad's assistants, that I'm working today and don't have time to chat. She gives me a pouty smile, then hands me a bag of saltwater taffy and says it's on the house.

"Thanks. That's really nice of you." I start to accept it, but she won't release the sack.

"I have an ulterior motive, Claire. I want you to go to a party with me Saturday night."

I'm guessing she thinks playing tug of war with me is seductive. It's not. Neither is the way she bats her lashes at me, thick with too much clumpy mascara. She's a friend at best, and there's no spark between us, at least on my side. But Dad expects me to be pleasant. Always.

"I'd really like to," I begin. "But I'm not sure it's a great idea. I mean, since our parents work together and everything."

"All the more reason we should get together. Come on, Claire. It's just one date. If I kiss you and you don't like it, that will be the end of it. I promise." She finally lets go of the taffy and winks.

I ought to leave it on the counter, especially since I didn't ask for it anyway. Instead, I drop it in my messenger bag and say, "I'll think about it. Thanks again." Courteous, that's me.

"I'll text you. It'll be fun," she calls after me.

I wave over my shoulder and spot Nora on a nearby bench. I have to admit I find her a lot more attractive in person, probably because she has that soulful, intense look I often see in Ethan. As I head in her direction, I can see her back's bent, her shoulders hunched. I take a seat beside her. The wood slats creak beneath my weight. Float planes rock gently against the dock in the harbor below us. It might sound screechy to someone unfamiliar with the noise, but to me it's a soothing sound I've always loved.

The sun peeks out from behind a puffy, gray cloud, and a man not far away drops his hat on the boardwalk and unzips a bag holding a steel drum. "Are you okay?" I say to Nora. "Would you like some taffy?" I pull the sack out of my bag and start to pass it over.

She lifts her head. A bead of sweat slips down her cheek. Her hair has come undone, cascading down her back. It's dark and rich, falling past her shoulders in soft, shiny curls. It makes her look less stern. More...*No, don't. Don't even think about it.*

Nora Thomas is a geek like me. Same with Amber. I sent her a follow request on Instagram, but she never responded. She's hardly said a word since we left the airport.

"Do I look okay?" She waves the candy away, her hands coiled tightly into fists.

Does she want me to be honest? "Not really. You look a little pale."

"Right. Then why ask?"

"Well, because—" I stop. The last text I got from Amber said that Nora was bright, but weird and not to pay any attention to her weirdness. I got the feeling I wasn't supposed to notice her at all. "Is there anything I can get you?"

"No. Please leave me alone."

"For how long?" I check the time on my phone. We're already running late, but I don't want to rush her if she isn't up to it.

"Would forever take care of it?"

I blink in semi-shock as she sticks out her jaw, looking angry and frustrated. The frustration, I get. This is a big day for her, and I'm sure she doesn't want it spoiled by being sick. But why is she angry? It feels like it's directed at me.

I start to rise and sit back down again. "Have I done something to offend you, Nora?"

"No."

"Then I have to say, you're coming across as rude."

"I don't feel well."

"That's what I asked you."

She lets out a sigh of annoyance. "And I asked you to leave me alone. Look, Claire. You're a flirt. I get it."

What? "No, I'm not."

"Fine. Have it your way. But if you think I'm impressed just because you're blowing kisses to every pretty girl you see, you're wrong. That's Amber's thing. I couldn't care less if you're the most popular girl in Juneau."

I can feel the back of my neck grow hot. This isn't fair. I'm friendly and polite, that's all. It's how I was raised. "I haven't blown a kiss to anybody! If you're talking about the girl at the taffy shop, she called me over."

"Sure. Let's stick with that. Why don't you go play with Amber. Look. She's waving at you."

I hardly know what to say, but I don't think I should have to defend myself to someone I've just met. Glancing up, I see Amber coming toward us. She's balancing a paper plate of sushi rolls in one hand, a twenty-four ounce cardboard drink cup in the other. She motions with the plate and almost drops it. It tips from front to back a couple of times before she steadies it.

"Yummy! You have to check this out, Claire. Spicy tuna roll on sale. They're leftovers from yesterday. I got enough for both of us. You want some?" She swishes her hips, then catches a glimpse of Nora. "Oh for heaven's sake, what's wrong with you? Please don't tell me you had another panic attack. Did someone say boo?"

"So adorable." Nora's nostrils flare as she stands up. "I'm going back to the car. I'll meet you there."

"Aren't you going to tell us to take our time?" Amber yells after her. Nora picks up her pace. She kicks up her heels like a runner as Amber slides onto the bench, taking her place. "I was hoping you wouldn't have to see that. I did tell you she's passive aggressive, didn't I? It's why I broke up with her. Not to mention how she was suffocating me with her neediness. It was like I couldn't have other friends. We had to spend all our time together, every waking moment. That gets old. You know what I mean."

I can see how it might. However, I'm also beginning to feel a little sorry for Nora. "She has panic attacks? You didn't offer her any of your sushi."

"She wouldn't want it. Spend five minutes alone with her, and you'll get it. Crowds. Loud noises. Things that go bump in the night. She's a nervous wreck. It used to happen more when she was younger, at least that's what she told me. She takes medication now and practices finding her 'safe spot,' whatever that means. You know about her parents, right?"

Amber bends her face to the plate and takes a bite of tuna between her front teeth. Somehow, she makes it look dainty. Seagulls scream and dive at us, but she manages to ignore them. "Sure you don't want one? They're delicious. Much better than anything we can get in Anchorage, or probably anywhere in Alaska." She holds out the plate.

Day old sushi? No, thanks. And I'm not one for dissing my home state even if I do get tired of halibut every now and then. "I'm good. What happened to Nora's parents?"

"It was all over the news. They died in a freak avalanche accident a few years ago. Tried to ascend Denali too early in the season."

"Both of them?"

"Yeah. Sad, right? Bad things happen to Nora, I'm telling you right now. I think she attracts disaster. She also lost a brother, which I probably shouldn't have mentioned when you showed us that picture of your friend. But honestly, she needs to get over it and get on with her life. She acts like it's some awful secret. He died at birth, and she thinks it's her fault. I've told her that's silly. It's really not that rare when both twins don't survive the birthing process. One is almost always larger and healthier."

Amber makes her way through the rest of the sushi talking about "disappearing twin syndrome." I've heard of it, so I know she doesn't have her information quite right. I'm a bit of a science nut. Dad got me a subscription to *Scientific American* for my birthday a couple of months ago as a joke, but I love it. From what I've read, fetal tissue from the vanishing twin is absorbed by the mother and the surviving infant. It usually happens early in a pregnancy, not at birth.

"We should go," I say as Amber stands, stretches, and tosses her trash in a metal can nearby. The gulls immediately swoop for it. We're late enough as it is, and I hate the thought of my civics teacher finding out that I made an unauthorized stop.

Amber belches loudly. "Squeeze me!" She puts her hand over her mouth and giggles. I wonder how long it would take before that giggle would start getting on my nerves.

Nora's propped with her butt against the rear passenger door as we approach the car. She's got her hair wound back in the twist, and she's polishing her glasses with the hem of her shirt. She glances up and squints, looking irritated again. But for a second all I can think is how beautiful her eyes are.

"It's about time," she gripes. "I hope you two are enjoying yourselves."

"We are. No thanks to you," Amber shoots back. She loops her arm through mine. "Come on, Claire. Let's go have some fun."

CHAPTER FIVE

Nora

Once we get in the car, I dry swallow half a Xanax and do a couple of deep breathing exercises a counselor taught me when I was younger. I inhale through my nose and let my belly fill with air. Breathe and count. Realign my focus and find my safe spot, currently a cool, brightly lit forest with sunshine peeking around tall leafless birch trees. It helps.

Claire starts the engine and enters tour guide mode again, talking about a place called the Glacier Gardens Rainforest Adventure with a panoramic view of Mendenhall Valley and the Chilkat Mountains she says is to die for. She keeps glancing at me in the rearview mirror with a concerned expression, so I guess Amber must have shared my dirty secrets.

My last anxiety attack happened at a school baseball game three weeks ago when our team unexpectedly beat last year's state champs. They got so excited they stormed the bleachers, and the pitcher, a guy I hardly knew, scooped me off my feet. When I pushed him away, I fell backward over a row of benches, banging an elbow and conking myself on the head. Before I understood what was happening, I was on my back with a dozen faces swimming in front of me. Everyone kept asking if I was all right. I didn't black out, but I came close. Amber was mortified at the drama I caused, furious with me for embarrassing her in front of friends.

Maybe that was the beginning of the end for us. I can only imagine what Claire thinks of me now. The thing is, I don't want to be *asked* if I'm okay. I want to *be* okay. I don't want to feel overwhelmed when a child steps on my foot and another screams like a banshee.

I was a kid myself, having just turned four, when a stranger attempted to abduct me at the Fifth Avenue Mall. It happened so fast I barely processed what was going on. One minute, I was with my mother. The next, a woman I'd never met was dragging me through the multilevel parking garage. I remember whiffs of gasoline, the sounds of far-off echoes of car engines, squealing tires and honking horns, and the high-pitched chattering of a child nearby. The woman told me my mother had been hurt. She said I had to come with her.

Mom called security and caught up with us. The mall guards surrounded the car before I was thrust inside it, but the woman got away.

It might not have been so traumatic if my parents hadn't made such a big deal of it afterward. The woman didn't hit me. She didn't even yell at me. The only thing that hurt was my arm socket from being yanked through the mall and out the back exit of one of the stores. In spite of it, I wasn't allowed to play outside alone all summer. When I went to school that fall, my father drove me and my mother picked me up. Anytime I was invited to a birthday party, they insisted on interviewing the parents first. It didn't make me popular, just weird, like Amber always says.

Three blocks past Glacier Avenue (okay, yeah, I've been counting), Claire makes a left on Main Street. "We're a little late, but it should be fine." She white-knuckles the steering wheel as if convincing herself of it. "The Capitol is half a block ahead. In half a minute, you'll see a sculpture of a grizzly designed by an artist named Skip Wallen. It's one of our more famous landmarks." She's in tour guide mode again.

She slows at the sight of flashing lights and cranes her neck to peer around the car in front of us. "Looks like ordinary construction. I'll see if I can get around it. If not, you guys can get out here and walk. I'll find a place to park and join you as soon as I can."

It sounds like a good idea to me. I don't want to miss another minute and definitely not the school funding vote itself. I'm hoping Senator Roth will give one of her famous RBG-type speeches about how no doors should be closed to students who lack access to a good education.

Tall, rusty scaffolding on the sidewalk obscures my view. Suddenly, the Jeep we're following screeches to a halt. Claire slams on her brakes. Amber braces herself with a hand on the dashboard, another on her belly.

She laughs. "Seriously, Claire. You're a terrible driver."

"Sorry."

"Oh, don't—"

"Don't what?" Claire spins the steering wheel to move into another lane, only half paying attention to Amber as she concentrates on driving.

"Don't jerk the car like that. My stomach."

That gets Claire's attention. "Are you sick?"

"I don't know. Crap, maybe. Let me out." Amber unbuckles her seat belt and scrambles to the sidewalk, clutching her waist and dropping to her knees.

Two men wearing hard hats and orange vests are jackhammering the walk beside a manhole cover. Concrete chips fly everywhere. The noise, louder when she opens the door, pounds my eardrums like a car engine in a closed-up garage.

At first, I think Amber's making fun of me again. Another joke to make me look stupid in front of Claire. *Nora got sick. Now it's my turn.*

When she doubles over and folds both arms around her waist, I understand this is nothing to laugh about and jump out of the car.

"Move out of the way," I shout at the men who stop and stare at us like we're performing a play. Groups of pedestrians pause uncertainly in their tracks. A woman with a fluffy cloud of russet hair like cotton candy takes out her phone and points it at us. Does she think this is something worth filming? How messed up is that?

I squat next to Amber and rub her back. "How can I help? Is it the sushi? Do you want water? I'll find some if you need it. Maybe Claire has a bottle in the car."

She gasps and leans into my arms. Tears spill down her cheeks. "Will you call my parents? I—I thought it was a cramp. I've got a sharp pain right here." She grasps my fingers viselike and points to the region near her belly button. "I feel like I'm being knifed."

Definitely no joke. "Get back!" I yell at the gathering crowd. I fumble my phone out of a pocket and call for an ambulance, and then I dial her mother.

Mrs. Abbott has a million questions, most of them irrelevant.

"We're on Fourth Street," I say sharply. "Claire says the ambulance will most likely take Amber to Bartlett Regional Hospital. It's not that far away." Claire gives a frantic nod beside me. I'm not sure where her car is, or when she joined us.

"I don't know the address. Look it up!" I shout. "The ambulance is pulling up right now." I cut off the call and stuff my phone inside my pocket.

Two paramedics emerge from the truck. The crowd parts for them. The woman taking video tries to move closer. Someone grabs her elbow and drags her behind the scaffolding. The workmen have disappeared, their tools abandoned a few feet away.

"What's going on?" asks a female paramedic. She kneels on the sidewalk next to Amber. "That's all right, young lady. Help is here. We're going to take care of you. Can you tell me where it hurts?"

Amber motions to her stomach and grabs my arm. "Nora. Don't leave me!"

"I won't," I promise, wishing I could sound as composed as the paramedic who checks Amber's pulse and mutters something about administering fluids, before deciding against it. Her partner pulls a flat orange board out of the back of the truck, and they load Amber inside.

"Can Nora come with me?" Amber sobs, still gripping my hand. I glance back at Claire.

Claire lifts her chin. "Go on. It's fine. I'll follow in the car. I'll be right behind you."

CHAPTER SIX

Claire

I've gotta say watching Nora spring into action was nothing short of amazing. Brilliant, really, especially after hearing Amber describe her as a nervous wreck. She didn't seem bothered by the situation *or* the noise. Like a traffic cop, she directed all the looky-loos to step back, then managed to keep Amber relatively calm by rubbing her neck and stroking her hair.

"You're going to be okay, Ambs. Don't think about your tummy. Focus on your breathing. I've got you covered. You're going to be fine," I heard her say more kindly than I thought Amber deserved.

I was a little surprised to hear her yell at Amber's mother, though honestly, the woman asked the dumbest questions.

Mrs. Abbott's piercing voice carried through the phone. "Why aren't you girls at the Capitol yet? What have you been doing? Can it wait until the legislators take a break? Where exactly is this hospital?"

"Look it up!" Nora shouted. It made me want to laugh. *Jeez, lady, your daughter's practically having a heart attack. Sorry if her timing's inconvenient.*

It takes me a couple of minutes to get back to the car, which I've double-parked on a side street, and another minute or so to navigate the heavy traffic. I park in the hospital's visitor lot and make my way on foot to the ER entrance.

I'm completely off script now, which I'm sure to pay for later with my civics teacher. He's going to be so disappointed in me, but there's nothing I can do. I should never have let Amber talk me into stopping for sushi. I knew it was a bad idea, but I'm the worst at saying no. I suppose I thought it would be bad manners to simply tell her she could pick it up later.

I step through the outside door into the coolness of the emergency center in time to see Amber, her jaw slack and her eyes still drawn in pain, being rolled down an interior hallway on a gurney. There's an IV bag hanging off a handrail of her bed. Nora and the Abbotts stand at the counter, talking to a petite Black woman in scrubs who's asking what Amber ate. She's short and muscular. Leather bracelets slide up and down her wrists as she takes notes on an iPad with a yellow daisy cover. When Nora mentions stopping at the harbor for sushi, Mrs. Abbott's lips pinch together in dismay.

"What in the world possessed you to do such a foolish thing? Nora, I'm especially surprised at you. You're usually more responsible. And you, Claire, clearly I don't know you, but I should think you'd know better too. Does your teacher know you did this? If you've given my daughter food poisoning, I swear…" She snorts but doesn't finish. Probably because she's considering different ways to have me drawn and quartered.

I want to say I didn't make Amber eat anything. But if she's sick, then technically it is my fault. Either way, my tour guide days are over. Goodbye A in civics. Hello mediocrity.

"It was both our ideas, mine and Amber's. Not Claire's, so don't blame her," says Nora. "The spicy tuna roll was just too tempting."

I glance at her, startled. Why is she covering for me when she obviously doesn't like me?

The woman with the bracelets looks up from her iPad. "Then you ate it too?"

Nora runs her tongue across her upper teeth, stalling. "Well, no. I changed my mind at the last minute. I had saltwater taffy."

"And you?" She turns to me.

"Me, too." I gulp. "I had saltwater taffy. Amber ate the tuna rolls by herself."

The woman shifts from one foot to the other in white sneakers with thick rubber soles. She sticks the iPad in a wide pocket on the side of her smock. "All right. I'll let the doctor know. Feel free to have a seat." She gestures to a row of plastic chairs bolted to the floor. A bald man holding an ice pack on his forehead sits nearby, facing the window. "Or if you prefer, there's a nice café attached to the building. I'll make sure someone finds you when we have more information."

"Do you have any idea how long it will be?" asks Mr. Abbott. His wife's still staring at me with her eyes crossed as if she'd like to eat me alive.

The woman at the counter shakes her head. "I'm sorry, I don't. If there's any change in your daughter's condition, we'll let you know right away."

That sounds ominous. What sort of change in Amber's condition are they expecting other than a semi-slow recovery? I had food poisoning once in middle school. The stomach cramps were the worst. Everybody who had pork for lunch got sick. My mom picked me up from school and took me straight to an urgent care, where they fed me ice chips and told me to take plenty of sips of water and clear broth, nothing with caffeine. I was up and about and completely well the next day. Rehydration is what's usually called for. Surely the I.V. bag attached to the gurney is supplying Amber with fluids and replacing her electrolytes. It ought to make her feel better soon. So why can't her parents stay with her? My mom stayed with me.

The gravity of the situation hits me full force, like a bucket of ice water sloshed in my face. How could I have let this happen? If Amber dies, I'm responsible. I'd hate myself. Why didn't I do as I was told and go directly to the Capitol? We ought to be there now, listening to Senator Roth talk about the new school finance bill. I've made a huge mistake.

Mr. Abbott makes a worried gurgling sound in the back of his throat and guides his wife to the chairs with a hand in the small of her back.

Nora hesitates as if she's about to follow them, then turns to me with the tiniest of smiles. "What do you say we try the café, Claire? It's almost lunchtime. If you're really nice, I'll let you buy me a sushi roll." She astonishes me again.

CHAPTER SEVEN

Nora

I almost told Claire she owed me. One look at her panicked face, and I knew she wouldn't get that I was joking.

I'm not worried about Amber. It's a good thing for her she's hardly ever sick because when she is, she's the biggest baby ever. When I was eleven, I broke my leg on a ski mogul. I sat in the snow for half an hour before being transported to the hospital. I was in excruciating pain, my tibia rubbing against my skin, as a rescue team carried me down the hill. Still, I couldn't wait to get the cast off six weeks later because I wanted to get back to skiing with my parents. When Amber caught the flu shortly after we got together, her mother nursed her like she was an invalid. Amber thinks I'm the frail one. Well, I'm not.

We head outside and around the side of the building by the hospital's main entrance. Claire pauses beside a leafy bush, saying she needs to call her civics teacher. I step over to the café door to give her privacy. Her voice is loud enough that I can hear her end of the conversation.

"I'm sorry. I know. I'm really, really sorry." Pause. "At the hospital. Yeah. I don't know. I'll ask her." She puts her phone away and joins me, aiming for a cheery expression. Her lips curl at the corners, but her eyes stay flat. "Would you like me to take you to the Capitol? I hate that you're missing the legislative process, the very thing you came to see."

"Are you going?"

"Just to drop you off. I need to come back here and make sure Amber's okay."

My gaze bounces between Claire's face and the parking lot. It's tempting. I've been looking forward to this excursion for months. My first real trip outside of Anchorage and a chance to meet my idol Senator Roth in person. On the other hand, Amber begged me not to leave her, and I promised her I wouldn't. What if she's alert and asks for me? I should stay. If she feels better by this afternoon, we can continue with our itinerary as planned.

"I'll wait and see how she is. Maybe go later," I tell Claire.

"Fair enough." We move on into the café, which is every bit as pleasant as the woman in the ER told us. It has kind of a nineties vibe with a beige tile floor, lots of oak and brass, and instrumental music coming from little round speakers high up on the wall. I ask for a bowl of tomato bisque and a glass of iced tea. Claire orders coffee, black, and a single shrimp tempura roll. We find an empty table near the window.

"If that's for me"—I scooch my chair closer to the table and point to the roll—"I should tell you I was kidding."

"It's symbolic." Claire cuts it in two small pieces with a plastic knife, scooping the larger section onto my soup saucer. "We're not sick. It's freshly fried. And it comes from Alaska, not Japan. But if you don't want your half, I'll eat it all myself."

"If you insist," I mock-grumble, then down it in a couple of bites. "Not bad."

"Amber said you wouldn't eat sushi. Are you making an exception for me?"

Why would I do that? I eye her for a moment, wondering if she's serious. "I avoid raw food because of bacteria risks and parasites. This is fried. Also, I don't get why anyone who lives in Alaska wants seafood from Japan. Just saying."

"Agreed." Claire shrugs and consumes her half, making little crunching noises with her teeth. She swallows with her eyes closed like it's one of the best things she's ever tasted. I'm fascinated, watching her.

"Can I ask you a question?" She sits back.

"Why I told Mrs. Abbott I wanted sushi?"

"No. I get that. You're nice, and you could see she was about to take my head off. I want to know why you called me a flirt."

I'm not nice or kind, or even particularly sympathetic. If anything I tend to be overly suspicious of other people's motives, another part of my strangeness Amber's always talking about. I do, however, have a sense of fairness. Mrs. Abbott isn't a bad person. But once when I went out for Amber's birthday with her parents, I watched her tear into a waitress because her jalapeño tacos weren't spicy enough. Excuse me, like that's the waitress's fault?

I spoon creamy tomato soup onto my tongue and think how I want to answer. "Do you know everybody in Juneau?"

"Of course not." She wags her eyebrows, grinning. "Only pretty high school girls."

Ha-ha. *Like you.* "You're outgoing then. When I see someone I barely know, I usually look the other way and go on about my business. I'm guessing you don't do that because you're a people person. You probably have a zillion friends who love you, people who look forward to seeing you every day."

Claire reaches for my iced tea as if to drink it. She must see my eyes widen in alarm because she stops herself and sips her coffee instead. "I hope so. I look forward to seeing them. Not you?"

"Nope."

"I figured. I sent you an Instagram follow request. You never answered."

"Maybe I didn't see it."

"Did you?"

"Maybe. Maybe not." Yeah, I saw it. But I didn't see the point in looking at a bunch of photos posted by someone I'd never see again after today. Also, Claire intimidates me. She's attractive, like Amber, the kind who'd have no interest in someone quiet like me. I'm introspective. A homebody. I enjoy baking cookies with my "aging" grandma.

"Amber told me your parents died in an avalanche," says Claire.

"True." A crevasse, actually. But I'm not going to argue.

"And that you had a twin who died at birth?"

"Also true." I can feel my fingers stiffening, the familiar ache I experience whenever I think of Nick.

"Do you live with an aging grandmother?"

"I do."

"What else?"

"That's pretty much it."

"Nora." She lets out an exasperated sigh. "The way conversations generally work is when one person asks a question the other answers, then asks something in return. It's a back and forth. That way people get to know one another."

I finish off my bisque and dab my lips with a napkin. "Oh. Is that the way it works." My voice comes off flat.

Claire rises from her chair. "You're impossible. I give up. I'm going back to the ER waiting room. Nice to meet you, Nora Thomas. I hope you enjoy your time in Juneau."

She's out the door before I realize this isn't what I want at all. I'm being recalcitrant, Gran's word for me when I work myself into a mood. Hastily, I deposit our dishes on a sideboard, thank the man in the hairnet who ladled my soup into a bowl for me, and hurry outside. I catch up with her on the sidewalk.

"Wait, Claire. I'm sorry. I'd like to say I'm not normally like this, but that would be a lie. Amber says I'm weird, and she's right. I wish I had an excuse. The trouble is I don't; it's just the way I am. This morning I repacked my perfectly fine suitcase twice, rolling instead of folding to save space because I had to do it right. I can get halfway to school on any given day, and then return home even if I might be late just to make sure I locked the front door. I doubt everyone and everything, more than you'd think. And"—I pause for breath because I'm speaking really fast—"I was rude to you at the harbor and again a second ago in the cafeteria. Is there any way you can forgive me? Do you have sisters or brothers? What do you want to be when you grow up? Do you like giving tours at the Capitol?"

Claire tilts her chin, her face set. "No. An architect or construction engineer. And yes." Then she softens. Her full pink lips fold into a smile. Her lower lip is slightly larger than the top. I want to touch it. She's really quite lovely. "I have two stepsisters. My parents are divorced. My father is a home builder. I love science, but I plan to be a builder because I want to be like him. He can take an empty space and turn it into a house people will discuss in dinner conversations. I give tours because I need an A in civics. Right now, it's my only B. I like showing students from other cities around the Capitol because the legislative process is astonishing. Tedious at times, but when a vote is about to take place, my heart pumps. Our government, the country's government, I mean, is the best in the world. Also, true confession time—I have a tiny crush on Senator Roth. She's…I don't know…" Claire's words trail off.

"Confident. Commanding. Absolutely gorgeous for an older woman?" I say.

"Stunning, right?" Claire laughs. It's a musical sound, low and throaty like a cool jazz piece. It gives me the shivers, a feeling I'm startled to find I like.

"Senator Roth is Jewish, you know," I say, allowing a hint of mischief to enter my voice.

Claire rocks back on her heels, with a mock-horrified expression. "Oh, no! I wish you hadn't told me that. Well, if that's the way it is, I'll just have to admire her anyway."

I'm pleased she gets my sense of humor. Amber often thought I was somber when I was only kidding, one of the many things we never understood about each other. Claire and I stand out on the sidewalk for another couple of minutes and then go back into the ER waiting room.

Mrs. Abbott has found an old *People* magazine with a photo of Ben Affleck on the cover looking puffy-faced and furtive. She sits sideways in a chair with her legs crossed, thumbing through the pages like she's speed-reading. Mr. Abbott stands at the counter talking to a large white woman wearing a smock covered with colorful umbrellas. When he sees us, he comes over.

"Is Amber feeling better?" Claire wears a worried look.

He shakes his head, his brows bunched together. "No news is good news, right? They're still running tests."

For food poisoning? My good mood dampens. "Can we see her?"

"Not yet. They're taking her in for a CT scan in a minute. Listen, why don't you two go on with your day as planned. There's nothing you can do here. I'll text you when we know something."

For the first time, I'm aware that Amber may not be all right after all. The man with the ice pack is gone. A woman furiously clicking knitting needles in her lap is sitting in his chair. A boy and girl, both with dark eyes and hair, roll yellow Tonka trucks at her feet. Nick and Nora with their grandmother; that could have been my brother and me. When the little girl catches my eye, I start to say hello and ask her name. Her eyes dart away from me. Maybe someone tried to kidnap her once too.

Claire lays a warm hand on my arm. "We should get out of here."

"But—"

"Consider it a mental health break."

"Go on, Nora. You deserve it," Mr. Abbott urges, waving at the door.

As a realist, I know I don't. Why would I? I haven't done anything special.

I let Claire drag me back outside before I shake her off. "Claire. I understand I'm missing out on something important, but I can't leave Amber. I promised her I'd be here for her."

She sucks in her cheeks. "Okay. I get that. But we don't have to sit inside, do we? We can at least walk around and get some exercise. There's nothing wrong with that. Say yes, and I'll buy you another sushi roll. You can have the whole thing."

Something in my chest loosens. My lungs expand. I like the idea of spending more time with her. "Ha, a whole roll to myself. Okay. But just around the parking lot. You know the area, so lead the way."

CHAPTER EIGHT

Claire

I could lead the way, but I'd rather walk side by side through the soft spring grass, inhaling the fresh scent of early blooming irises and holding Nora's hand. The notion is so foolishly romantic I have to give myself a mental shake. *Blech.* Even in my head I sound like a bad movie.

Truthfully, I don't have a lot of practice with girls, although I've done my share of dating. The last girl I went out with told me I was picky. The one before was, I hate to say it, shallow. How much time can one person spend obsessing over hair products? I prefer spending time in groups, or with Ethan who has no expectations of me.

Nora's different from other girls I've known. She's intense. Like, even when she isn't looking at me, she's listening, sifting carefully through my words and not just waiting her turn to talk. All I could think about in the café was kissing her. I imagine the feel of her lips. Soft. Gentle. Unsure, at first.

Good grief, I am a flirt! I keep trying to come up with ways to make her smile. I want to be silly and clever and make her laugh. Maybe I should swish my hips like Amber did at the wharf. Is that how she first attracted Nora's attention?

I realize now that Nora has the kind of substance Amber lacks. Not many people would help a woman carry her baby's things and assist a doddering old man off an airplane. Or stand by an ex who gaslights her every chance she gets.

As we head through the parking lot past my car, I ask her about her brother again. At first, I don't think she's going to answer.

"Are you sure you want to know? Amber used to hate it when I talked about him. She was always telling me I should let it go."

"Well, I'm not Amber." *And I'm not going to undermine you like she does either*, I add silently to myself.

Nora hesitates, bobbing her head from side to side. "His name was Nick."

"What like Nick and Nora in *The Thin Man*?"

"You've read it?"

"Not the book. I've seen a couple of the movies based on it. Nick and Nora Charles were detectives in a bunch of mystery-comedy films from the 1930s. My dad went through a phase of watching black and white movies on TV when I was younger. I used to watch with him. *The Thin Man. After The Thin Man. Shadow of the Thin Man.* There were several others. Not important, though. Sorry. I interrupted you. Go ahead."

"That's okay." She grins. "Not many kids our age would know that." She pauses again, and I can't help staring at her muscular shoulders. She's got an athletic build. Not sure why I didn't notice it before. Probably because I was too focused on her eyes.

"Anyway, I think about Nick all the time. Too much. Even today, when I saw those two kids in the waiting room...the little ones with the dark eyes and hair? Is it weird to wonder what he would have been like? I mean, if I'm gay, would that mean he would have been, too?"

"It's not weird. And not necessarily," I reply. "There might be a greater likelihood if you were identical, but even that's not a guarantee. Scientists call it epigenetic. Siblings—twins, that is—can both carry gay genes, but aren't necessarily attracted to the same sex due to certain environmental factors."

"How do you know that?" She moves up beside me. The backs of our hands brush, sending a thrill like an electric spark shooting through me. She doesn't seem aware of it.

"My father gave me a subscription to *Scientific American*. There was an article about twins in it last month. Different placentas might not transfer the same level of hormones to each fetus. Here. Hold on a sec, let me look something up."

We've reached the sidewalk by a stand of white bark birch trees. Magpies chatter on the back of a bus stop bench, scattering when a city bus pulls up trailing a cloud of smoke. The doors open with the pneumatic hiss. The driver gives me a questioning look.

Taking out my phone, I wave him on and Google "How can twins have different sexual orientations?" I scroll down the screen to an article I read last week from Indiana University.

"Check this out. It's about identical not fraternal twins, but it's interesting. It says if one twin is heterosexual and the other isn't, the lesbian may have an index finger that's shorter than the ring finger on her left hand, which could mean a higher exposure to testosterone in the womb."

Nora peers over my shoulder at my phone. "Really?"

"That's what it says. It probably falls under the realm of anecdotal or non-causational evidence, like drinking two cups of coffee or a glass of wine every day will make you live longer, but who cares? Here, you can see it for yourself."

I feel her warm breath on my neck, her steady gaze on my face. "You have beautiful hands by the way. Your fingers are long and slender." Her hand is making its way to my phone. The moment the words pop out of my mouth, she puts both hands behind her back.

"You have nice hands too."

"Well, thanks, but there's no need to deflect a compliment just because you feel uncomfortable receiving it."

She frowns. "Don't tell me what to do."

Is that what I did? I sigh. "Sorry again. All I'm trying to say is that I know myself. My fingers are adequate. A little on the short side, but they work. I also know I have nice hair, a cute nose, a pretty smile."

"So adorable," Nora mutters out of the side of her mouth.

I ignore that. "Tell me what you think is special about you."

"Well, I'm smart."

"Yeah. I know that. You're a straight A student. You wouldn't be here if your civics teacher didn't think you were worthy of the opportunity to visit the Alaska state legislature. It's quite an honor if you don't live in Juneau. Even kids here aren't invited on a regular basis, especially not for dinner. Tell me something else. Do you like the way you look?"

"Well enough." She blushes.

"All right. Then I'll tell you what I see. You have lustrous hair. Soulful eyes. You have the kind of angular face that will be as striking as Senator Roth's in a couple of years." Nora opens her mouth.

"You're also more loyal to Amber than she deserves," I go on before she can argue or tell me why I'm wrong. "Putting aside what you did for me, you saved Amber from her mother's wrath when you said you wanted sushi." Nora gives a tiny smile of acknowledgment at that. "So, are you an artist?"

"What?"

"Your hands. Your fingers. Do you paint or work with clay?"

Slowly, she draws them out and gazes at them as though seeing them for the first time. "I wouldn't call myself artistic. I took piano lessons until I was fourteen, if that counts. We had a piano in our old living room. Unfortunately, there wasn't room for it at Gran's place."

"Well, then. We'll have to find one so you can play for me this afternoon. What's your favorite kind of music?"

"Jazz. I know, don't say it—nerdy."

"I wasn't going to say that. The bluesy kind or where they sound like they're tuning instruments, preparing for something else?"

Her lips twitch again, no doubt fighting back another grin. "Anything by the Dave Brubeck Quartet. But really, I like all kinds. Look, my index finger is shorter than my ring finger. Let's see yours."

I hold my hands out and have to catch my breath as she strokes my palm. "Not much different. Maybe a little shorter."

"What kind of music do you like?" she asks. Our eyes meet, and she holds my gaze with a thoughtful expression.

"That's easy. Hip-hop, pop, early aught's rap. Not much headbanger stuff. Almost everything by Eminem." Her eyebrows pull together. "Wait. You don't know who Eminem is? Please tell me you're kidding. I was starting to like you," I tease.

"I've heard of him," she says defensively. "Tell you what. If we can find a piano, I'll play 'Take Five' for you. It's Brubeck's most famous piece. Do you know it?"

"I don't."

"Come on, seriously? Please tell me you're kidding. I was starting to like you," she teases back. "Anyway, how about this? I'll play piano for you and you can introduce me to your favorite Eminem song. Do you have it on your phone?"

"I do and you've got a deal." I take her hand and shake it. "Should we head back to the hospital and check on Amber first?" I glance in the direction we've come. We've been walking several minutes, heading slowly toward the wharf. I didn't realize we'd come so far.

"We could." Nora bites her lower lip. "Or, we could look for a piano. It's up to you."

"Let me think about it." I tap a foot, taking in the top of a nearby birch tree that's just beginning to leaf out. I'm pretending like I have a choice, which I don't because I want to get to know her better.

"Well?" She's still holding my hand.

"I vote piano."

"Okay, then." My heart warms as she breaks into a beautiful full-watt smile.

CHAPTER NINE

Nora

Claire says there's a piano bar along the harbor and that it's actually a pizzeria but it's too far away from here to walk. We hike back to her car.

"Is it called Marco's, by any chance?" I slide in on the passenger side and buckle the seat belt, noting clean floorboards at my feet. Evidently, she throws her fast-food trash behind her when she drives. Usually that kind of thing bothers me, but today I don't mind.

"It is. You've heard of it?"

"From the old guy on the plane. Funny coincidence."

"Very." Claire fires up the engine. "I haven't been there, but I've heard the food's pretty good and cheap."

I'm glad to hear it. Gran expects me to wait until my senior year before I get a job so I can concentrate on my schoolwork. She gives me a small allowance. I brought emergency cash with me, not much, because we're supposed to be having dinner in the legislature lounge. This morning I was looking forward to dining with Senator Roth, even hoping I'd get to sit beside her, but now I want to be alone with Claire. I regret not accepting her Instagram follow request a couple of weeks ago. It occurs to me I need to be more open to new experiences.

Claire smells good. Like a really nice shampoo. I wanted to keep holding her hand after we shook, but it would have been super awkward walking back to her car with our fingers linked together. After all, we just met. We're not dating, and we never will, living so far apart. The thought descends on me like a heavy blanket, weighing down all others.

By the time Claire edges her car into a parallel parking spot in front of a glass shop with beaded curtains hanging in the display windows, I've worked myself into a mood again. Why am I doing this when I should be back at the hospital with Amber's parents?

"Everything okay?" Claire asks.

"Fine."

"Are you sure?"

"Of course I'm sure! I can't believe you're asking me that again. Have you learned nothing about me?" I know I sound fussy, but this isn't going to work. We're too different. I'm lying to myself if I think this is anything more than a silly flirtation. I'm wasting both our time.

Instead of getting frustrated and giving up on me as Amber would have done, Claire opens her phone and thumbs through her apps. "Here it is. This is called 'Cleanin' Out My Closet.' It's old, but it's my favorite Eminem song."

We listen to it in silence.

Instantly, I identify the tempo. Allegro, in the key of A minor. A good beat and thought-provoking lyrics. And although I don't fully understand the context, I find it calming. Once it's over, I say, "I kind of like it. I'd probably need to hear it several times before I can say for sure."

Claire nods. "I feel that way about a lot of music. Eminem, the artist, is singing to his mother about how he wants the truth to come out about the horrible way she treated him."

It sort of makes sense. It makes me like the song even more. I turn my head to find Claire staring at me.

"Nora." She takes a beat. "Asking a person if she's okay isn't an insult."

Is she for real? "I know that, Claire. It's like saying 'Have a good day.' You're supposed to answer 'fine' like I did and move on. It means absolutely nothing." I'm beginning to wonder if she thinks I'm mentally challenged. Why on earth does she feel like she has to explain a simple phrase to me?

She sighs and drops her phone inside her bag. "It can also be genuine and well-meant from someone who cares about you."

Now that part I don't buy at all. "We don't know each other well enough to care how the other's feeling." I open the car door and step out to the boardwalk, happy for a breath of fresh air.

She locks the car behind her and follows me around the corner into an alley. A sandwich board on the sidewalk advertises the day's specials: three different kinds of pizza toppings. A swinging sign over the entry shows a round-belly guy balancing a thick, flat crust on fat, flat fingertips. "You're dark," she mutters, stepping inside.

"Don't I know it." I wished I hadn't let it show.

She comes back with a harsh, "How would I know?" and storms ahead of me.

The place seems crowded for early afternoon. We find a table halfway in the back. I spy a dusty upright piano around the corner in a smaller room. This isn't a piano bar, I realize, disappointed. It's a restaurant that happens to have a piano, like the practice ones we have at school. Musical instruments ought to have a place of honor. On a stage, or in the center of a room.

Half a dozen men in shorts and silky green uniform tops with stripes are chugging beer at the bar, evidently celebrating a soccer game. Several women with nearly identical short gray haircuts sit at a table with empty mugs and a pitcher of frothy beer in the center. The place smells of too much forced joviality, with equal parts piss and beer. I don't like it.

Claire signals a waitress who looks a few years older than us. "Hey. How's it going? I'll have the Wolf Pack Pilsner. I noticed you've got it on tap. Make it tall. What would you like, Nora?"

The girl has braids down her back and an apron with a line drawing of the chubby pizza guy on front. She pecks Claire's cheek with her lips.

"How's it going?" She laughs. "Claire, you devil. Just look at you. Love your new haircut. What a heartbreaker you've become!"

"Thanks."

"Don't mention it. Listen, if I serve you alcohol, you have to promise me you won't tell my boss. Lucky for you, he isn't here."

Claire makes a zipped-lip motion. "Mum's the word."

Braid Girl winks, takes my order for a glass of sweetened iced tea and departs.

Claire taps the table with her knuckles and purses her lips. "I'll have a beer, and then we can head back to the hospital because that's obviously what you want. That's Blanca, by the way. She was a few years ahead of me in school. Pretty, don't you think?"

"Not my type," I grumble. I know what she's doing. Blanca didn't card her, so they must have been tight. Maybe they still are.

Claire gets her beer and orders a mushroom pizza with extra cheese and a thin crust. She tells me I can have some if I want it. I don't intend to eat a bite, even though I'm hungry, and it's what I would have ordered.

I sip my tea and glare at her, thinking it's a good thing we don't date. We can't get along for more than a few minutes at a time. "What's your type?" I say because now she isn't talking, just staring past my shoulder with her pretty green eyes narrowed.

She waves a hand dismissively. "Oh, you know, anything with a pulse. I'm not particular. We flirts will go with anyone. Not the dark ones though."

Obviously she means me. I slurp more tea and crunch an overly large ice cube in my back teeth. I'm feeling sorry for myself. "Too bad you got stuck with me instead of Amber."

"My thought." She pauses, then shakes her head. "No. Forget that. I don't mean it. It's just that I don't understand you."

"You want to like me, but you don't." I get it. I'm difficult. I'm weird. Amber tells me I don't fit in. I do well in school, but I spend most of my time with Gran because she's one of the few people willing to put up with me.

Claire turns her gaze to the bar where one of the soccer players with a scruffy beard tells a joke that ends with, "That's what she said." The others roar and slam their mugs against each other's, sloshing most of their beer on themselves.

"Men are stupid." She runs a finger down the side of her glass.

"Not all of them," I say reflexively. Not because she's wrong, but because I feel like arguing with her, when, in fact, hetero guys in groups can take on a herd mentality. The leader doesn't have to be the smartest, or the most attractive. Only the most confident. They'll follow him like bison leaping off a cliff. It's a scenario played out every day at school.

I'm expecting Claire to change her tack in support of her friend, Ethan. Instead, she eyes me like a bio specimen. "Do you really think that, Nora?"

"That men aren't stupid?"

She snorts a laugh that comes out like a cough. "No. That I don't like you. Because the thing is, I like you a lot. But like I said, I don't understand you. You run hot and cold, as if half the time you're angry about something, though I have no idea what. I told you I think you're sexy. What part of that don't *you* understand?"

I can feel my eyebrows inching up my forehead. Does *all of it* cover it? And she never said I was sexy, just that she liked my hair. The tips of my ears heat. A blush crawls up my neck. "Are you going to offer me a sip of your beer, or are you going to hog it all for yourself?"

Her eyes widen. "Are you going to offer me a sip of your iced tea?"

She has me again. I'm not a sharer. It's an only child thing, I suppose. No one to share food with. I shove my glass across the table. "Help yourself." She downs nearly half of it.

"So?"

"You help yourself." She passes me her mug. "Have you ever had a beer?"

I take a huge gulp, stifle a belch, and wipe my sleeve across my lips. Of course I have. Amber and I used to go to weekend parties all the time. *Sometimes.* "Gran doesn't allow beer in our cave. It attracts bears."

Claire eyes me for several seconds, and then she bursts out laughing. When Blanca arrives with the pizza, she begs her for two more pilsners. One for each of us.

"See?" she says after Blanca's come and gone again. "I don't know what to make of you. Will you play me that song on the piano? The one you mentioned earlier?"

I'm being given a second chance, which I don't want to waste. "Only if we can start over again."

"Deal." Claire extends her hand across the table. "I'm Claire Tucker. I've lived in Juneau my whole life. Dad says we may be moving to Anchorage in a couple of months."

"Really?" My heart beats faster, flip-flopping like a baby seal inside my chest.

"Really. Your turn."

"Okay. I'm Nora Thomas. I've lived in Anchorage my whole life. I'm anxiety prone and weird beyond reason."

"No, you're not—"

"Let me finish, please." I have to say what's on my mind before I lose my nerve. I draw a ragged breath. "I would be thrilled if you moved to Anchorage because I find you enormously attractive, Claire Tucker. I want to kiss you and touch you in places that make me blush. You are a flirt, whether you acknowledge it or not. But it's actually something I find I really like about you. You're not my type because I don't have a type. Except maybe you."

Claire gazes at me silently until her phone buzzes. I lift my chin at her bag. "Go ahead."

"I don't have to get it."

"Please. I don't mind."

She unclasps the snap on her messenger bag and digs around inside it until she comes up with her phone. "It's Ethan. The guy

I told you about? School just let out. He wants to know if he can join us. He—I texted him your picture earlier. I hope you don't mind. He says he'd like to meet you. But we don't have to."

"I don't mind if you don't." I'm curious about this guy who supposedly resembles me.

Claire hesitates. She unlocks her phone and presses a couple of buttons. "I'm saying no."

"Why?"

"Because, Nora Thomas, I want to keep you to myself."

CHAPTER TEN

Claire

Excuse me, who's the flirt? Nora just told me she wanted to kiss me. I nibble around the corners of a slice of decent mushroom and black olive pizza. I can't even begin to think about finishing the beer because I don't want it anymore. I only ordered it to shock her. I mean, yeah, I'm not going to lie. I like an occasional malt at a party. But in the middle of the day?

The minute I saw Blanca, I knew I wouldn't have any trouble getting served and something told me to go for it because Nora seemed to be doing her best to piss me off. Why not hand it back to her? Look, Nora Thomas, here's your attitude on a silver platter. You can shove it up your ass.

I wasn't kidding when I told her she ran hot and cold. Just when I thought we were beginning to get along at the hospital— bam. She's back to acting as if she wants to hurt my feelings for no good reason. I wasn't expecting her to turn it around again.

"Piano time?" I ask, watching her polish off a third slice of pizza.

She wipes her mouth with a crumpled paper napkin. There's a smudge of pizza sauce on a corner of her lower lip, but I'm not about to mention it. The truth is, I'd like to lick it off myself. "If I have to." She pushes her chair back reluctantly.

"'Take Five.' You promised," I say cheerfully.

"I remember," she grumbles. She's one of the grumbliest people I've ever met, except when she isn't.

I traipse after her to the piano tucked in a quiet corner. She hesitates, then pulls out the bench. "You can sit too, if you'd like." She motions to the empty seat beside her. "Just not too close."

"Right. I'll try not to touch you."

"It's not that! I just need room to move my arms a little."

"I get it. I'm teasing." I smile and gently knock her elbow. "Go ahead. If I recognize the lyrics, I'll sing along."

She glances up. "There are no lyrics. Well, actually there are, but no one ever sings it…Oh, you're teasing again."

Trying. "I'll just hum or whistle to myself then."

"Very funny." She takes a deep breath and leans into the keyboard. At first, she's nervous. She fumbles a couple of notes, then she shuts her eyes.

It turns out, I have heard the piece, I just didn't know the name. Something opens up inside me. I'm swept back to an era of smoky lounges and dirty martinis in long-stemmed glasses. Pretty girls in cocktail dresses with updos and tiaras, like you see in the old *Thin Man* movies on TV. It's incredible.

Nora doesn't just "play" the piano; she's a gifted musician. She feels it in her bones, I can tell. I wish she'd go on playing all night. When she finishes, she folds her hands in her lap.

"Well." She swallows noisily, like she's got a bite of apple stuck in her throat. "What do you think? It's really better with all the instruments together. Dave Brubeck was one of the biggest stars in the history of jazz. His sax player, Paul Desmond, composed the music. It crossed over to the Billboard pop charts in 1961."

I ought to say I'll probably like it better after hearing it a few times like she did, but I can't. This isn't a tease-worthy moment. "It's beautiful. It makes me feel like I've transcended to another planet. I wish you had a piano at your Gran's house so you could play all the time."

"Thank you?" She gives me a questioning look. "Why do *you* want a piano for *me*?"

I'm beginning to realize Nora takes things more literally than I do. I brush that aside because my nerves are on fire with desire for her. "Never mind," I stammer. "You know...I'd really like to kiss you. If you don't like it, that will be the end of it. I won't do it again."

Oh, my gosh. Did I just say that? The same cheesy words Dina expressed to me at the candy shop? What was I thinking? Was that the best I could do? It's too late to take them back.

Nora stretches her neck to take a look around the corner at the men in their soccer uniforms and the women drinking beer. "Um. Okay, I guess."

It's not exactly a ringing endorsement, but she did tell me she wanted to kiss me first, so I'm moving forward with this come hell or high water. I press my lips to hers, gently at first. Then she opens her mouth and lets me slip my tongue inside. My heart thumps wildly in my chest. My body expands. "Nora. That's one of the best kisses I ever had."

"I liked it too." The words are plain, but the meaning behind them is filled with something else. A longing for more. She wraps an arm around my waist and starts to kiss me again.

All at once her phone rings, a jangling sound that startles both of us.

"I'd better get this. It could be Mr. Abbott." She drags her phone out of her back pocket with obvious reluctance, unlocks it with her hooded gaze on me and says hello. Her eyes go wide as she listens. "Yeah. Okay. They can do that? Really? I'll be right there." She shuts it down and sets it sideways on the empty music stand.

I'm fearing the worst. "They can do what? Was that Amber's father? Is she *dead*?"

Nora takes my hand and massages my short index finger. "Amber has appendicitis. She needs an appendectomy, and her parents want it done in Anchorage. The hospital is advising against moving her, but the doctors say she's stable enough for transport if we can get the next flight out. She's scheduled for surgery in Anchorage later tonight."

My heart sinks. "You're leaving. Well, shoot. I'm sorry you didn't get to meet Senator Roth. She's cool. Even more so in person." My voice sounds wooden. I should be saying that Barbara Roth is majestic, or better yet telling Nora that I don't want her to go, that I want to spend more time with her. A lot more.

She traces my jawline with a finger, making my heart stutter. "Claire. Don't you get it? I don't care about Senator Roth. Not anymore. I got to meet you."

PART TWO

CHAPTER ELEVEN

Three Months Later-Nora

"Red or blue?"

"Blue."

"Chicken or beef?"

"Pork."

"Sunshine or rain?"

"Rain."

"Rom-com or suspense?"

"Please." I make a silly face into the phone.

"You do realize you picked the last answer on every question." Claire collapses on her queen-size bed, her head hitting the pillow with a muffled thud. Her bright yellow bedspread and clean white furniture are sunny and warm, like her.

"Coincidence." I shrug. "Your turn."

"Red. Chicken. Sunshine. Rom-com."

Of course. In other words, the complete opposite of everything I chose from her online love match quiz.

Against all odds, we've been texting, FaceTiming, and inboxing each other the entire summer without any major disagreements. I love our visits, although it didn't take long to understand how truly different we are. Claire is cheerful, spontaneous, and optimistic—not a single quality I possess.

"Coincidence," she repeats, likely reading my mind. "Food, movie choices, none of that matters when you like someone."

"If you say so."

"Well, I do. I think we're a great match. Let's try again. Compliments, physical affection, or acts of kindness?"

"All three."

"See? That's exactly what I would have said."

I so want to believe her. Heat rushes through my spine at the thought that tomorrow I'll get to see her again. I doubt I'll sleep ten seconds tonight. It's been three months since we kissed at Marco's.

A text comes through from Amber. *Are you ignoring me?*

I most certainly am, but she's making it difficult when I'm FaceTiming Claire. "What time does your plane arrive?" I say to Claire, taking a seat behind the tiny desk in my bedroom and logging on to my computer with my phone cradled awkwardly against my neck.

"Early. Seven a.m. By the way, you have a beautiful ear. Will you still be able to meet Dad and me at the airport?"

"Absolutely." Gran has given me permission to miss my morning classes, something I wouldn't normally do, but this is a special occasion. My dreams are coming true.

Two weeks ago, shortly before school started, Claire informed me that her father had rented a house in Seaford Gardens, a neighborhood on the northwest side of town where the road splits and ends at a park. It's one of the swankiest parts of Anchorage with three-car garages tucked discreetly out of sight behind monster mansions. The house, a pale green two-story Tudor with a golf course-type lawn, is a temporary place to stay until Mr. Tucker can design and construct something of his own. He's moving his business here. The best part, the part that keeps me up at night like a kid looking forward to a birthday party, is I'll get to spend real time with Claire, not just phone calls.

Amber sends another text, her third today. *"Why haven't you called me back?"*

Um, because I've been over you since spring break last year when you dumped me?

I don't feel bad about it anymore. I visited her a couple of times at the hospital after a surgery that left her with a three-inch scar on her lower abdomen. She keeps telling me she wished she'd never broken up with me. Too late for that. Besides, I never felt about her the way I feel about Claire.

"I'm coming to your house. You have to stop ignoring me," she continues to text.

I heave a sigh. *"No, I don't."*

"I'll be there in 20."

"I won't open the door."

"Then I'll wait until you do."

"You do know Claire's moving here?"

"So? Why would I care about that?"

I've told her that Claire and I are a couple now. Amber has decided to treat Claire like an inconvenience, like she doesn't exist.

Claire's silvery voice pulls me back to a much better conversation. "You seem distracted. Don't tell me Amber's texting you again. Is she?"

I suppress a grin, simultaneously deleting the stream with Amber and setting the phone on my desk as I realize Claire's been looking at a close-up of my ear. "You told me not to tell you. Which is it?"

"You're adorable." She uses one of our favorite catchphrases. "I love to see you smile."

"Why, thank you. You're not so bad yourself." I blow a kiss at the phone, wishing I knew how to be more effusive. I hope it's something I can learn.

The next morning, I reach the airport with an hour and a half to spare because I can't bear the idea of being late to meet Claire's plane. When I push through the revolving outside doors, I accidentally inhale the odor of ammonia from the freshly mopped vinyl floor. I snort and choke as the astringent scent fills my nostrils. I hope it's not an omen. Shoeprints in the wet streaks catch sunlight streaming through the windows. My stomach churns as doubts about how this morning is going to go start to surface.

I've seen Claire's face every day on my phone all summer so I'm not concerned that I won't recognize her. "See how odd you are? Nobody else would think of that," Amber would say if she could hear my thoughts. But what am I supposed to do when we meet? Shaking hands would be too formal. Kissing her cheek might be all right. On the other hand, I don't want her to think I view her as nothing more than a friend.

The fact is, I've been fantasizing about doing much more with her. But what will her father say? I wish I'd just come out with it and asked her yesterday. "Will your dad mind if I kiss you?"

We hugged when we parted at the Juneau airport. I might have done more—I certainly wanted to—except that Mrs. Abbott stood nearby and watched us with one of her wrinkled nose expressions, the one that said she'd like to vomit. Blowing through her nostrils like a horse didn't help. Honestly, what did she think Amber and I were doing in Amber's bedroom with the door closed last fall?

Maybe I should let Claire take the lead when we see each other. But what if she's waiting for me to do it?

By the time the plane lands, I've worked myself into a state. *Come on, Nora. Get a grip.* Claire doesn't think I'm strange. As least she says she doesn't. But how well does she really know me? What if she's forgotten how moody I can get? Maybe I should go home and wait for her to call. She and her father will want time to settle into their new house. I'm just about to leave when I hear her call my name.

She steps off the jetway, her face lighting up the second she lays eyes on me. "Nora! There you are. Oh my gosh, you have no idea how glad I am to see you. I was afraid you'd change your mind and not show up. I've missed you! Aren't you going to kiss me?"

"If you insist." I mean it as a joke, but it comes off sounding stiff. "Sorry. That was supposed to be funny."

"I get it. I'll kiss you." She presses her lips to mine. When I taste her tongue, I forget for a moment that we're in an airport lounge surrounded by other people. My head pulses, and my hands grow damp as my heart fills with something extraordinary—she's here, and she still wants to kiss me!

Reality comes crashing back when a guy with dreads in a purple Nehru jacket behind her clears his throat. "Hello? I say, do you mind moving out of the way?"

Claire draws back breathlessly and gives him her dazzling smile. "Sorry, sir. I haven't seen my girlfriend in a while." *Girlfriend*, wow. I like that.

Apparently he isn't bothered by it either as the corners of his lips turn up. "I understand the feeling. You two enjoy yourselves. Just do it over there, okay?" He gestures to a couple of rows of empty seats in the waiting lounge.

We giggle and head away from others. "Oh, Nora." She laces her fingers with mine. "That's better. So much better. Were you worried we wouldn't click?"

"A little. You?"

"Not at all. But I know how you are. You probably worried about it half the night. I couldn't sleep because I was so excited. Now we can see each other every day. And guess what? North sent me an updated schedule this morning."

"Do we still have classes together?"

"Yep. But different ones. First and last."

AP Chem and Honors English are two of my favorites. More importantly, I'll get to start and end the day with her. "That's even better," I say.

"That's what I thought, too. Dad?" She turns to a model-handsome man with well-toned muscles who has moved up beside her. "This is Nora Thomas, the girl I've been telling you about. Isn't she gorgeous? Don't you think she looks like Ethan?"

Mr. Tucker takes a quick peek at his phone, then slides it in a hidden breast pocket of his custom-tailored suit. He flashes bright white teeth in my direction. "Ah. So this is the famous Nora who has captured my daughter's heart. Pleased to meet you, Nora. Do you know Claire's talked of little else all summer?"

Really? I feel myself grinning. "Hi, Mr. Tucker." I manage a blushing wave.

"Don't you think she looks like Ethan?" Claire asks again.

"Mmm. A little." He shoves the duffel bag he's dropped aside with a polished wingtip, and offers up another flash of pearly whites. "You're lovely, Nora. And positively brilliant, too, by all accounts. Ethan's..." His face takes on a pained expression.

"Oh, Dad, don't start. You promised," Claire cuts in.

"And so I did, although you asked." He pats her shoulder indulgently. "Let's leave it at that then, shall we? I imagine you have a car, Nora?"

"I do."

"That's fine, then. I've ordered one for our luggage. An Escalade. I hope it's big enough. I'll buy something in a day or two once we settle in and get a car for Claire as well. Maybe in the meantime you can drive her to school and show her around the city?"

"I'd be happy to." This time my voice sounds fairly normal because it's exactly what I want. Claire gives me a not-so-subtle shove with her elbow to let me know she's on board with the idea too.

"All right, then. Excellent. Claire has our new address. So, why don't we meet up there in say, half an hour? That should give you and Claire time to get reacquainted. Does that sound all right to you, my beautiful daughter?"

"Perfect." Claire looks at me. "Okay with you?"

"Sure." I can't imagine anything better.

Mr. Tucker tells us to go on ahead of him. He has to wait for their bags.

We head to my old Suzuki in the long-term parking lot. It's a beautiful day for once. Warm and not a single cloud in the sky. A good sign. Even the air smells fresh and clean, which is really something when you're surrounded by the bitter odor of jet fuel this close to the landing strips.

"Here's what I know about Anchorage," Claire says as we walk. "The population sits at around three hundred thousand, making Anchorage roughly ten times larger than Juneau. Captain James Cook was one of the first explorers to map the coastline. The inlet bears his name. He turned one way and called it Knik, then turned the other way and called it Turnagain because he was searching for the Northwest Passage and finally realized his ship couldn't get through."

"Thank you, Wikipedia." I laugh. "So, what don't you know?"

"Everything else. How to get around. How far away our school is. Are the classes harder than the ones I'm used to. What's the best coffee shop. Will I like the new house. When will I get to meet your grandmother. And will she like me." She pauses at the last and chews her lower lip.

"Of course she will. What's not to like?" Gran's going to love Claire. I can guarantee it. She's humble, a trait Gran values and one that Amber isn't familiar with in the least.

"Are you sure? I mean, what if she doesn't? Will she let me come to your house and will she let you visit me?"

I find Claire's anxiety endearing, mostly because it's something I experience myself. "Stop worrying. I can do enough of that for both of us."

She lets go of the tension building in her shoulders and relaxes. "One more thing. You'll introduce me to your friends, right? It's going to be weird not knowing a single other person."

"I will. I promise." I don't mention that I don't have a ton of friends like she does. She'll figure that out soon enough.

When we reach my car and get inside, Claire leans across the seat to me. "Good. We're finally alone, so I can kiss you properly. You didn't say, have you missed me as much as I've missed you?"

"I have. More." I mean it. I've thought of little else the last three months. But I can't help asking, "What was all that stuff with your dad about Ethan?"

She knocks her head against the headrest. "Oh, nothing. Dad seems to believe Ethan's a bad influence on me."

"Is he?"

"No, not really. But did I tell you that he got in a bit of trouble a few weeks ago? Nothing serious. He and a couple of guys got caught spray-painting one of the portable classrooms behind our school one night. Dad found out I emptied my savings to get him out of jail. He was furious for half a minute, but he got over it. And anyway, it wasn't Ethan's fault. He lets others talk him into stuff because he wants to get along. The thing is, his home life is truly awful. His mother—don't get me started on Alice—is a piece of work, and his stepfather may be worse, although at least he's hardly ever around. It isn't fair. Ethan's sweet. He wouldn't hurt a fly. I wish you'd had a chance to meet him. I think you would have fallen in love with him. He's kind and very handsome." She takes my right hand, massaging it with her thumbs.

My heart softens in my chest. My fingers, all the way up my arm, tingle with desire. "You talk about him a lot. Should I be jealous?"

Claire's eyes twinkle. "Certainly. If it will make you kiss me like you mean it."

How can I say no to that? I press my lips greedily to hers. Longing surges inside me. I want to caress the parts of her skin that I can't reach sitting in the car.

Claire's hand inches up my shirt. "Too soon?" she breathes into the crook of my neck.

"Definitely not. Except…your dad's waiting for us."

"Spoilsport." She pretends to pout and takes out her phone to check the GPS. "Presuming that's International Airport Road ahead of us, take a right on Minnesota Avenue, then keep going until it curves. From there…"

"I know it," I admit before she can go any further. "Would it creep you out to know I've been by your new house?"

"What? I have my first stalker! I love it. Nora, I don't believe there's a single thing you could ever do to creep me out."

If only she'll go on believing that.

CHAPTER TWELVE

Claire

Three weeks after moving into the Seaford Gardens house, I'm finally beginning to learn my way around Anchorage. "Just remember, mountains on the east," says Nora. It keeps me from heading the wrong way entirely but doesn't help if I'm looking for a certain street without a sign, or a house without a number, or a bakery that's been recommended to get a cake for her birthday, which is a week away next Monday. I'd like to bake one myself, but we're still waiting for our pots and pans to arrive from Juneau. All our stuff's been delayed.

My classes are about the same. Not terribly difficult, with some more interesting than others. The main thing is I find my new history teacher, Mrs. Hicks, more approachable than my junior civics teacher back in Juneau.

"Everyone in my class starts out with an A." She beckoned me to her desk as I was getting ready to leave class the first day. Everyone else had already left. "Nora speaks very highly of you, Claire, so I don't imagine you'll have any difficulty maintaining it. Will you be joining our LGBT club?"

I guess that was her way of asking if I was gay.

"If they'll have me," I eagerly replied.

"Oh, they will. You needn't worry about that. Welcome to North, by the way, if I forgot to say it earlier. Now run along. You don't want to be late for lunch."

On the way out, I spied an eight-by-eleven framed photo of two girls on the wall above the light switch. "Are these your daughters?"

"Heavens, no." She chuckled, tossing her pen on her calendar blotter. "Oh, dear. That didn't come out right! Those are two of my all-time favorite students, Virginia Eaton and Katie McRanes. They graduated...now, let me see, the year before last, I believe. They gave me that picture because they didn't want me to forget them. Like that would ever happen!"

I waited, thinking she'd elaborate. When she didn't, I moved on to the cafeteria to join Nora for lunch.

People at school like Nora, and she really isn't as antisocial as she thinks she is. Friends greet her in the halls and ask her about tests she's taken that they'll have later in the day. I'm surprised, though, that she and Amber Abbott still eat at the same table, given their dating history.

Amber entertains a group at one end, occasionally inviting Nora to comment on some funny story she's telling. Nora and I sit at the other with two girls who are both in National Honor Society. Often our conversations revolve around school projects with the four of us doing our best to ignore Amber's attempts to make Nora notice her again. I'm not going to ask what Amber did to Ellie and Samantha, but it's clear they care even less for her than Nora does.

"Never again?" I said to Nora the other day when she was avoiding Amber's latest attempt to engage her, this time about a test.

"Never." She gave me one of her serious looks, then broke it up with a somber smile. "I'm with you."

All in all, things are going well, except I didn't realize how much I would miss my friends in Juneau. Dad says I'll adjust, but it's harder than I expected. I'm used to chatting with folks who work in local shops. To talking to the guy who mowed our lawn about his six-year-old who'd lost her baby teeth. To waving to hikers on trails I'd walked every day of my life. To visiting with my friends at the airport. I don't have a dentist or a hairstylist here. I don't know which restaurant to stop and pick up dinner when Dad plans to cook, then finds he doesn't have time for it. We had a housekeeper in Juneau. Here, for the time being, we're on our own.

I know I shouldn't complain. That's usually not me. But let's face it, I miss having Ethan to pal around with. For three years he was my go-to guy, the one to whom I could confess my thoughts and crushes. The one who didn't laugh when I pinned a ginormous poster of Senator Barbara Mills Roth on the wall behind my bed.

"So, what is it you like about her? I just don't see it," he used to say, putting his feet up and crashing on my bed like he owned it.

"Um. Because she's intelligent and beautiful?" Duh. Nora gets it.

I haven't heard from Ethan in nearly a week now, and I'm starting to worry. Granted, his school attendance has never been that great. He'd often disappear for days after arguments with his mom. They'd usually start with something silly like who put the empty milk carton back into the refrigerator, then deteriorate into a yelling match with him calling Alice awful names and her throwing ashtrays at his head. Eventually, they'd make up. But more than once I woke up in the middle of the night hearing a tapping at my window—Ethan pleading for a spot on my floor when it was too cold to sleep outside. I wish he was here now so I could tell him about Nora, how much the sound of her voice excites me and how I find the depths of my feeling for her kind of scary. I've never felt like this with anyone till now.

Lucky for me, Nora's gran doesn't hate me. Our second day in Anchorage, Dad took the four of us out to an expensive seafood restaurant with windows facing the water and a big shiny mirror behind a polished wood bar. Before, when I'd imagined

Nora's grandmother, I pictured an upright gray-haired lady in a color-coordinated pantsuit with perfect posture and exquisite manners. I was right about most of it, except her hair is snowy white.

"Oh, goodness. I haven't been here in ages," she exclaimed. "I'd forgotten how…lovely it is."

She seemed about to say something else. Dad must have thought so too because he immediately steered us to a quiet little bar adjacent to the restaurant that was less ostentatious.

"What do you say we eat in here, Mrs. Thomas? More relaxed, don't you think?" My father always manages to put people at ease. It's one of many reasons he's good at his job.

We ordered appetizers of shrimp, spinach, and smoked salmon instead of full dinners. Before long she was telling him to call her Sarah and inviting me to call her Gran. Dad even got her talking about her son, Nora's father, who had worked as an environmental attorney for one of the big oil companies.

"Anchorage is a bit landlocked," she said when the conversation worked its way back around to the reason for our moving here. "Nora says you build houses from scratch?"

"Custom homes, yes, most of the time." Dad sat back, crossing his knees and sipping chilled white wine in a glass he held between two fingers. He ran a thumbnail down the crisply ironed fold of his pants. "I'm looking forward to expanding into commercial work, meaning office buildings, once I get my business off the ground."

Nora and I exchanged worried looks, neither of us wanting to consider the possibility of what would happen if his business didn't take off. "Gran" patted the table with long, slender fingers like Nora's and said, "Oh, I'm sure it will. I have no doubt. I'd be willing to bet you are a very capable and competent businessman."

"He is," I agreed enthusiastically.

She left much of her food untouched, but wanted to split the check. When Dad refused, she insisted on leaving the tip, rooting around her handbag and coming up with three carefully folded fives for the hundred-dollar tab he'd put on his credit card. Dad gave me a raised eyebrow because I'm sure in his mind it wasn't enough. Still, he didn't say a word.

On the way out, she lingered by the table. When Nora and Dad were out of hearing distance, she called me back, placing a gentle, crepey hand on my arm. "You seem like a good girl, Claire. Are you?"

I wasn't sure what she meant. I wasn't going to swipe her tip off the table. Was she asking if I was kind or clever or a good daughter to my father? I settled on, "I try to be."

"Yes." She nodded thoughtfully. "I imagine you do. You may or may not know that Nora's quite taken with you. She thinks she's in love with you. The only thing I ask is that you don't hurt her. She's been through quite a lot in her seventeen years, more unhappiness than someone her age should have to know."

I opened my mouth to tell her I had no wish to ever hurt Nora because I was falling in love with her as well, but she stopped me with a soft tap. "When you break it off, will you promise me to respect each other's feelings?"

"Yes, of course, but we won't break it off," I said at once. When I put my hand on hers, she slid hers out from under it, letting go of my arm with a *we'll see* expression. It had been a pleasant evening, one of the best I could remember. But her request struck me as somehow sinister, putting a pall on the earlier conversation, a foreboding of something bad to come.

* * *

Honors English is our last class of the day. I've been staring at the clock for the last twenty minutes, wondering if I dare take my phone out and text Ethan again. The last message I sent said, "*This has gone on long enough. Where are you?*" I'm just about to reach inside my messenger bag for it when Eminem sings out, "I'm sorry, Mama. I never meant to hurt you."

I grab the phone and mute the volume. Nora's head bounces up across the room. We've been separated for talking too much.

"Claire," says Mr. Cooper with a harried expression. "We don't allow phone calls during classes here at North."

"I know. I'm sorry. It won't happen again." I drop the phone in my lap. He goes back to looking at his computer, and I mouth at Nora, "Ethan. Tell you later," then wait until I'm absolutely positive Cooper's gone on to something else, before peeking at my cell screen.

"Got a big surprise for you. Can you look out the window?"

It happens that I can. I half-rise in my chair, craning my neck. I'm totally stupefied to see Ethan leaning casually against the concrete base of the twenty-foot Tlingit totem pole in North's circle drive. He has his feet crossed at the ankles, phone in hand. Ours eyes meet. He lifts his chin, tossing thick dark hair out of his eyes.

I'm stunned. I can't wait to get out of here as a thousand questions pour through my thoughts. Why is Ethan St. James in Anchorage? How did he get here? How did he know where I'd be?

The last one I can answer. Sort of. Ethan's grades suck, but he's smart. Smarter than most people give him credit for, including my father. You give him any sort of problem—math, geography, life—he'll figure it out. If he applied himself to school, everyone would know he's a genius.

Nora keeps looking at me. I shrug because I don't know any more than she does. When the bell rings, we meet at the door and dash outside, not bothering to drop our books off at our lockers.

Ethan, grinning like the delicious fool he is, lets me hug him as if he's doing me a favor. I don't care. My chest heaves with shameful sobs because I thought I'd never see him again. Yet here he is, a genie sprung from a magic lamp.

"I missed you too." He pats my back. Then he turns to Nora with his wicked smile and says, all innocent-like, "Hey, sis. Nice to meet you. How about a hug for your long-lost brother?"

CHAPTER THIRTEEN

Nora

The guy I'm gawking at is a couple of inches taller than me with ropey muscles and thick, dark, unfashionably long hair. He's got a hooked nose, prominent cheekbones, and a triangular chin in need of shaving. I can't name fashion designers to save my life, but I do know when I'm looking at expensive clothes. Jeans that fit just right. Brown leather sneakers with off-white soles and fancy logos on the sides. A tailored black shirt conforming to a flat, slender waist.

The second I heard the "Cleanin' Out My Closet" hook, I knew something was up. Claire never mentioned her favorite song is also Ethan's ringtone. The suspicious side of me wonders if they had this planned to shake me up. I toss the ridiculous thought away.

Claire steps to my side away from Ethan as he drops his arms, looping thumbs in perfectly pressed front pockets and splaying longish fingers on his thighs. "So, no hug then?"

"I don't know you," I say plainly.

His face stiffens, then relaxes. "Sorry. Of course you don't. Bad joke. I'm Ethan. If Claire has told you anything about me, then you already know I'm kind of a goof. She kept saying how much we look alike. Personally, I don't see it, but once she gets a thought into her head, it sticks like glue to paper."

I nod and clamp my jaw because I can't think of a single thing to say.

Claire fills the gap. "Ethan, why are you here?"

"Wow." He bounces a brow in what has to be mock bewilderment. "I mean, wow. Not the happy greeting I was hoping for, but okay, sure, I get it. I go to school here. Well, not yet. I start tomorrow. Can you believe it? I'm an exchange student. Got my schedule and everything. I thought I'd surprise you guys. So, aren't you glad to see me, Clarice?"

"Don't call me that. You know I'm glad. But you had no right to startle Nora."

"Yeah." He drops his chin. "Said I was sorry."

"It's okay." I manage to unlock my jaw and speak. "Nice to meet you, Ethan. I guess I sort of feel as if I know you too. I've heard a lot about you. And for the record, we probably do look a little alike, just not like sister and brother. Anyway, welcome to North Anchorage High School. Can we give you a tour?"

"Sure!" He beams. "I'd love it."

Students stream out of the building, moving past us, some giving Ethan an extra-long look. He waves and nods like a king at a coronation as we head back inside the building. Claire asks him where he's staying.

"With my host family, an elderly couple named Bob and Edna Sinclair. Their kids graduated from North a few years ago. Do you know them?"

"I don't." Claire drops back beside him.

"I don't either," I say.

"I guess they go to college somewhere else. Idaho State, I think. Something called the Woogy program?"

"WUE," I correct him. "No 'g.' It stands for Western Undergraduate Exchange. It's a program that allows students from participating states like Alaska and Idaho to attend out-of-state universities at a reduced cost. It's a great way to save money and still attend the college of your dreams."

Eyes twinkling, Ethan pulls up short, giving me a look like he thinks I'm trying to be funny. "Gosh, Nora the Explorer. You really *are* smart. Got yourself a keeper here, Clarice. I mean Claire. It's one of my nicknames for her from—"

"*Silence of the Lambs*. I've seen it." I'm annoyed when I have no reason to be, so I do my best to stuff it back inside me. I point out the cafeteria on our right, the double doors of the gym beyond that, the trophy cases along the wall in between. A few students are still milling about. "The media center is on the second floor. Do you need to check in at the main office?" I gesture to the set of interior windows across from the front doors.

"Nope. Already taken care of. Let me see"—Ethan pulls up his schedule on his phone—"I've got bio with a Mr. Henderson first period. Can you show me where that is?"

"Around the corner on the left," I say as we head in that direction. "I didn't know Mr. Henderson was teaching biology this year. Oh, look, he's in his room. Do you want me to introduce you to him?" Henderson is a North High School institution, like Mrs. Hicks and our assistant principal Mrs. Pugh. He's been around since the school opened a decade ago. He's known as a decent teacher, although he has a no-nonsense reputation when it comes to tardies. Three, and you earn yourself an automatic after-school detention.

I start to tell Ethan this. He shakes his head to stop me. "That's okay, but thanks. I'm a big boy. I like to figure out stuff for myself. But if you guys don't mind waiting, I'll say hello to him right now."

"We'll put our books in our lockers and be back in a minute," says Claire.

We walk in the other direction past the front office. I place my things neatly on a locker shelf, grab what I need for tonight's homework, and then join Claire as she shuts her locker with a double-sliding click. "Did you know?" I hope I don't sound accusing, but I've got to ask.

"That he was coming here? No. I would have told you if I did."

"You don't think it's strange that he showed up in Anchorage less than a month after you moved here?"

Claire blows a noisy breath. "Not really. I'd call it a happy coincidence. I've missed him. Please, Nora, give him a chance. He doesn't know about Nick. All I said was that I thought you two looked alike." She shoves her backpack up her shoulder and pecks my cheek. A custodian nearby dumps trash from a can into a larger barrel stationed on a dirty dolly. Leftover fried chicken odors waft around us. *Yuck.*

Give the guy a chance? "Okay. I can do that." I push my stupid suspicions back inside me.

When we get back to Mr. Henderson's chem lab, Ethan is just coming out. "Pleasure to meet you, sir." He spins back to the room and waves. Henderson lifts a hand in return, then goes back to whatever he was doing at his desk. "That's weird." Ethan pulls the door shut behind him.

"What is?"

He glares at his phone. "My schedule. It's effed up. Apparently I'm supposed to have chemistry, not biology. And it's second period, not first. But Henderson, can I ask? Is he kind of a dick?"

"Not too bad, but he will mark you if you're late," I say as Claire holds out a hand for Ethan's phone to see his schedule. He doesn't notice and slips it inside a back pocket.

"Shall we see if we can get it fixed?" she says.

Ethan cuffs her upper arm, curling his lips into a goofy smile he shares with me. "Dear Clarice. You're too nice. Both of you, I mean it. I've taken up enough of your time this afternoon. I'll take care of it first thing in the morning. No biggie. Chem. Bio. It's all the same to me. Now orchestra or band, that's something I'd get out of bed on time for, even in a rainstorm. Do you like music, Nora? No, don't answer that. You're a pianist. A virtuoso. See, Claire Bear? I do listen when you talk. And by the way, Nora, I absolutely love Dave Brubeck's work. 'Take Five' is my favorite, but 'Blue Rondo Ala Turk' is a close second. You're familiar with it too, I suppose?"

Is he kidding? That's like asking if I'm familiar with the taste of chocolate cake. "I know it," I say shyly. "I love it too."

"Awesome. So we have something in common, after all. I mean besides the twinks thing." He wags a finger back and forth between us.

Claire asks if he's headed to the Sinclairs' house.

"I guess I probably should. Not exactly looking forward to sitting through a hundred Matlock reruns with the Olds, though. Any chance I could talk you guys into having a smoothie with me first? Claire loves smoothies, but I'm sure you know that, Nora. Is there a good coffee shop nearby?"

"Caseo's?" Claire and I turn to each other and say simultaneously. She gazes at me fondly, and then looks back at him. "It's a few blocks away. Have you got a car?"

"Not yet. I Ubered over from the Olds..." He draws a breath and glances at me. My cue, I guess.

I gesture to my Suzuki, one of the last cars remaining in the parking lot. And a few seconds later we're on our way.

CHAPTER FOURTEEN

Claire

Ethan tucks his legs into the Suzuki's cramped back seat. With his chin resting awkwardly atop his knees, he assures Nora he's completely comfortable. He even sounds like he means it because he doesn't want to be rude any more than I do. I know this because we've talked about how being gracious is important.

We head down UAA Drive past the turnoff for Goose Lake Park. Ethan points out buildings, stores he remembers when he lived here as a kid, a small sculpture that looks like a tilted wineglass.

"I don't want to intrude on your time together. I really appreciate you guys letting me hang with you today," he says as Nora expertly spins the wheel into the back parking lot at Caseo's, Anchorage's number one gay-friendly coffeeshop.

She shuts off the engine, glancing at him in the rearview mirror. "No problem. We're happy to have you along. I can't imagine how hard it would be to be the new person in an unfamiliar school. Especially after the semester's started. If you'd like, you can sit with us at lunch and if the Sinclairs don't live too far away, I'll drive you to school until you can get a car or find somebody to carpool with."

I squeeze her knee in silent thanks. She's doing this for me because Ethan's my friend. He's a guy who means well, but doesn't always make a good first impression.

I unclasp my seat belt to get out, thinking this is what it means to have a perfect life. My beautiful and talented girlfriend on one side of me, my longtime buddy on the other. For the last three years, Ethan's been like a brother to me. When my cat got run over by a car, it was Ethan who consoled me while I sat in the street, crying my eyes out. When my tears finally ceased, he directed me to go inside the house, while he cleaned up the mess that had once slept on my pillow, my kitten, Sampson, that I adored. If you don't know him, Ethan can come across as flippant. I'm telling you you'll never meet a kinder person.

"Okay. Love it," he says, taking in Caseo's motherboard ceiling and the flyover videos of Denali playing on the walls when we get inside. "Smoothies on me, folks. I insist. Are the strawberry scones any good? Let's have some of those. And sandwiches. The Olds are planning an elaborate dinner of cheese and crackers tonight. I'm going to need a snack."

"Just a vanilla smoothie for me," Nora calls after him as he makes his way to the counter for our drinks.

"Me, too," I say.

"Cheese and crackers for dinner?" she whispers when we take a seat at a table with a plastic chessboard in the center. Dinging sounds from the pinball machines in the arcade in back escape through the doorway behind me.

"I know," I say, eyeing Ethan talking to a girl with pink-tipped hair at the counter. "Makes you wonder if the Sinclairs are up to feeding a growing teenage boy."

Nora follows my gaze. "Are you worried about him?"

"Not really. He'll figure it out." Secretly, though, I have my doubts. I may have mentioned that Ethan can be a handful. Getting out of bed each morning can consume every ounce of his energy. I doubt the Sinclairs have any idea what's in store for them.

Nora picks up a black pawn and rolls it between her fingers, before replacing it in a corner of the chessboard. "Speaking of wondering…"

"What?" I sit forward so I can touch her wrist.

She hesitates. "Oh, never mind. It's not important."

"It is if you say it is."

"It's just that I never heard of an Anchorage-Juneau student exchange program."

"Well, I'm sure there is one if Ethan's part of it."

"Yeah. Of course there is. Of course. Only, I got the feeling from things you've said that he struggles in school? I mean, wouldn't the most successful students be the ones invited to participate?"

I don't like what she's implying. My neck heats with irritation. "Oh, so only the best get opportunities? Is that it? How about those who deserve second chances, the students who don't come from good homes, kids who don't make good grades. Shouldn't they be allowed to make something of themselves?"

"Claire." She eyes me, crestfallen. "I'm sorry I mentioned it. I need to keep my mouth shut. Let's don't fight."

"I don't want to either." I nod, aiming for a more conciliatory expression. "And I get that you were put off when he called you sis. But he doesn't know your history, I swear. That's just his way of making a joke after I kept saying you guys look alike. Give him a chance, and I promise you'll come to love him as much as I do."

"No problem." Nora shrugs.

I'm debating whether we should discuss it further when Ethan slips up behind me, taps my right shoulder, and then moves to the other so I'll look the wrong way. "Girl at the counter? Here's the scoop. Her name's Karen. She's a senior at Bartlett. And drum roll, please"—I tap the table with the sides of my fingers obligingly—"She gave me her number."

"Good for you," I say.

"Are you going to call her?" Nora asks.

"Sure. Maybe not right away because I want to spend time with you two, but I will in a day or so. Cool place, did I already say that? Great suggestion. Karen says she'll bring our food and drinks in five minutes or everything's on the house. How awesome is that? Hey, Clarice. That reminds me, although I don't know why it should. Did you notice my new Derbies?"

"I did," I say, wishing for the hundredth time he wouldn't call me that. "Very chic."

"I know, right?" He props a foot on the table, showing off a brown leather Porter City Derby sneaker. "These babies retail for three hundred bucks. How's that for bobo? I got a pair for you, but then I went off and left them back in Juneau. What the heck was I thinking? Guess I wasn't. I'll ask Riley to send them. I'll ask if he can get you a pair too, Nora the Explorer."

Nora stiffens and her eyes go wide. She looks about as lost as I've ever seen her. "Derbies? Riley? Three hundred dollars?"

"It's the way they're stitched," Ethan starts to explain.

I place a hand on the table to slow him down because this is what I do for Ethan. Translate him for others when they can't keep up with his frantic pace. I turn to Nora. "Riley—Riley Crew, that is—is Ethan's stepdad. He's an entrepreneur of sorts. He finds stuff and sells it. Ethan works for him."

She still looks lost. Karen, with the pink-tipped hair, brings our tray of food and drinks. She sets it on the table. Ethan gestures to an empty chair, inviting her to join us.

"Thanks, but I can't. Monica would skin me alive." She giggles, covering her mouth with bitten nails. "It's Ethan, right? Just wanted to make sure I caught your name. Anyhow, you've got my number. I'd love to see you again."

"Me, too." He waves as she departs, and then turns back to us. "Cute, right?"

I see Nora's lips forming the word "adorable." She bites it back. "I'm sorry, I still don't understand. Your stepfather *finds* merchandise, like your shoes?"

"Yeah. Only Claire's making it sound more respectable than it really is. Dude's a dumpster diver. You've heard of that? At night when stores are closed, he sneaks out back to pick through merch they throw away. He only takes the good stuff. He's got an eye for it. Electronics. Linens. High-end shoes and clothes. You name it. Once he found an electric fireplace in mint condition. It's the kind of stuff store managers are too lazy to send back to wherever they got them in the first place. Anyway, he brings it home to Alice—she's my mom—she figures a price and lists it, like on Marketplace or eBay, whichever site fits best. eBay for the spendy stuff. Marketplace for the smaller stuff. I box and mail, for which they pay me and sometimes give me extras, like the shoes."

"I see." Nora rotates her smoothie on the napkin while playing with her straw. "And that's how your parents earn a living?"

I frown. Why does she have to sound so disapproving? Just because her father was an attorney, that makes him better? People like Riley don't always have the means to go to law school. I remember being baffled the first time I heard Ethan talk about the family business. I hope I didn't sound like her. Granted, it's not the kind of work I'd want to do, but it's not illegal.

Instead of addressing Nora's tone because that's something to discuss in private, I turn to Ethan. "You don't have to give me shoes. I have plenty."

What I'm really trying to say is there's no need to buy my affection. I give it freely because I love him.

"I know that, Claire Bear. But I want to." He takes a huge bite of a sandwich, talking with his mouth full of what looks like chicken salad. "And yes, Nora Lee. Get it, like Sara Lee desserts?" Nora barely hides a snort that he misses. "That's how my folks make money. Dumpster diving. It's kinda gross, I know. Thing is, they've tried plenty of other businesses that haven't worked. Gift cards. Magazine subscription upsells. You name it. This one's their best so far. Now, please don't say you wouldn't like new shoes? I promise they'll be clean." To his credit, his eyes don't stray to the old, worn Vans she's got tucked neatly under the table.

Nora sips her smoothie, likely stalling. "It's really sweet of you to offer. But I wouldn't feel right taking money out of your parents' pockets."

"And if I just gave you new shoes anyway?"

"Well, then maybe. But can we get to know each other a little better first?"

I cut in as Ethan swallows, "Sounds like a solid plan to me."

They both nod. Ethan finishes off his sandwich with a happy smile. He wants to do this for her and for me.

Nora, with an apologetic look, shrugs and takes my hand.

I can't stay mad at her for long. I'm crazy about her. It's not the introduction I'd have planned if I had a choice. But for the two slightly strange individuals I care about, it's not too horrible a start.

CHAPTER FIFTEEN

Nora

We bag up Ethan's scones and head out to my car. He directs me to a white, nondescript house not far from the park at the end of Claire's block. How convenient.

"See you in the morning," I say, pulling my seat forward to allow him to unwedge his legs from the back. He stands by my door, shaking them as if to make sure I know they fell asleep.

"And be out on the sidewalk ready to go at a quarter past seven because we're not waiting for you if you're late," Claire warns through the open passenger window.

I'll wait if we have to, but I'm glad she said it. I've never been late to school a day in my life, and I certainly don't want to start now.

"Your wish is my command, Clarice." Ethan bows. "So good to meet you, Nora the Explorer. Good things happen to those who believe, and I believe you and I will be best friends."

Ha. I pull away from the curb.

Ninety seconds later, I cut the engine in Claire's driveway. The house her dad's renting is unfurnished, but the owners keep the grass trimmed and watered, so it looks nice from the outside.

Inside, it has an open floor plan with two large living areas in front, a kitchen and dining room in back. Hardwood floors with massive, ornate baseboards lead to creamy textured walls and soaring ceilings. Claire sleeps on an inflatable mattress in one of four big bedrooms on the second story. She's still waiting for her bedroom set to be delivered from Juneau. The moving company says it may be a while.

We sit in the car for a second. She doesn't invite me in like she has the last few weeks. "So," she says eventually.

"So?"

"What did you think of Ethan?"

I try to frame my thoughts into words that won't sound harsh. "Energetic. Friendly?"

"Hmm. Energetic and friendly like a puppy? You say it like a question. I'm going to go out on a limb and guess that you don't like him."

Am I that easy to read? "It's not that. I just met him. I need more time to form an opinion." What I really mean is that something about Ethan St. James seems off. Like he works too hard to impress people. And what's with the nicknames? Clarice? Claire Bear? Nora the Explorer? Do I seem like the type of person who'd be into that?

Claire gazes out the window as a man pushing a baby carriage and dragging a reluctant Doberman that clearly needs to squat walks by. "I don't get it. We hit it off in Juneau right away. Big time, wouldn't you say?"

Not at first. I'm a little surprised she's forgotten how we argued. "That's different. You're a girl. I like girls. You're also unbelievably sexy."

She disregards my flattery. "Meaning you don't like guys?"

"Well, not to date. I will say Ethan's fun and generous. And like you said, he has a good attitude. I'm sure I'll grow to appreciate him. Do you really still think we look alike?"

She sighs and puts her hand on my leg, massaging my upper thigh. It instantly distracts me. "I'm surprised neither of you can see it. The qualities I like about Ethan are some of the same I see in you."

"Such as?" I wish she'd go a little higher.

"He's talented and funny."

That stops me in my tracks. "Seriously? Nobody has ever called me funny."

"Then they don't know you. You have a sly sense of humor that I'm betting Amber never understood. You're also more optimistic than you're willing to let on. Ethan may seem a little over-the-top to people who don't know him, but what I like most about him is that he doesn't let life get him down. All that stuff about his parents' business? Most of the time they don't have enough money to pay the rent. Or at least until recently, I should say. Riley's often gone and Ethan hates his mother. Still, you'll never hear him say a bad word about her. Nora, I know having him show up without warning wasn't ideal, but I'm glad he's here. You get that, don't you?"

Now, I feel ashamed of myself. "Yes. Of course I do. You missed him. I can't imagine starting over in a new city and only knowing one or two people. It would be incredibly difficult, even for somebody who doesn't mind being alone, like me. I'm happy he's here for you, Claire. I'll make room for him, I promise. Starting tomorrow, we'll be a happy little threesome."

"Wait. A threesome like a throuple?" She drops her jaw, pretending to be appalled. "Let's don't go overboard. Lean over this way and kiss me. He's not going to get in the way of that now, is he?"

I love kissing her. In fact, I love everything about her. "He'd better not."

Since we both have a test coming up in history tomorrow, we make out for a couple of minutes, and then say goodbye.

When I get home, I wander around the kitchen until I can't help myself. I take out my phone and Google the address of the house where I dropped Ethan off. And guess what I find?

The people who own it aren't named Sinclair.

The next morning I'm still preoccupied with the results of my Google search. I find myself on autopilot, fixing Gran's bacon, eggs, and hash browns. The sink is full of dirty plates because it's pretty much impossible not to make a mess with multiple skillets, even when I wash each pan directly after using it.

I've picked up my phone a dozen times, thinking to text Claire and tell her what I learned. But what if I'm wrong? Isn't it possible Bob and Edna Sinclair are renting the house where Ethan had me drop him off? Or the one next door to it? I never actually saw him go inside. And anyway, if I'm right that something's off about his story, the smartest thing to do would be to let Claire figure it out for herself. I could tell by her reaction when we parted that I'd already slipped a few points in her estimation. She might not see my meddling as well-meaning. I go back and forth so many times I almost miss what Gran's saying.

"Honey, it's only for a few nights, four at most. I'll leave Thursday afternoon. Are you sure you'll be all right by yourself?"

"I'll be fine," I say, setting her plate on the table. "I might invite Claire to stay over. What would you think of that?"

I hold my breath as Gran picks up a fork and makes a stab at an egg cooked over easy. Yolk slides like slime into the bacon and potatoes, making my stomach queasy. Personally, I like my eggs cooked hard. Yolk broken, nothing runny whatsoever. I've had to overcome my urge to fix her meals the way I'd like them. She dabs her fork into the hash browns and lifts it to her mouth.

"Mmm. Delicious, sweetheart. You're so good to me. Claire staying over? I think it's an excellent idea. I may still ask one of the neighbors to check in on you from time to time. I'll be back Monday in time for your birthday. Just make sure Claire's father knows. You can always call me if you need anything."

I exhale and promise her I will. Once a year when Gran goes to see her oncology specialist in Seattle, she stays with an old college friend, a woman she roomed with years ago. They go out to eat, see a couple of shows, and shop. The last two years I've gone with her, missing school, which I hate. I've been begging her to let me stay by myself. This will be a first. Inside, I'm jumping with joy especially since she's okay with Claire staying with me. We'll have an entire weekend alone together… unless you-know-who interferes.

Fifteen minutes later, I find Ethan waiting out on the front walk as promised. I have to bite my lip from saying something stupid like asking if we'll ever get to meet the Sinclairs. When we get to school, he peels off for the office to get his schedule straightened out. It gives me a minute alone with Claire to share my good news.

"Do you think your dad will let you?"

"I'll ask. I may not tell him your grandmother will be out of town."

"Oh. But—" Her eyes twinkle with mischief, and I stop myself in the nick of time from being so annoyingly straight-laced. I need to get over that. "What he doesn't know won't hurt him, right? Any chance he'd stop by to check on us or think to call her?" Gran and Mr. Tucker exchanged phone numbers the night we all went out to eat. Giving each other their numbers was my grandmother's suggestion, naturally.

"Stop by? Definitely not. He's way too busy. I don't think he'll call, either. He doesn't expect me to misbehave."

"Misbehave. There will be plenty of that going on." I bounce my eyebrows at her like a cartoon character on a kids' show as Ethan makes his way back from the office. Locker doors bang all around us as kids start heading for their morning classes.

Ethan rakes a hand through his hair. "Bad news, girlfriends. My classes are still effed up. How hard is it to get one schedule right?"

"I wouldn't think too hard." I gaze over his shoulder at the office where it looks like business as usual inside.

"I know, man. That's what I said. Did you know your school has like, two thousand students? Bay Charter had four hundred, so I guess I should cut Principal Foster some slack. She said it was something about old man Henderson not having room for another student in his second hour. I didn't follow the deets, other than I have to go back and wait while they sort things out. This could take some time, so you guys go on to first period without me. Hopefully, I'll see you around later. If not, how about we meet out front by that totem pole thingy after school? There's something I want to show you."

"What?" says Claire, looking curious.

"A secret, Clarice. You're just going to have to wait."

She opens her mouth, probably to say, "Fine," but I sneak in with, "What about lunch? You don't want to sit with us?"

Ethan grins. "Are you kidding? I wouldn't miss it. Apparently, you have two lunch periods. Which one is yours?"

"First."

"Ha. Doesn't that figure. Mine is second."

Yeah, I think. *It figures.*

"Anyhowser, after school? What do you say?"

"Sure." We nod.

"We'll keep an eye out for you in the halls," I add with a phony smile. Like I've said, I have a suspicious nature. I can't seem to help myself.

CHAPTER SIXTEEN

Claire

No matter how many times I pass Ethan's locker over the next few days there's never any sign of him. It annoys me to no end. Ethan has to know teachers expect him to bring his textbooks to class with him. I'm worried he may be skipping his harder classes, putting his position in the exchange program in jeopardy. Back when we were freshmen at Bay Charter, he proudly proclaimed himself a school super slacker.

"Triple S. Triple Threat," he shouted, pumping his fist in the air like he was cheering on his favorite sports team. I wish education was as important to him as games and music.

He plays guitar (not as well as Nora plays piano), then again he never took formal lessons. He's entirely self-taught. The other afternoon when we visited the woods where he'd been storing his guitar—the something special he wanted to show us—he sat on an overturned tree and played a jazz song for Nora called "Moondance."

She knew it and loved it, immediately identifying the key as A minor, explaining to me it had been written by an artist named Van Morrison fifty years ago. The next day the three of us signed up for time in one of North's music rehearsal rooms after school. Ethan and Nora practiced the song together once to get a feel for one another's rhythm, then Ethan pulled up the lyrics on his phone and asked me to sing along. I did for a time, but honestly what I really wanted to do was sit back, listen, and enjoy spending time with my two favorite people.

Ethan says the "Olds," as he calls them, won't tolerate unnecessary noise in the house, which is why he keeps his guitar in a waterproof bag in the woods. They like TV, it seems, but have to turn it up way too loud because neither of them can hear a blessed thing. He's always hungry, and I hate the thought that they aren't feeding him enough, so I finally asked my father if he could stay with us.

Dad's reaction was predictable. "What the hell, Claire? Why is that boy here?"

He grumbled for most of the night, then relented the next day. Again, predictable. Dad has a soft spot for the downtrodden. He used to give pocket change to people living on the streets of Juneau even though the mayor went on TV and asked everyone not to.

I think Dad likes Ethan more than he wants to admit. The day my parents' divorce was finalized, Ethan showed up at our door with a hamburger pizza and a sack of buttered breadsticks. "I feel your pain, dude. Families can be grueling. I should know."

Dad rolled his eyes at me as soon as Ethan's back was turned. He still ate the pizza, and later, after Ethan left, I caught him smiling to himself.

It's also helped that Dad managed to get our furniture delivered and set up, so Ethan will have his own fully furnished bedroom right down the hall from mine. He had to work out the housing transfer with the administrators of his exchange program, but evidently when they saw our address it didn't turn out to be a problem. He's moving in after school today.

What I haven't told either Ethan or Nora is that I've ordered two DNA test kits from an online site. Last year, Dad and I spit into a couple of tubes on a lark and learned we have a third cousin who lives in Norway. She's married to a podiatrist. They have a nine-year-old son. We started following each other on Instagram, and she's invited me to visit and stay with her family when I graduate. What a hoot it would be to discover Nora and Ethan share a distant relative like that. Some great grandfather who staked a claim at the Yukon River or an aunt who's musical like they are.

I head to the cafeteria after a history test, noting Nora in an intense conversation with Amber by the water fountain between the cafeteria and gym. Nora bends to push her water bottle in the stream. Amber eyes her wolfishly, like she'd love to jump her bones. She's ignored me since I got here, pretending like we don't know each other. It pisses me off. I don't know why I was ever attracted to her. She's so basic with all her selfies, pouting into her camera phone.

"Just come over so we can hash it out. You owe me that much," she hisses to Nora as I approach.

"I don't owe you anything. You broke up with me, remember?"

My breath catches in my throat. I'm glad Nora feels no obligation to her ex, but if she's simply angry that Amber initiated the break up…I refuse to complete the thought.

"Hey, Amber. What's up?" I lift a hand to get her attention like we're pals. Nora raises her fingers to her mouth, covering a smirk.

"Why are you here?" Amber's nostrils flare at me.

I'd like to slap her face, but I smile. "Because it's lunchtime? Or is that a broader question? If you mean why am I here on earth, I'd guess I'd have to answer, 'Why are any of us here?' 'Why do we exist?'"

"Shut up."

"Well, that's harsh. Wait. Aren't we tight? Nora, help me out here. Am I misreading the situation? Is this…"

Amber walks away, leaving me in midsentence. Which is fine because I've run out of lame adlibs. I turn to Nora. "She wants you back."

Nora sighs. "It appears so, although I don't know why. We were never right together. I couldn't keep up with her."

"Because that's the way she made you feel. But can't you see that that's wrong? She destroyed your self-confidence by making you believe you're weird."

"I am weird."

"You're different. It's not the same thing. You're not sunny."

"Stormy. Got it. Let's go to lunch." She loops her hand around my arm, and we march into the cafeteria.

I still don't get why everyone can't see Nora for the beautiful person she is. Although maybe it's because it's not how she sees herself. I'm going to change that. When we get close to our table, I can feel a smile light my face because there sits Ethan with a grin that surely matches mine.

Nora draws a quick breath like a sniff that I pretend not to notice as he tosses his hair out of his warm, dark eyes. "Yo, besties." He rocks back. "Come on over. Let me introduce you to Ellie and Sam."

Ellie winks and Sam giggles as he throws his arms around their shoulders.

I sigh. *Why, Ethan? Why do you do this?*

CHAPTER SEVENTEEN

Nora

Several months after the incident at the mall I heard my parents whispering about me when they thought I couldn't hear them. "She's got to go out at some point," said Dad. "She's shy, Miriam. It'll be good for her." They were in the kitchen; I was in the broom closet as I'd taken to squeezing myself into small places that felt safe.

"But I could teach her. I was planning on it," Mom argued halfheartedly.

"I know, and you'd both probably love it. But then she wouldn't get outside. Listen, if you stay with her I'm sure it will be fine."

It was to be my first piano lesson. I wasn't keen on it because by then I was used to spending time alone. Nevertheless, Mom faithfully accompanied me to every lesson, usually waiting in the car outside, checking her phone and reading magazines while I ran scales on the upright on my teacher's glassed-in porch.

Mrs. Boyer was ancient. She lived two blocks from my elementary school and one street over from Nick's gravesite.

She had a severe, uncompromising expression, especially if I hadn't practiced, which was most of the time at first. I liked her anyway because she smelled like Snickerdoodle cookies hot out of the oven. While she demonstrated the proper way to hold one's wrists, cupping her hands like she was capturing a butterfly and lightly touching keys with her pale, thin finger pads, I studied the way the blue veins on the backs of her hands popped out. I wanted my hands to look like that when I was her age.

Each spring Mrs. Boyer held a recital on the Steinway grand in her formal parlor. Parents attended, perched on rented folding chairs, passing store-bought pastries and sipping punch in tiny cut-glass cups. Everyone wore their finest outfits. We were preparing for the day when we would play our pieces on a real stage with famous musicians who'd grown up just like us. Mrs. Boyer's equally elderly sister kept us, the students, on the porch while we took turns performing by ourselves. That first year, I was too nervous to eat or drink. I was scared to death I wouldn't find middle C on a piano I'd never played. When it came my turn, I burst into tears.

"I can't do it. I just can't! Please don't make me."

Mom came out to find me because by that time I'd planted myself behind a fake bamboo tree in the corner. She wasn't cross or disappointed. She pressed a cool palm to my cheek.

"Darling, no one's going to make you do anything. But wouldn't you like to see how it goes? Just do your best and who cares how it turns out. Whatever you decide, your dad and I will love you."

I wiped my eyes behind my glasses, steadied my sturdy little legs, marched out and found middle C on my first try. All in all, I acquitted myself pretty well, despite nerves that have never entirely left me. Playing with Ethan the last few days has brought back memories like that.

I never wanted to be a concert pianist, and I wasn't terribly upset when I couldn't fit music into my senior class schedule. All I really want is to play whenever I feel like it because that's when I experience an alternating warmth and chill that comes with creating glorious harmonies. They begin in my fingertips and travel up my arms, filling my soul with cosmic elation.

Ethan gets it because he loves music too. Although, if he bungles a note he doesn't let it get him down. He just tries harder the next time. We've played together every day since he got here, and I'm starting to understand why Claire likes him.

That said, seeing him cozy up to my lunch friends is alarming. Why is he here? I sat across from Ellie and Sam for a month before I really knew them.

"Are you skipping class?" Claire says, her tone turning cool, likely for my benefit.

"Got a sub." He shrugs. "Dude doesn't even know I walked out. Sit. Take a load off. When I asked around, people said this was your table. Have you met my friends?"

He introduces us to the girls we sit with every day, telling us about their classes and NHS responsibilities, making a big show of how much he's learned in the minute and a half since the lunch bell rang. Sam and Ellie are clearly flattered. Who wouldn't be by someone who actually listens and remembers what you say? He's like Claire, instantly making friends everywhere he goes.

When he finishes with, "Got a girlfriend now, Karen at Caseo's. Almost sorry about it after meeting you two. Tell you what, though, if that expires you're up next," I'm betting I'm the only one who finds it strange.

He excuses himself and heads to the à la carte line, giving Claire a chance to say, "He's new here. He can be a little much to take at times."

Ellie follows him with her eyes. "I don't mind. He's sweet."

"And funny," Sam adds, scooping up her sandwich.

Great, I mumble to myself. Am I really the only one who finds his behavior off?

The air in the cafeteria is thick with testosterone after last night's football game that ended with a narrow victory for North. I didn't see it, but I've been hearing about it in the halls all morning. Hockey and football players arm wrestle across a nearby table, trading jokes about which sport requires more physical strength. Dollar bills slip from one hand to the next when the quarterback bests our star hockey forward.

Out of the corner of my eye, I see Amber, a few seats down, throw a sketchy look at Claire. She motions to her phone. Mine pings in my lap.

"She brought her boyfriend to Anchorage. Where does that leave you?"

"*MYOB*," I text back.

"You're not concerned? Who the hell is he?"

I mute my cell and shove it firmly into a side pocket of the backpack at my feet, then take out my leftovers from last night's dinner, beef and broccoli casserole. I keep an eye on the unruly group of athletes lest they spill over to our table. When Amber gestures to her phone again, I ignore her.

Ethan returns from the line with a large chocolate milkshake and several snack-size bags of Cheetos. He tosses one to each of us at the end of the table. "Don't say I never gave you anything, girlfriends."

Claire catches hers with one hand and lobs it back. "Junk food, bro? Consider this your last crap meal. Have you called your parents with your change of address?"

Ethan huffs a dramatic breath. "Yes, *Mommy Dearest*. Alice said to give you a smack on the lips in thanks for looking out for me. Is that okay with you, Nora the Explorer?"

I clench my teeth. Yes, I like him better than I did a few days ago. Nevertheless, I don't find most of his jokes amusing and this is the kind of exchange I particularly dislike. Honestly, I'm not thrilled with the idea of him moving in with Claire either. Claire's father called Ethan a bad influence. I wonder if he's right. Just because he's here in the cafeteria doesn't mean he's attending classes.

Claire and Ethan talk about transferring his stuff to her house after school. When the bell rings, Amber makes a beeline for our end of the table to introduce herself to Ethan, following up with a decidedly pointed remark that she hasn't seen him around before.

"Well, I've seen you." He winks. "The infamous Amber Abbott, Nora's ex."

"Not for long," she slips in slyly, letting her heavy-lidded gaze drag up and down my body. Oh, please.

He replies with, "Better give it up, sweet thing. You don't stand a chance against my Claire Bear."

"Claire what?" She scoffs. "What are you, seven? You have no idea what you're talking about."

For a split-second Ethan's eyes harden into something unrecognizable, then he releases a chuckle and holds his palms out as if weighing pros and cons. "Let me just say I'm putting my money on Claire because seeing you…I'm thinking Nora has better taste."

Butterflies take flight in my stomach. Amber blinks in shock. She's not used to being dissed. She clicks her tongue as if she's got a bad taste in her mouth and says slowly, "Ethan St. James. You know, I believe I have heard your name. And I'm certainly going to remember it now."

"Please do. Bye-bye now," he sing-songs as she walks away.

Ellie's and Sam's eyes finally stop bouncing back and forth. They pick up their trash, mutter something about NHS, and scoot out fast. Ethan says he has to get to class, which leaves Claire and me alone at our table. The cafeteria is clearing out, with football and hockey players fake-punching each others' shoulders as they leave.

"Well," I say. "That was interesting."

Claire stares after Ethan, flustered. "He's very protective of me."

"Yeah. I noticed."

Wolverines, I recall, are solitary animals. They're clever and playful, about the size of domestic cats. What a lot of people don't understand is how dangerous they become when hungry or protecting their young. They can kill a full-grown black bear.

I think of the feral look that slipped in and out of Ethan's eyes. Did I just witness the human equivalent? I think of a line from a movie. What was it?

Something about them not making good pets.

CHAPTER EIGHTEEN

Claire

Ethan drags his guitar and suitcase through the front door after school and drops them on the marble floor of our house.

He looks around. "Dang, girl. Dis place is da bomb. It's even bigger than your last house. Who'd your dad have to kill to score this crib?"

"Don't say that. It makes you sound deranged." I cuff his arm with fond irritation before directing him to the shower on the second floor. It's all I can do not to wrinkle my nose because, frankly, he smells like cheap cologne covering up some very ripe B.O. Which I tell him.

He lifts his arm and takes a whiff. "I don't know what you're talking about. Smells pretty good to me." Then he clomps upstairs with his things.

"Don't kid yourself. Use soap. Plenty of soap," I call after him, following his lissome figure with my eyes. Ethan's an attractive guy, and not just to me, his friend. Straight girls like Sam and Ellie see it too.

I spent most of the afternoon thinking about how he went after Amber to defend me. In Nora's circle that counts as an outright challenge, and although I'm glad he cares about me, it wasn't necessary. I don't need a guy to look after me, and more importantly, I'm not sure it was a good idea. Amber carries weight at North. People tend to listen when she talks. I don't need Ethan getting into trouble for my sake, not when he just got here.

"Towels in the little closet halfway down the hall?" He leans over the balcony a little too far for my comfort.

"Yep. Help yourself to whatever you need. But if you decide to shave, don't leave hair in the sink."

He salutes. "Clean up after myself. Got it, Sarge."

Sarge. Better than Clarice or Claire Bear. I don't mind nicknames once in a while but Ethan goes overboard. Clarice. Claire Bear. And occasionally Clairy Toons. I have no idea how he came up with that one. Each time he calls Nora "Nora the Explorer" I see a flicker of annoyance cross her face. He doesn't understand that she's not used to that kind of casual intimacy. I may have to have a talk with him about it later.

Dad's going to be working late again tonight, and I don't feel like fixing a big meal, so I call a local Mexican restaurant and place an order for the beef enchilada plate. "How many?" says a guy with an unexpected British accent on the other end.

"Three—no better make it four." One for Nora, one for me, two for Ethan with his enormous appetite. "And maybe add those doughy things with honey?"

"Sopapillas, love. You've got it." He names the price. I read him Dad's credit card number, adding a healthy tip because I'm my father's daughter and giving memorable tips is what we do. I ring off just as Nora sticks her head in the front door that Ethan left wide open.

I slide the DNA kits that arrived today on top of the microwave and go out to the hall to meet her. "How's Gran?" I ask because Nora had to stop by her house after our afternoon music session to drop off a travel shoe bag her grandmother wanted for her Seattle trip.

Nora greets me with a kiss. "I think I understand where my OCD comes from. Gran has packed and unpacked three times. She doesn't leave town till Thursday night."

I lead her to the living room couch. "She's well prepared. Can't fault her for that. Ethan's upstairs in the shower, so we have a couple of minutes to ourselves."

"Ah." She sighs, dropping her head on my shoulder. "More perfect words have never been spoken." She snuggles up against me, and for more than a minute I forget what I was about to say. The couch is extra wide and long, a one-of-a-kind special purchase from a store down south and shipped by freight truck to Alaska a couple of years ago. It smells of fish and salt water now, looking worse for wear after a journey across the Gulf of Alaska on an open ferry. I still love it. I used to fall asleep on it, trying to wait up for Dad when he pulled all-nighters back in Juneau.

"Actually," I say, getting serious and smoothing my hair with a hand. "There's something I wanted to talk to you about before Ethan joins us."

"Okay." She pulls away, her face taking on a guarded look.

"You may have noticed he can be a bit naïve when it comes to interacting with others. And because he's new to North, he doesn't understand that Amber can make trouble for him with his classes."

"You know about that?" Nora's cautious expression gives way to relief.

"Know about what?"

"Nothing. I interrupted. Sorry. About his classes?" She folds her hands in her lap.

"I'm worried he may be skipping them. I've been by his locker and he's never there, which tells me he's either not taking his books to class or he's not going at all. What I'm saying is that when something gets too hard, Ethan's first inclination is to quit. And if Amber decides to make trouble for him before he has a chance to find his footing, it could put his position in the exchange program at risk."

"I see. And you want me to ask her to leave him alone?"

I eye her with surprise. "No! Gosh, no. I don't want you to have anything to do with Amber. I'm just hoping you can help me persuade him to take school more seriously. He respects you, you know that. If we work together, like maybe the three of us do our homework together, maybe he'll start to see it's worth the extra effort."

"Oh."

There's obviously something she's not saying. I'm pretty sure Ethan's growing on her, but she probably doesn't want him cutting into our time together. I don't either, but I don't know what else to do. "I would never ask you to intervene with Amber on my behalf. Ethan's either. You get that, don't you?"

"Sure. Of course." She doesn't sound convinced.

"So, all I'm asking is that you help me provide a good example for him. Alice has some college, I think, but Riley barely finished high school before enlisting. They're making money now, but what kind of life would Ethan have spending his evenings going through other people's trash—"

"I get it, Claire! You don't have to keep repeating it!" Nora interrupts abruptly.

This isn't going the way I want. I sit back, wishing I hadn't mentioned it.

Ethan trots downstairs barefoot, toting a big black Hefty trash sack. He's shaved and combed his wet dark hair off his forehead. "Do you mind sticking this in the washing machine for me?" He holds out the sack.

"Not at all." I get up and start for the laundry room behind the kitchen at the back of the house.

Nora says, "The Sinclairs wouldn't let you do your laundry at their house?"

He shrugs and shakes his head. "They didn't want to pay for extra water. Can you believe it? How those two raised kids with that kind of attitude, I'll never know. They told me to use a laundromat. Thanks, Clairy Toons. I owe you."

I toss in a pod after he dumps his clothes in the machine. Then he rubs his hands together like he's warming them before a fire. "I'm hungry, girlfriends. What time's dinner?"

CHAPTER NINETEEN

Nora

No, I don't believe it. A laundromat, seriously? But what am I going to say? *Hey, bud, Amber told me you're not enrolled at North, and I think you've been living in the woods because the Olds you're always going on about don't exist?*

Again, I could be wrong. Amber could very well have been lying when she texted that a friend who works as an office aide looked up Ethan's schedule and discovered there wasn't one. That there's no Ethan St. James enrolled at North.

When I stopped by the house to drop off Gran's new shoe bag I spent an extra minute looking up Juneau-Anchorage exchange programs. Just because I couldn't find a record of any doesn't mean there isn't one, I keep telling myself.

Driving to Claire's house, I spent some time pondering my ex-girlfriend's motive for texting me rather than notifying the school of an unauthorized student in the cafeteria. Doing it would have brought security down on Ethan immediately. She's obviously working to drive a wedge between me and Claire. I have to wonder if part of it is because back in Juneau she was attracted to Claire and Claire chose me over her. There was also the whole appendicitis thing that upset the balance of our relationship. I don't know...Perhaps she sees me as her savior, or in some warped way thinks she owes me another chance.

If I'm honest with myself, though, I also have to consider that there might be something else going on that has more to do with Amber than me. For months, I showered her with attention, getting only scraps in return. Once my adoration faded, she wanted me again—her hopeless little gopher willing to do anything she asked. I was the one she could make fun of, as if that made her better than me.

Whatever the case, I don't need it. I love Claire, and I like Ethan well enough. Neither has ever said a word to hurt my feelings. I'm not keen on our trio dynamics, but if I'm right about him, Claire will either figure it out on her own, or someone else will expose him.

Dinner arrives in four cardboard cartons smelling of ground beef and refried beans. My stomach rumbles. I haven't had a bite to eat since lunch. Claire doles out a carton to each of us and two for Ethan, who opens the refrigerator and starts to grab a beer.

"Don't!" she yelps.

"I'll pay for it." He glances over, looking hurt.

She sighs. "It's not that. Oh, here. I was going to wait until after dinner to show you this."

She slides off her stool and steps back to the microwave, tossing a package marked as a DNA test kit between us. "The instructions say you shouldn't drink, smoke, or chew gum thirty minutes before you take the test. Come to think of it, you probably shouldn't eat first either, so I guess we need to finish dinner and wait anyway."

Ethan eyes the kit, uncomprehendingly. "You want to see if Nora and I are related?"

"Well, yeah. I thought it would be fun."

"Huh. Fun. Shouldn't there be two kits?"

"There are. It's a double pack." She removes the cellophane wrapper to show us. "We can do a rush and find out the results in a day or two. What do you say?"

She goes on about taking the test with her father and discovering a distant cousin in Norway and how it will settle any doubts we might have about each other if we learn we're related. Finding out Ethan is my long-lost cousin twice removed isn't going to alleviate the kind of uncertainties I have, but I don't see the harm.

"We both like music." Ethan returns to the table, picking up a test.

I shrug. "I don't mind, if you don't."

He squints to read the label and despite myself I start to feel excited. Is it possible he's farsighted too?

"Honestly, Nora Lee, I would be thrilled to learn I'm related to you. Even if it's only distantly. You're gorgeous and awesome, just like me. Shall we?"

I don't know about all that, but I shrug again and say, "We shall."

We hurry to finish dinner, and then have to sit and wait. Claire prepares the kits, which basically involve a plastic tube for each of us where we'll spit and a blue vial that screws on top. She takes another minute to register us to receive the results, putting in her address so they'll come back at the same time. Meanwhile, Ethan and I play the silly match game she found online last summer.

"Red or blue?" I say.

"Purple." It's silly, but I have to smile because he's figured out a combination that can work for both of us.

"Chicken or pork?"

"Fish," he answers right away. "Did you ever see that movie where nearly everybody on the plane gets food poisoning? A lady says, 'We had a choice of steak or fish.' And the guy says, 'Yeah, I remember. I had lasagna.'"

Claire is laughing so hard she almost drops a kit.

I wave a hand. "One more. Sun or rain? No, wait. I already know what you're going to answer—snow."

Ethan does a fake eye roll. "Please don't second guess me, Nora the Explorer. I was going to say tornadoes!"

Claire checks her watch and places a tube in front of each of us. "It's time."

Filling them isn't a speedy process. I spit until my mouth runs dry, then we add the solution to the top and shake for five seconds before packing them back up in the box.

"Are you nervous?" Ethan asks me.

"Not at all. What's the worst that can happen? I find out I'm a horse and you're a donkey?"

"I was thinking more along the lines that we're both aliens from Mars sent to spy on unsuspecting humans."

"That must be me," says Claire. "Come on, guys. Let's take this to the UPS office. I'll overnight it." She links arms with both of us, and we head out to my car.

Ethan and I wait outside the UPS store on Dimond while Claire takes the boxes inside. He leans against the car facing me with his feet crossed at the ankles in his ridiculously expensive shoes. "Seriously, Nora. Will you be upset if we do share blood?"

It seems like kind of a strange question. Why would I be? I know who I am. I'm not going to start skipping school or raiding dumpsters if Ethan St. James and I have a distant relative in common. It might be fun. I haven't told him about Nick, but I have no reason for withholding it. I'll share the story later. "Absolutely not," I say. "How about you?"

"Like I said, I'll be honored." He holds out a hand the way Claire did back at Marco's last spring in Juneau when we finally decided to be honest and tell each other how we felt.

We shake, and I think Gran is going to get such a kick out of this.

I'm wrong about all of it, but I won't know that for a while.

CHAPTER TWENTY

Claire

Nora and I went back and forth over inviting Ethan to stay at her house while her grandmother was out of town. I wanted to be alone with her, but I felt guilty leaving him by himself at my house.

"He can sleep on Gran's couch if you want to ask him," she offered kindly.

I'm not normally wishy-washy, but the situation was unique. Ethan had just moved into my house, and here I was leaving him to fend for himself. He probably won't have my father for company either. Dad's likely working late again.

Ethan ended up solving the problem for us when he decided to take Karen bowling. That night, Nora and I rushed through our homework and spent the rest of the evening watching movies nestled together.

"You pick one, and I'll pick the next," she suggested.

I chose a romantic comedy about a couple of millennials who lived on opposite coasts. Him, a flight attendant for a major airline. Her, a large animal vet. Every time he flew out to see her, she was out on call. She'd come back in time to wave as he boarded his next flight. It was funnier than it probably sounds, and of course in the end everything worked out fine.

Nora chose a thriller about a group of badass women spelunking for missing treasure. A society of malicious cave dwellers picked them off one by one until there were only two left. I thought they'd both get out, but at the last second a cave dweller grabbed one by the ankle and pulled her back. It was disappointing after investing an hour and a half of fright, but I loved sitting close to Nora and squealing each time a shadow advanced across the screen. Nora kept an arm around me and told me when it was safe to open my eyes and watch.

We were up late and didn't get much sleep, tangling ourselves in the sheets of her narrow bed and exploring one another's bodies. I awoke with a smile, puffy lips, and her warm arm thrown casually across my back. My energy was delightfully spent. And still I wanted more.

Ethan's pacing the front steps when we arrive to pick him up for school the following morning. "How was your date?" Nora asks as he comes running out to the car.

"Great. Fine. We didn't go bowling. Never mind that. They're here." He's so excited his voice squeaks.

We don't have to ask what he means because it's what the three of us have been waiting for. Proof that Nora and Ethan either do or don't share a few threads of DNA.

She parks the car facing into the cul-de-sac and we get out. It's seven o'clock and my neighbor next door is mowing again, making broad checked patterns in his yard. "You didn't open it?" Nora asks, following Ethan as he trots inside the house.

"Of course not. I've been waiting for you."

I'm bouncing on my toes in anticipation. "Is Dad here?"

"I haven't seen him. I don't think he came home last night."

Ethan picks up two envelopes from the kitchen island, one addressed to him, the other to Nora, both with my address. "I want to go on record as saying it's my belief we're related to Senator Roth. Here's the proof. Nora and I are her grandkids. You're her maid's illegitimate daughter, Clarice."

"What? Why do I have to be the maid's kid? Maybe Senator Roth had a love child and gave me up for adoption. Or we're triplets. We basically look alike."

Nora bobs her head in agreement. "If you mean we all have arms, legs, eyes, and ears, you're absolutely right. We're mirror images of one another."

"And noses. Don't forget we all have noses. Does anyone want donuts or coffee? I could make a coffeecake," Ethan adds to our rambling conversation with an unmanly giggle.

We're making stupid jokes and stalling for the big moment. We're enjoying the anticipation. Sharing sixteen percent or more could make Ethan and Nora cousins. Twelve and a half might mean they have a great-aunt or uncle in common. A random thought passes through my head. Maybe I'll invite Nora to go to Norway with me and meet my cousin. Why not? I think I will.

She hands me her envelope and says, "Will you do the honors? I guess I am a little nervous after all."

"Of course." I carefully tear off one end of the envelope and tease the paper out. Ethan slides an index finger under the seal of his and rips it open. We press the creases with our thumbnails and lay them side by side on the kitchen counter.

For a long moment, Ethan, Nora, and I stare at identical results. The only thing different is the names. Ethan St. James on one. Nora Thomas on the other. Nora takes off her glasses and polishes them with the hem of her shirt. "This can't be right."

I swallow the saliva building in the back of my throat. I pick up both sheets and turn them over, my eyes skimming the ethnicity charts about Russian and Mediterranean descent without taking in the details because I can't get past the front side. "It's the same test Dad and I took, and it was right. We share fifty percent."

Ethan scratches the back of his neck, clearly perplexed. "But that's what this says. Fifty percent. Pretty sure you're not my mother, Nora."

"And you're definitely not my father," she muses, examining the numbers for herself.

Ethan picks up his paper. "Okay. So, what does it mean? Fifty percent. That's a lot, right? Like half siblings?"

"Full siblings. It means you're my brother. But like I said, it can't be right. He…my brother…" Nora's words drop off.

"You have a brother?"

"He died right after he was born."

"Oh." The color drains from Ethan's face.

Nora's looking pale as well. She rubs her hands as if she can't decide what to do with them. I lead them both into the living room, spying a crumpled bag of corn chips, seven empty beer bottles, and the butt of a joint under our imported inlaid coffee table. In my head, I'm thinking I need to clean this up before Dad gets home. My voice is saying something else. "Nora's twin was a still birth."

"Not quite. Nick…Nicholas was his name, he took a single breath, then passed." Nora untwines her long fingers and turns to Ethan. "Ethan, what's your birthdate?"

"Monday."

This coming Monday?"

"Yeah, the thirtieth."

"No. Is it? But that's my birthday. Here's my driver's license. May I see yours?" She pulls hers out of her phone case and passes it over.

Ethan runs a hand across his jaw. "I don't have it."

"You don't—"

"It's upstairs in a dresser drawer."

I can feel my eyebrows draw together. Now is not the time for games. "Ethan. Go upstairs and get it, please."

He hesitates, then jogs up to his room.

"This is just too weird," I say. "It makes no sense."

Nora nods. "I don't know what to make of it."

When Ethan returns and hands her his driver's license, she holds it out, her arm seesawing as if she's having trouble reading it. "In what hospital were you born?"

"AC. Amicus Care."

"Here in Anchorage?" Her voice drops an octave.

"Right. You?"

"Same, but that would mean…Ethan, is this a joke? Because if it is, it isn't funny."

"I was going to say the same to you," he blurts, shifting from one foot to the other. "If you're messing with me—" He stops and turns his frustration on me. "Claire, you did this. It was your idea. You mailed the kits. Tell us why you did it."

"Me?" I'm startled by his anger. "I didn't do anything. I'm in the dark just like you are. I thought it would be fun to figure out if you shared a relative. That's all. You guys know I don't do pranks."

I'm not sure they believe me. Ethan clenches his jaw. Nora eyes me, bewildered.

She starts to stand. "We're late for school," she says, then sinks into the wrinkled cushions of the smelly couch. "I'm just…I don't…This isn't…" She keeps starting and stopping and finally lands on, "I'm calling Gran."

CHAPTER TWENTY-ONE

Nora

My fingers are shaking. I can barely hit Gran's name plugged into my phone. She picks up on the second ring.

"Hi, sweetie. Everything okay? I'm at the doctor's office, and I only have a minute. Can I call you back when I'm done?"

I can't find my voice. A strange guy named Ethan looms in front of me. A girl I barely know sits beside me. She's too close. Her proximity makes my skin itch. My pulse pounds in my ears. "We took a test. One of those things to find out where you come from—"

"I'm sorry, honey. Can you speak up? They've got the TV on. I'm sitting right beside it. Never mind. Hold on a second and I'll step into the hall."

I pull the phone from my ear and gaze at it in awe. How do they cram so much *stuff* into such a teeny tiny package the size of a sandwich? It's a computer. That's what it is—a computer.

Claire touches my wrist. "What did she say?"

"She's watching TV."

"What?"

"At the doctor's office."

"Do you want me to tell her?"

"Of course not. I can do it myself." Dazed, I hand Claire my phone.

"Hi, Gran. This is Claire…No, we haven't left yet. No. Late start. Teachers' meeting. Listen, Nora and Ethan took a DNA test. They're looking at the results right now. It says he's her brother. Ethan St. James. No, sorry. He's my friend. I thought I said that. She's right here." Claire holds out the computer sandwich to me. "She wants to talk to you."

A joint rests at my feet. An earthy, dried apple scent I failed to register when I came in wafts up. How did I miss it? Did Karen spend the night with Ethan?

Gran is speaking into my ear. "Nick," she says in a quaking voice.

"My brother. He died. I remember." I don't remember. Mom and Dad told me about it. My grandmother isn't making sense.

"Honey, listen to me. That's not what happened. Nick was kidnapped from the hospital. We only assumed he died after a couple of years went by without finding him. The police looked and looked for him. They thought it might have been an inside job. Someone on the AC staff, perhaps. Your parents offered a reward, but nothing came of it. In the end, they decided it was best not to tell you. I don't mean ever…They just wanted to wait until you were older. I'm sorry. I should have mentioned it myself. But this Ethan boy—how do you know him? Claire said he's a friend of hers. How did you meet?"

Claire takes over the phone again. "It's probably a mix-up. We really don't know anything yet." She glances up at Ethan, who's gone completely still. His face is as white as a sheet. "No. I don't think that would be a good idea. Why don't I call you back once we've figured a few things out. Yeah. This afternoon, I'll call."

She hangs up. When I don't accept the phone from her outstretched hand because I can't make myself, she sets it on the table. No one speaks. The white walls of her house make me dizzy. I worry I might throw up. Each time I tilt my head, bile rises in my throat.

Ethan slides to the floor against the wall across from us, propping his elbows on his bony knees. Claire says, "I'll be right back." We sit in silence.

She goes upstairs, comes back with her laptop and opens it on the coffee table. Then she steps into the kitchen and returns with two water bottles. Her sandals make smacking sounds against the hardwood floor. She hands a bottle to Ethan and sets the other by my hip. I down a couple of Xanax from my backpack and take a couple of sips of water.

Claire opens a browser, making little noises to herself.

After a minute, I close my eyes. None of this feels right. It doesn't make sense. Nick, my brother, is dead. I've visited his grave. My parents and I went once a year on my birthday. On *our* birthday. Mom and Dad used to talk about him. They always said how much they missed him.

After more time has passed—I don't know how much—I hear Claire talking on her phone. My eyes slit open.

"Hello. Hi," she says in an adultlike voice. "This is Claire Tucker's mother. Claire isn't feeling well today. She won't be at school." She punches off and hands me the phone.

I've never done this before, but I understand what she expects. I go to *Recents* and tap the school's number. I clear my throat and assume what I hope sounds like a creaky, older tone.

"Good morning. Hello. This is Nora Thomas's grandmother. She isn't feeling well. Oh, thank you for asking. Just a stomach bug, I think. I'm sure she'll be back on Monday."

Did I just do that? Did I just lie to a school secretary? Will I be struck by lightning?

I hang up and hold the phone out to Ethan, who hasn't moved from the wall. "Your turn."

He lifts his shoulders lethargically. "They won't miss me."

Claire glances up from her computer screen. "You don't know our attendance clerk. Believe me, they'll know if you aren't there."

He scratches his neck, his dark eyes wide but unreadable. "Believe me, they won't, Clarice. I'm not enrolled at your school."

She tilts her head. Her jaw drops in disbelief. "What are you talking about?"

"I'm saying I'm here under false pretenses. I'm not enrolled at North. There's no student exchange program. I made the whole thing up. I had to get away from Alice and I couldn't stand how pitiful I'd look showing up at your door again, begging to sleep on your floor. We had a fight. I stole some cash from Riley and took the first flight I could get to Anchorage."

"But the Sinclairs, the people you were staying with—"

"Don't exist. I was sleeping in the woods down the street. The Olds are a product of my imagination. I'm a fraud."

I don't feel the satisfaction I thought I would in learning I was right. Instead, I'm thinking that my brother's been sleeping in the woods. *My brother.* It's just not possible. Is it?

Ethan watches Claire's eyes go soft. "Don't feel sorry for me. I'm not up for it. I lied. Not the first time, right? And don't we have more important things to worry about?" He waves a hand at her laptop. "Are you looking for a phone number for the DNA kit company?"

"I'm looking for evidence of Nora's brother, Nick. You're both going to want to see this."

Ethan struggles to his feet and comes over, perching on the edge of the couch. She angles her screen so we can both see it.

The browser is open to an article in the *Alaska Daily* dated seventeen years ago. October first. "BABY KIDNAPPED" is the title. My face is numb. I fear I might be permanently paralyzed.

'*Baby Boy Thomas, born yesterday morning, was abducted from Amicus Care Hospital. The infant, weighing seven pounds four ounces, had been fed and was resting comfortably in the hospital's level one nursery of the maternity ward. Moments earlier, his twin sister had been taken to the parents, Mr. and Mrs. Joshua Thomas, at their request. An emergency phone call distracted the nurse in charge who reported there was no one on the line when she stepped out of the room to answer it. When she returned, Baby Boy Thomas was missing. A heavyset woman, approximately five foot two, one hundred sixty pounds, with shoulder-length black hair was seen entering the unit in hospital garb moments earlier. Helicopters circled above the medical complex on Unga Street while officers on the ground searched vehicles leaving the hospital's numerous exits and each floor, room-by-room. The airport, bus terminal, and taxicab companies throughout the city have been alerted. The kidnapper, who is believed to be between twenty-five and thirty-years-old, could have been wearing a wig, police said.'*

Ethan is the first to look away. He drops his head into his hands. "Alice."

Alice, his mother? *Breathe and count*, I tell myself. Find my safe spot. Everything I've ever known and believed is a lie. My parents. My poor, poor parents.

Claire sits forward on the couch. "You lived in Anchorage, Ethan. You told me so when we first met. When did you move to Juneau?"

"I—the summer before kindergarten. I'm going to kill her. I swear I'm going to kill her." He squeezes his left hand into a fist, then stretches his long fingers, his gaze riveted to his appendages as if counting to be sure everything's in place.

Claire pats his arm. She's good at offering comfort. Kind, I think, but not too kind. Gentle, but not overly sympathetic. The female officer who reported my parents' death to me three years ago was like that. She came to the door and offered me water. I wanted to scream and punch the wall but couldn't bring myself to do it in her presence.

"Don't say that, Ethan. You don't mean it," Claire murmurs. "Do you know, did Alice work at the hospital?"

"She ran a home daycare center. Four or five kids usually. Mostly my age."

"Do you remember their names?"

He shakes his head. "They came and went. The other kids and me weren't friends."

"You were young. It's understandable." Claire's hand comes to rest on his forearm. She turns to me. "How are you handling this?"

I'm stunned. I can't process any of it. Who's buried in the grave I thought was Nick's? "I'm fine," I say.

She lifts her other arm as if to hug me, then lowers it as I shrink into the roomy cushions of the couch. *Get a grip*, I tell myself. *Don't panic.*

Claire nods. "Okay. All right. You know, truthfully, we don't know anything yet. This could simply be a weird coincidence. What I propose is that we go to the hospital and check your birth records for ourselves."

"They won't let us. HIPAA regulations," I say dully.

"Normally true, but you're interested parties. You may have to fill out a form or two, but they can't deny you your own records."

She's probably right. And I don't want to sit here doing nothing. Without school, the day expands before me like a mountain trail begging to be explored. *My brother. Is it really possible I have a brother?*

My phone rings. It's Gran calling me back.

"Nora, honey. I'm finishing up here. I'll take the first flight out this afternoon. I should be home by bedtime. Will you be all right until I get home? Are you at school?"

"Yes. At school," I lie. "But don't come home, Gran. Claire and I are going to the football game tonight. You're not going to believe this…it was all a misunderstanding. I wasn't wearing my glasses and I misread the report. It said five percent, not fifty. Turns out, that makes us, like, not related at all."

She releases a small sigh of relief. "Honey, I'm so sorry I never told you the truth about your brother. You have to know your parents never gave up looking for him. Your father spent hundreds of thousands of dollars on private detectives who searched the country for him, following up on every lead they had, no matter how inconsequential it seemed. And your poor mother, I don't think she ever accepted it. When a boy turned up in Ohio, we thought we'd found him. He was older though. It wasn't just—"

"I've got to go, Gran. Sorry. The bell just rang, and I don't want to be late for my next class."

"Ding," Ethan murmurs.

"Oh, right. Yes, of course." She pauses. "Are you sure you don't want me to come right home?"

"I'm sure."

"We'll talk about it Sunday afternoon then. I won't stay for the cruise. Honestly, I wish you'd come with me to Seattle. You know there's a fun little vintage bookshop I only just discovered."

"Gran."

"Right. Sorry. I love you."

"I love you, too. I'll call you later. Oh, how was your physical? Does the doctor have your test results?" Ethan stomps his feet like a racehorse at a starting gate. No, I'm the horse. He's the donkey. Claire sits patiently beside me.

"Not yet. But he says I'm the picture of good health. Go on to your class, sweetheart. I'll talk to you after school."

We hang up. Thankfully, the Xanax is starting to kick in. I lift the corners of my lips to Claire and Ethan, hoping what I'm about to say will come off cheerful even though it's the opposite of what I'm feeling. "All right then. No worries. Let's head over to the hospital."

Neither replies.

CHAPTER TWENTY-TWO

Claire

Ethan's eyes are glued to his phone in the back seat, and Nora is eerily quiet. We head south on Minnesota Avenue. Four weeks ago I didn't know this road. Now I realize it's one of Anchorage's main arteries with moose fencing running along the sides on the northern end and open fields peppered with retail shops and housing developments farther south before you reach downtown. I watch the road awhile, then glance at Nora behind the wheel. I'm trying to imagine what she's feeling.

What would it be like to believe your twin brother's dead, and then suddenly learn he's not? To find out that he might well be a boy you met days ago?

Nora doesn't care a lot for Ethan. I suspect she only puts up with him because of me. When he admitted there was no student exchange program, she didn't look surprised. I caught her expression change and the short nod she gave afterward as if she'd been questioning his presence in Anchorage all along.

And Ethan, my best friend...I don't know what he's going through either. I understand why he wanted to get away from the toxic relationship with his mother. Things have always been difficult between them, more so recently after the vandalism incident this summer. It wasn't a big deal really. Ethan and a couple of his friends spray-painted a few swear words on the portable classroom behind our school. Alice, however, blew her lid and made him leave the house. Like she hasn't done a few things she's ashamed of? And now, to find out she may not be his mother after all? What would that be like?

I keep telling myself not to jump to conclusions. It's most likely a mistake. I've been running scenarios through my head of how supposedly scientific DNA results could have gotten confused. Is it possible Nora's and Ethan's spit was contaminated either here or at the lab where it was processed? Or that Nora's and Ethan's names went on other people's reports? There has to be a logical explanation, something that doesn't involve a seventeen-year old abduction. In science, it's called falsifiability when a conclusion doesn't support the hypothesis.

The hospital is an attractive three-story red brick building with a rounded front and a bank of windows on every floor. Nora parks in one of the visitors' parking lots not far from a revolving glass door. The sign above it, reads, "Administration."

She leans over me to dig through the glove box. "Alternate ID, just in case," she explains, coming up with her car registration and slipping it into the back of her phone case. "I just want you to know that I don't blame you for any of this." Her fingers brush the back of my hand.

I fight the urge to protest. *Blame me for what, Nora? I haven't done anything wrong.*

Ethan drops his phone into the breast pocket of his black silk shirt and inches out of the car. He follows us up the sidewalk to the door. "Let's find out if I should call you sis."

"Right." Nora stiffens. His tone is too cavalier.

An elderly security guard directs us to an office on the second floor. "Turn right when you get off the elevator. You'll find birth records at the end of the hall. They'll ask for your identification. A driver's license or social security card will do."

"How much does a job like yours pay?" Ethan asks with false joviality. I know him. He's clearly attempting to regain the emotional footing he's lost.

"Second floor," the unsmiling guard repeats.

"Jesus. What's with that guy? Is it a state secret?" Ethan complains when the elevator doors slide shut.

Neither of us answers. Nora stares at the lighted numbers beside the door. I turn my gaze to the carpeted floor, imagining a scene where happy parents learn their newborn son is missing. How their joy would give way to unfathomable panic. Disbelief first, then anger and grief. I've had occasion to wish I was born to different parents, especially after my mother divorced my dad. I hate that she broke up our family. This is worse. Much, much worse.

A woman with a blond shag cut and a name tag reading "Lori," listens to Nora's request and pushes a clipboard and a pen at each of them, then asks to see their identification. She checks something on her computer and disappears through a door behind her. A moment later, she returns with a single piece of paper: a copy of Nora's birth certificate.

"That will be three dollars, cash or credit. I'm sorry, young man." She hands Ethan back his driver's license. "Is it possible you were born at another hospital? People often confuse us with Providence, off Spirit Drive." She gestures to the right as if we can somehow see another hospital through the wall if we only look hard enough.

Ethan shakes his head, his dark hair obscuring his expression. "Look again."

She sucks in both her lips and punches more keys on her computer. "Sir, you're not in our system. I don't know what to tell you. Have you had a name change?"

"No."

"Then do your parents have different last names? Sometimes, people only register one name. Although…" She frowns and holds out her hand to take another look at Ethan's driver's license. She asks again for Nora's.

Nora, Ethan, and I glance at one another. This can't be good.

"I'm Nora Thomas," Nora blurts. "My twin brother was kidnapped from this hospital seventeen years ago. This is him!" She flaps a hand, knocking Ethan hard in the chest.

Lori pats the counter with polished nails. "I didn't work here seventeen years ago, but I remember seeing the story on the evening news. Such a tragedy. It's why all newborns' ankles are banded now. If the band is cut or the infant removed from the hospital without authorization a building-wide alarm goes off. I'm terribly sorry. Why don't I get a supervisor? Maybe she can help. Do you mind waiting a moment?"

She vanishes through the back door again. Nora and Ethan mutter simultaneously, "Why bother?" They eye each other suspiciously.

I feel like I should say something calm and encouraging, but I can't come up with anything that won't sound trite.

I'm still thinking there has to be a reasonable explanation. Maybe Alice did tell Ethan the wrong hospital. It's probably Providence, I tell myself, still desperately clinging to the notion that everything will work out like a happy rom-com in the end.

Strains of instrumental music echo down the hall. A child gets off the elevator and runs to a window, pressing dirty little fingers to the glass. A father's voice calls him back. Presently, a large Black woman returns with Lori. My heart sinks when she immediately starts offering apologies, saying there must be a muddle because they've recently switched to a new software system.

Ethan cuts her off. "Did a woman named Alice St. James work here seventeen years ago?"

Her uncertain smile reveals a gold front tooth. "I'm sorry, hon. I wish I could help, but employment records are confidential."

She really does look sorry, but Ethan isn't having it. "You're useless! You let babies get stolen, and you don't do anything about it. Christ, I'd like to come right over this counter and—"

I grab his forearm, giving it a good hard yank to stop him before he gets us thrown out. This woman is a cog. She doesn't deserve his anger.

"How about the nurse who was on duty at the time of the kidnapping? Can you at least tell us her name?" I plead. One look at her sympathetic face and I know that isn't going to happen. "Then, will you point us in the direction of anyone else who might have worked in the maternity ward?"

"I'm—"

Nora's eyes glisten. "Please don't say you're sorry again."

"No. No. I won't. But I also can't help you, I'm afraid. Have you tried contacting the police? If you have an attorney, he or she can likely get you a copy of the investigation report. Hospital records can be unsealed, you know. I'm just not in a position to do it." She gazes at Nora with obvious compassion.

"I understand." Nora's chin quivers as she nods.

The woman steals a glance at Lori, and then turns back to us. "You know, if you're hungry, the vending machines on the third floor of C wing aren't half bad. Nurse Edith Berg is usually around if you need change. She's been here forever. They all wear name tags, so she should be easy to find. Again…no, never mind. I won't say it. Good luck."

We thank her and head back down the hall to the elevator. "Vending machines? What's wrong with her?" Ethan scoffs.

Nora's eyes clear once the doors slide shut. "Oh, come on, Ethan. Don't you get it?" She points to the vertical row of elevator buttons and the designations beside them. "Third floor, C wing, is the maternity ward. Edith Berg? She's the one with answers."

CHAPTER TWENTY-THREE

Nora

Back at records, I made a point of wiping a hand across my eyes. I even honked into a tissue. I wasn't crying. I'm too frustrated by bureaucratic hospital nonsense for tears. Why can't people be straightforward? We're not asking for the combination to a bank vault. We want to know how someone allowed my brother to get kidnapped.

Claire gives me one of her *Are you okay?* looks. I tap her elbow with a finger to let her know I'm glad she's here. When we get off the elevator, Ethan starts toward a vending machine as if he really thinks we're here for candy, then hastens to catch up when he notices Claire and me making our way to the nurses' station. A middle-aged woman in light green scrubs sits behind a faux oak desk. I've got a story planned for getting her to locate Edith Berg for us, but it turns out I don't need it.

"I'm Edith Berg. How can I help you?" she says pleasantly when I ask if Nurse Berg is working today. I revise my estimate of her age, adding ten years, as I examine her more closely. She reminds me of my piano teacher, Mrs. Boyer. Same hands. Same beautiful translucent skin.

"Did you work here seventeen years ago when Baby Boy Thomas was kidnapped?" I ask, not sure how to start except to come right out and say it. I lack Claire's tact, her way of putting others at ease. Lucky for me, Nurse Berg doesn't seem to find the question strange.

"Yes, indeed." She stacks the keyboard under her computer and switches it off. "As a matter of fact, I was here that day although I'd taken a shift in the NICU, so I didn't see it happen."

It's a good start, better than I had reason to hope for. I take a breath, aware of Ethan's eyes darting to my face. "I'm Nora Thomas, Baby Boy Thomas's twin. And this may well be my brother Nicholas who was abducted the day after he was born."

"I see." Her voice is calm. She takes a long look at Ethan. "How interesting. I imagine there's a story behind that."

"There is, yes. Although it maybe not be as interesting as you suspect. What we'd like to know is if you remember a woman named Alice St. James working here at the time of the abduction."

At that, Edith Berg's expression turns cautious, her eyes pinching at the corners. "May I know why you're asking?"

Her tone stays pleasant, but her gaze shifts back to Ethan.

"Alice St. James claims to be his mother." I blink as Claire's fingers touch my wrist. I'm not sure why. A warning?

"She raised me," Ethan puts in quietly, then shuts his mouth. I'm glad he's letting me handle this and not threatening to jump the counter and hurt her.

"I see," Berg says again.

"Well, did she? Was she a nurse?" I lean in, not thinking to intimidate her as Ethan might, but because I wore the wrong shoes for hiking through a hospital. My school flats have no arch support.

Berg takes a mint from a jar below the counter. She unwraps it and sticks in her mouth. "I don't suppose there's any harm telling you that Alice St. James worked in housekeeping. She adored babies, so the maternity ward was her favorite place in the hospital. She spent quite a bit of time up here, often talking about how she wanted children but couldn't conceive. Something to do with her ovaries, she said, although the way

she put it didn't make a lot of sense. She'd been working here…
now, let me think…four or five weeks before the incident and
turned in her notice a week after, saying she couldn't stomach
the notion of an infant's disappearance. I remember she made
a big deal about how hospitals ought to be better guarded. You
know, she was quite popular with some. The staff threw her a
party when she left."

My heart flutters in my chest. Ethan blows a loud breath
beside me. "Forgive me for being blunt," I say. "It almost sounds
as if you didn't like Alice." Which isn't exactly true but I want to
keep Berg talking.

"Hmm. I wouldn't put that way. Although I'll admit I
didn't care much for the way she spoke of our security staff
who searched every inch of the hospital. Alice was thoughtful.
Considerate. She made an effort to get along with people."

"But?"

She hesitates. "Well, now, since I've started down this path
I might as well continue. She made too much of an effort, in
my opinion. No one is that agreeable all the time, offering to
take on extra shifts and running personal errands for doctors.
When I heard the description of the woman seen entering the
ward, short and heavyset, I went straight to my supervisor. In
my mind, the timing was fishy, what with the kidnapping and
her quitting so abruptly afterward. Not to mention, all her talk
of wanting a baby. Unfortunately, my supervisor didn't agree.
He reminded me that the mysterious woman had dark hair,
almost black. Alice was a blonde. I even talked to the police
about it a couple of days later, reminding them the newspaper
had mentioned she could've been wearing a wig. But nothing
ever came of it."

Berg sighs, helps herself to another mint and holds out the
jar. "So, you're little Nora and this"—she looks again at Ethan—
"is Baby Boy Thomas. You two look alike."

Claire straightens her shoulders. Ethan sticks his hands in
his pockets. It's a pretty satisfactory interview, I think. Except
my head feels heavy, no doubt thanks to my double dose of
Xanax back at the house.

"So, what now? Where do you go from here?" Nurse Berg glances at us questioningly when we decline her offer of a mint.

I wish I knew. "We probably need to reconnoiter and chat."

"Think about it and assess the situation." She nods. "I can understand that. Good luck."

"Thank you."

"Can I see the babies?" Ethan asks.

"Why?"

"No reason. Just to look, to see where I was born. Before… you know…"

I get it. I feel the pull as well.

Berg steps out from behind the counter. "All right. Come with me. You know, you two really do look alike."

"See. I told you," Claire whispers in my ear.

Not the time, I want to tell her. I can't though, because I'm having one of my delayed reactions. All at once, I'm dizzy and out of breath. *Is this guy beside me really my brother?*

I barely make it to the wall of windows. Claire steadies me with a hand on my back as we gaze at row upon row of bassinettes with newborns. Two elderly women sit in rocking chairs in the back. They hold babies swathed in blankets.

"They're volunteers," Berg explains.

"Can we go inside?" Ethan asks.

"I'm afraid not. These ladies have been cleared by security and trained on proper infant handling. You can stay out here however, and watch as long as you like. I go off duty at four."

We thank her and she returns to her desk. The babies look like dolls, most with bald heads and nondescript, blobby features. The one directly across from me has a tiny fist in her mouth.

After a while, Ethan takes out his phone.

"Jeez, buddy. We can leave if you're bored." Claire gives him an irritated look.

He doesn't look up. "I'm not. I'm texting Alice. She's flying in tonight. I didn't think you'd want her coming to your house so I suggested we meet at Caseo's. Will you guys go with me?"

It's then that it truly hits me. However hard this is for me, it's a hundred times worse for him. Obviously, my life has been turned upside down. On the other hand, I had two parents who fed me, dressed me, paid for my piano lessons, and took care of me for fourteen years. They made sure I got to school on time. They cared about my grades. They loved me. And yeah, it's awful they're gone now having never told me the truth, but I still have Gran who'll do everything in her power to protect me.

Ethan isn't nearly as lucky. He has a crazy lady who tore him from the family he should have had. He's got parents who taught him to sort through trash, but who couldn't care less if he went to school. They probably didn't know he lived in the woods in Anchorage for nearly a week before Claire's father took him in. It's possible they wouldn't have cared about that either.

I feel like I need to meet this Alice St. James. Not necessarily to give her a piece of my mind because I'm certain Ethan will do that. Rather to wrap my head around how all this went down.

"I'll go with you." My voice sounds creaky like Gran's. This time I'm not pretending.

Claire, my innocent girlfriend who unintentionally nudged a pebble off a cliff and started an avalanche, wraps an arm around Ethan's waist. "I'll go too," she says.

CHAPTER TWENTY-FOUR

Claire

All my thoughts of IVF gone awry, stolen eggs, stolen sperm, and erroneous DNA reports flew out the window the minute Edith Berg admitted knowing Ethan's mother.

Only Alice is not his mother. I have to keep telling myself that. She's a stranger who committed a terrible crime because she wanted a baby of her own. What kind of excuse is it for stealing someone else's child?

And poor Ethan. He never got the chance to know the kind of love most kids take for granted. I know what a manipulative bitch Alice St. James can be when she doesn't get her way. She can be as sweet as ice cream to folks she's conning, then scream at Ethan for no good reason. Like I said, poor Ethan. And poor Nora who's been without him all these years.

We head back to the house without a plan except to wait until Alice gets to Anchorage. I make sandwiches from our leftover enchilada dinners, and we sit on the couch to eat and watch a movie. My mind wanders. I can't follow the plot. Ethan goes upstairs for a while, which gives Nora and me a chance to talk.

"What's Alice like, I mean other than the stuff you've already told me?" she asks, smoothing a crumpled napkin on the coffee table in front of us.

I don't even have to think about my answer. "Crazy. Alternately mean and nice. Possibly bipolar." I read up on the disease in *Scientific American*, actually because of Alice. In manic phases, sufferers have an extraordinary amount of energy and tend to act impulsively. Other times, they're depressed, moody, listless. It's Alice to the letter.

Although, thinking about it now, I realize abducting a child must have taken quite a bit of planning. No way could it have been an impulsive, spur-of-the-moment act. It would have taken Alice weeks to ingratiate herself with the hospital staff while waiting for the right opportunity to present itself. Or, quite possibly, she created one by calling the nurse away from the nursery with a fake phone call, and then sneaking in and lifting a baby from its bassinette. What then? Hiding in a linen closet until the coast was clear? Whisking the infant out in a laundry basket hours later? Did she drug Ethan to keep him quiet? These thoughts whirl and spin through my mind like a blender, each worse than the one before.

When one movie ends and another starts, Nora sits forward on the couch and gazes around the living room restlessly. After a minute, she gets up and starts clearing away Ethan's trash. "You don't have to do that," I say, rising beside her.

"I want to. I need to. It's a symptom of my OCD, I guess. I can't stand a mess. It gets inside my head." She gives me an apologetic look and carries the empty beer bottles to the recycle bin in the garage and asks for a mop. Together, we clean the entire first floor of the house. Nora straightens items on pantry shelves and wipes down shelves inside the refrigerator, then stands on her tiptoes and dusts the top. I call a halt when she suggests scrubbing the inside of the oven.

"Pretty sure it's self-cleaning, and it's hardly been used. Come sit with me and tell me what you're feeling." I take her by the hand and lead her to the couch. I get a soulful look in return.

"My life is utter chaos. I have a brother I thought was dead and a beautiful, kind girlfriend I don't deserve."

"Don't say that, Nora. You deserve the best."

"Sure. Sure." Her eyes take in the TV fretfully. "It's not what I mean anyway. Do you ever think you're attracted to broken people?"

"Me?" I'd never thought about it like that. Nora and Ethan aren't broken, but they've definitely hit a bumpy road.

I kiss her cheek. "I prefer to look at it this way. If you're broken, then so am I because I care about you and I want to help. Let's review the things we have in common instead. Music, books, school, sexy girls." That wins me a tiny smile. "Why don't we wait and see how this plays out before we jump to the whys and wherefores of our relationship? Then, if we decide we aren't meant for each other, I'll throw myself at Amber and convince her to toss you aside." That earns me the full-on chuckle I've been hoping for. "Deal?" I hold out a hand.

"Deal." She shakes it warmly.

Dad calls a minute later. "Sorry I've been AWOL. I've found a great plot of land just this side of Potter's Marsh. The owner wasn't keen on selling it so I let him talk me into going hunting while we discussed it." Dad hates hunting, meaning it's got to be a pretty sweet piece of real estate if he's agreed to go.

"Stay as long as you need to. I'll spend another night at Nora's."

"Okay. Everything all right at your end?"

Not really. "Fine. Have fun, Dad."

"You, too. Be safe. And tell Ethan he'd better not leave a mess for me when I get home." He's only half-kidding.

"No messes. Got it. See you later."

No messes. No messes in the house, I should have added because what happened next I couldn't control.

At eight-fifteen, Ethan takes a shower and comes downstairs wiping his shiny dark hair with a towel he tosses on the kitchen counter. Nora discreetly folds it and sets it by the sink.

We get in the car and drive to Caseo's through a light mist that drips off trees and lampposts, creating a swirl of fog hanging low and gloomy on the streets. It's the perfect atmosphere for a horror movie. I feel like I should be keeping an eye out for malevolent cave dwellers who wish to drag us to the bowels of the earth.

Dark roast coffee scents swirl around us as we make our way to a table by the door to the arcade in back. Between the noise of machine beeps, honks, and roars, and a slam poetry session by a Goth girl who's coming very close to plagiarizing Alex Dang's *Times I've Been Mistaken for a Girl*, I can't really hear what anyone's saying until Karen comes over with a dishrag slung across one shoulder and her fists clenched on her hips.

"Dude," she hisses at Ethan. "You stood me up."

"Couldn't make it," he mutters, barely glancing up from his phone. He's playing a game. His thumbs race across the screen as if his life depends on winning.

"Then the least you could've done was texted. Not cool. Not cool at all."

"Whatever." He shrugs. "Can I get a double shot of espresso?"

She taps a foot. "Go up to the counter and order it yourself. And while you're there, go to hell."

She takes off. For once I don't have the energy to reproach Ethan for being impolite, but Nora says, "You stood her up? Why?"

"No reason. What's it to you?"

"Forget it."

We're all tense. I push back my chair. "I'll get the drinks. What does everybody want?"

"Just the espresso," Ethan mumbles.

"I'd like a smoothie." Nora wrinkles her upper lip, gazing at him like he's a mosquito in need of squashing. "I'll go with you."

The poetry girl takes a break, and loud music fills the café so it's still hard to hear much of anything. Nora presses her fingers to her ears and stands beside me wordlessly.

When we get back to the table, Ethan growls, "Forget the drinks. Alice is here. She's in the parking lot out back."

CHAPTER TWENTY-FIVE

Nora

I pivot to the counter to tell Karen to give our drinks to someone else so they won't go to waste, then scuttle out to the sidewalk and around the corner after Claire and Ethan.

I'm trying not to think too far ahead, but I can't imagine a scenario where this goes well because Ethan is obviously upset and Claire's told me about Alice's infamously bad temper. What will Ethan say? Will Alice admit what she's done? I may need another Xanax. The two I had this morning are wearing off.

A couple of employees in aprons and hairnets stand outside the back door taking drags off a shared cigarette. Two girls who look a little older than us are making out in the alley beside the sports memorabilia shop next door. A man getting in his car locks the doors with an unmistakable click. He checks his phone, his face in shadows but his silhouette illuminated through the mist by a dim streetlight overhead. The scent of fresh roast mixing with dumpster odors is sour and unpleasant.

Being me, I'm busy identifying different meat and rotting fruit smells as a middle-aged woman steps away from the wall.

She's got an apple figure, bleached blond hair with a reverse skunk stripe, and a snake tattoo encircling her neck. Plastic flip-flops trim her feet. A gray ribbed tank clings to the folds of her waist like a life preserver.

"Ethan, over here!" she calls out in a friendly tone, tucking her phone into the back pocket of her tie-dyed yoga pants. "I'm so glad you texted. I've been frantic with worry. You're a naughty boy running off to Anchorage without telling me. You're *so* grounded."

Her bright eyes slide over us. The streetlight hits her cheek with a sickly glow. "Hello, Claire. Good to see you again. What have you been up to?"

Claire nods politely, but doesn't get a chance to answer when the woman's sly gaze lands on me. "Oh! Hi, there. I don't believe we've met. I'm Alice, Ethan's mother."

She shifts forward as if to shake my hand. I draw back. That is *so* not happening, lady. I fight off a wave of dizziness.

Ethan steps between us, his spine rigid like a scarecrow. "Grounded? How exactly do you plan to do that, *Mother*? Send me to my room without my supper? Throw an ashtray at my head if I don't do exactly what you say? I know all about how you kidnapped me and made my real parents believe I was dead. Like I told you on the phone, I took a genetic test. I know who I am."

His jaw grinds as Alice takes a tentative step forward, like she wants to comfort him. To give him solace for the pain *she* caused. The irony would be rich if it weren't so tragic.

"Don't be silly, son. I don't know what you think you know. For seventeen long years I took care of you. I wiped your ass when you shit. I fed you soup when you got sick. Remember that time you rode your little trike into the street and I ran out of the house in my underwear to save you? We're a team, baby. Let's don't do this here. I'm staying with our old neighbor, Della Rhodes. You remember her, on Boniface and Camelot? That awful green single story with the crumbling roof? Why don't you come with me to her house, just the two of us, so I can explain."

"No. Fucking. Way," Ethan says succinctly.

"Don't you dare speak to me like that!" Her words sound funny, as if she thinks it's what a mother's supposed to say.

Neither has actually raised a voice, but something about their stance alerts the guy in the car. He rolls down a window. "Hey, everything all right here?"

Alice stomps a foot. "Mind your own damn business, asshole." He hastily withdraws his head and starts the engine. So much for our good Samaritan.

"Come on, baby. I can explain. Let's get out of here. Do you have a car? Della is really excited to see you. She didn't know you were in Anchorage either."

"Bullshit," Ethan snaps. "I'm not going anywhere with you. I just wanted to give you a chance to explain yourself before I go to the cops."

"No. Don't do that! No cops, you know that."

"I don't know anything. You've got three seconds to start explaining. I'm counting."

"Okay! Okay!" Alice fumbles with a cigarette from a crumpled pack that appears out of nowhere. "Listen, baby. I didn't want to say it in a text, but yeah, of course I worked at the hospital. The pay was shit. That's why I started daycare. That, and the horrible kidnapping. How could those people be so negligent? Maybe people don't care when it's not their child—" The cigarette drops unlit at her feet. She stoops to pick it up.

"Talk faster." Ethan glares.

Claire and I stay back. I steal a quick glance at her face. She looks as clueless as I am.

I feel like a voyeur to one of the strangest encounters I've ever witnessed. Is this really happening? I can't yet wrap my head around the notion that this has anything to do with me.

"You heard me. I said speed it up," Ethan repeats.

Alice throws her hands in the air as if she's the one who ought to feel put out. "I'm trying! Why don't you try being patient for once?" She flaps a hand at Claire. "That girl has put bad thoughts into your head. What does she know? Her and her bastard father staying out with his slutty girlfriends all night… What kind of role model is that for you?"

Claire's eyes pop.

"Two seconds." Ethan motions to a nonexistent wristwatch.

"Yeah, okay. Look, I get it! I'm not your biological mother, I admit that. But it isn't what you think. When you were barely three weeks old, long after I'd left my job at the hospital, a woman calling herself Oliver—Mrs. Olivia Oliver, in fact—left you in my care. Baby, she begged me to take you in. But only for the day, she promised. You were sick and underweight, running a fever, which frankly wasn't good for the other kiddies in my care. She seemed so desperate I just couldn't turn her away. Too softhearted, I am. People say it all the time."

Ethan huffs an impatient breath.

"And you know, this Mrs. Oliver was a bit of a Raggedy Ann herself. Bad teeth. Hair unwashed. I won't talk about her clothes. I didn't think much of it because I'm not one to judge. She told me she'd be back for you that night. But when six o'clock rolled 'round, and all the other kiddies had been picked up, she didn't show. Imagine that. She didn't show! I tried calling the number she gave me. It didn't work. The next day I hunted for her. And for a long time after that I looked. You gotta believe me. I had no idea you were Baby Boy Thomas, even if it's true, which I doubt. I mean, how could I know? After all, it had been three weeks, long after everyone stopped talking about him. Anyway, I decided to keep you and raise you as my own because that's how much I loved you. Ethan, baby, let's get out of here. Come on. I really don't like this place. It's creepy. This can't be a very good neighborhood."

She's right about that. A coat of greasy slime spreads outward from the dumpster. A week ago, a fire burned a house on the next street over to the ground. Alice shivers, enfolding heavily-ringed fingers across her flabby upper arms. The rain is starting to come down harder. I find myself trembling with shock. Could any of what she said be true?

"One second." Ethan flips damp hair off his forehead.

"One second?" she repeats.

"That's all you have left. I'm still waiting for the truth."

"What? You don't believe me?"

"Not a single friggin' word. Tell you what, let's go to the cops together. They'll be curious about this mysterious Mrs. Olivia Oliver, don't you think? There ought to be a record of her somewhere, right? And of a baby she abandoned? While we're at it, why did you tell me I was born at AC on September thirtieth? Did Mrs. Olivia Oliver share that detail with you in the minute and a half you must have spent together seventeen years ago? Or did you come up with it from some gothic romance novel you read on the plane this afternoon? I'm guessing the latter. It's all lies, and we both know it."

Ethan's doing a decent job of staying calm, so I don't know what I'm expecting to happen next. Maybe Alice to double down with better details? Or backtrack with a more plausible explanation?

Clearly, I don't know her. I'm stunned when she draws back her fist and hits him in the jaw. Ethan's whole head bounces backward. The noise of her hand connecting with his face explodes across the parking lot.

He staggers likes a drunk. Claire makes an *oof* sound and reaches out to catch him, but he jerks away, shoving Alice with both hands into the dirty yellow garbage bin behind her. She stumbles, dropping something. Ethan picks it up.

Then they really go at it. Screaming, punching, clawing at each other's faces. Claire yells at them to stop, and suddenly I'm nauseous like I felt in the maternity ward this afternoon.

I squat and tell myself to breathe, glancing up in time to see Alice snatch a metal rod beside the trash bin. She slams it like a baseball bat into Ethan's leg. He shrieks and yanks it from her fist. Tosses it aside.

It's crazy. At this point, if I were her, I'd be getting the hell out of Dodge. She lunges at him again with a murderous glint in her eye. He shoves her one more time. She falls on her butt with a crack. It sounds like her tailbone broke.

"You're not my son!" she screams. "You're a crack baby loser. I never should have taken you in, you ungrateful piece of shit!"

"And you're a nasty, lying cunt. I should have drowned your ugly face in the bathtub a long time ago," he yells back.

Claire takes hold of his arm. For a second his expression is so contorted, I fear he's going to hit her too.

I struggle to my feet. I've got to help Claire.

"Ethan, stop," says Claire. "That's enough! You knocked her down. She isn't getting up. We've gotta get out of here."

Thankfully, the guy in the car is gone and the two girls who were making out are running through the alley away from us. I look around for the employees, but there's no sign of them either.

"Don't you leave. Don't you dare leave," Alice calls out faintly as we scrabble for my car. The last words I hear from her are, "You're dead to me, boy. You hear me? You're dead."

Ethan spins around and pauses, his tone all at once detached. "Bitch. You're the one that's dead."

CHAPTER TWENTY-SIX

Claire

"We need to get Ethan to the hospital," Nora says, slinging one of Ethan's elbows over her shoulder. I grab the other. Between the two of us, we drag him to her car.

Ethan plops down in the passenger seat. "No hospital. Just get me somewhere I can lie down. Christ Almighty, that bitch. I think she broke my leg."

His knee is swelling through his jeans. His jaw bears an angry, fist-sized mark. We ease his feet inside. I shut the door and hurry around to climb in back behind Nora. She peels out of the parking lot without watching where she's going.

"Nora, slow down," I shout. "Do you want me to drive?"

"We left her, Claire. We left Alice. My god, what just happened?"

I have no answer to that. It certainly wasn't a good idea to leave Alice injured and alone. Nevertheless, I can dredge up little sympathy for her after what she's done to Ethan. What matters now is getting him away from her. "At least turn on the windshield wipers, will you?"

She does, calming herself and slowing to a more reasonable speed.

A minute later, she takes a route I'm not familiar with and we wind up at her grandmother's house. Nora pulls into the gravel drive. She sits and takes a deep breath through her nose, blowing it out through her lips. "There's a rolling chair inside, Ethan. Do you want me to get it?"

He groans. "I don't think so. But could you help me out of the car?"

The rain, pummeling the car with icy pellets moments before, has slowed to a drizzle. We go through reverse motions getting him out. Ethan hops into the yard on one foot.

Nora kicks open the gate. "I really think we should take you to a hospital."

"You got insurance to cover me, Miss Moneybags?" he replies, shooting me a grimace.

"Well, no. But—"

"Right. Then case closed, got it? I'm banged up. It's not the first time and likely not the last. By the way, love your house. It's adorable." He eyes the paint-chipped door and the row of kitschy garden gnomes along the edge of the front stoop.

Nora ignores that. She unlocks the door and a second later we're inside.

The air is warm and suffocating. My head hurts. How did I not know about my father? I feel so betrayed. The son of a bitch. Naturally, I knew he dated after the divorce. But before? Is that why Mom left him? *Her father and his slutty girlfriends staying out all night.* Is that where he's been the last two nights? And how would Alice know unless she saw him?

This isn't about me, I have to remind myself. Nora and Ethan have been through much worse. And Ethan, for all his silly ways, has no way of knowing that "adorable" has special meaning to Nora. But I do, so here's what will happen next. Nora will go quiet because she finds Gran's house embarrassing not cute. She'll think I told him how we say it when we mean something else, and then it will be up to me to smooth things over.

I give myself a mental shake to stop my unproductive thoughts from spiraling as Ethan hobbles to the old brown sofa in the living room. While Nora's gone to get some towels, I sit beside him and in my best adult voice, say, "You're a guest, Ethan. Please remember that and behave like one."

He makes a face around his pain. "What did I do?"

"Never mind. Just be polite. Can you manage that for five minutes?" I'm not going to tell him how sensitive Nora is. She'd never forgive me. "Do you want ice?"

"Sure." He sucks a breath. "And if there isn't any vodka, you can fix me a Tom Collins."

"Ice for your knee, jackass." Still, I snicker, mostly because he expects me to.

Ethan lifts his shirt, revealing a red mark on his abs to match the shadow forming on his jaw. His knuckles are scraped. Blood drips down his wrist.

"Hey, Nora the Explorer," he says, when Nora returns. "I was serious about your house. It's homey, not like Clarice's grand manor. Last night I had to leave a trail of bread crumbs just to find my way to my room. Hope I didn't offend."

There's the guy I know and love. I throw him one of the towels she's set on the coffee table and use another to dry my hair and face.

Nora's dark eyes crinkle at the corners. Not quite a smile. "You didn't. Let me go grab you a bag of ice."

"Frozen peas or corn would be better if you have any," he calls as she disappears into the kitchen. "Claire." He whispers with a new and unfamiliar note of panic. "What am I going to do?"

"For now you rest. First thing in the morning, we'll go to the police. You're not letting Alice get away with this."

"But my real parents, what will they think? Will they want to get to know me? I mean, I'm not smart like Nora and seventeen years is an awfully long time. What if they don't want anything to do with me?"

It's only then that I realize I've never told him the other sad story. My heart breaks.

"Ethan, this is Nora's grandmother's house. Her parents… *your* parents…They passed away three years ago."

CHAPTER TWENTY-SEVEN

Nora

True confession time. I used to fantasize about Nick being Nicki, my sister who was also my best friend. That summer before kindergarten when I wasn't allowed to play outside, I spent long hours in my room, often under my bed or crouched on the closet floor. I told her stories and sang songs I'd made up. They always rhymed because that's what Nicki and I liked best.

Behind my back, my parents called my fantasy life a quirk. They tolerated it for a while before deciding I needed a more productive hobby, which is how they came up with the idea of piano lessons, a wise choice since it brought me out of my shell.

What would they think of Ethan, this version of Nick? He's not the sibling I want. He definitely isn't Nicki. *Come on,* I wanted to say, *no one finds this house adorable.* Putting it like that was just plain snarky. And bread crumbs to his room at Claire's house? Didn't he leave enough of a mess in her living room with his beer bottles and marijuana roach? I'm back to not getting what Claire sees in him or understanding why she hasn't suggested calling the police.

"Bitch. You're the one that's dead." Ethan's angry words echo in my head.

I pop another Xanax, then drop a dozen ice cubes in a Ziploc, wrap it in a kitchen towel, and hammer it into chips with Gran's meat tenderizer because no, I'm not going to waste frozen vegetables when ice will do. When I return to the living room, Claire's by the door, shouldering her messenger bag.

"I'm going to the store to pick up pain meds for Ethan. Can I borrow your car?"

I set the towel Ethan used to wipe his face on a doily on the coffee table as I frame my reply. "Of course. No problem. Pain meds?"

If either one of them had asked, I would have happily given Ethan one of my Xanax, which are good for pain as well as anxiety. But if Claire thinks Fred Meyer has something better, so be it. An odd, almost angry expression flits across her face. It's gone before I can process it.

"Just ibuprofen," she replies as if to assure me she's not after weed or something stronger.

"And Coke. The real thing," Ethan sings out. "You know, the commercial?"

Of course I know. The ad has made another comeback. *Thanks, Ethan, for unnecessary clarification.* "I've seen it."

I start to tell Claire I wouldn't mind going with her, but it occurs to me she may not think it wise to leave him on his own. I agree, but probably for a different reason. I toss her my car keys and bite my lower lip to keep from adding, "Drive safely," because I know she will without my advice.

Once she's gone, Ethan and I don't seem to have much to say to one another. I stand between the kitchen and the living room. He lies with his knee propped up on the couch.

"My parents." He runs a hand through his thick damp hair.

"What about them?"

"I don't know. How did they die?"

"They disappeared in a crevasse three years ago."

"That's it?"

"That's it."

"Were they—were they nice people?"

"The best," I say. "Dad was a lawyer. Mom was an administrator with the parks department. They loved hiking. They were on a Denali expedition when they died."

"I like to hike," Ethan says softly. "Were they musical?"

"Mom was. She could hear a song one time and play it."

"On the piano?"

"Yup. Neither played guitar. I can make you a cup of tea, if you like."

"Sure, if you're having one. That would be nice." Ethan gazes at his hands in his lap. The ice bag has slid to the floor. I resist asking him to pick it up.

"Chamomile?"

"I don't know what that is. But if you like it, I imagine I will too."

He's trying too hard again, as if he can't decide to be courteous or something else, this guy who fell instantly in love with a barista, then stood her up. I wonder why. Was he hoping someone better would come along, like Sam or Ellie, the girls he spent ten minutes with at lunch?

I head for the kitchen, feeling absurdly grateful for the opportunity to have something to do in another room away from him. While I wait for the water to boil for tea, I force myself to reexamine my feelings.

Truth, Nora. He has a right to ask questions about his parents. It's only natural he'd want to know about them. So why do I feel resentful? Why am I unwilling to share my memories?

Bitch. You're the one that's dead.

His words keep coming back to me. Did he mean it? I was shocked to the core when Alice punched him. How much other abuse has he had to endure?

I still think we ought to call the police, but there's no reason we can't wait until tomorrow when he's feeling better. I pour hot water into cups with matching saucers, dunk the bags, and hang the strings on the edge to let the tea steep.

When I return to the living room, Ethan's gone. The checkered towel wadded on the table. The ice bag is on the couch. A damp stain pools around it.

I remove it to the kitchen sink and take a seat in one of the straight-back kitchen chairs I pulled in earlier. I wait, sipping my tea. Ethan reappears a couple of seconds later. "Nature called." He limps unconvincingly to the couch. He spots the tea on a coaster on the coffee table and squeals, "Thanks, man. That looks great. I mean, really *really* great."

"You're welcome."

I wake the next morning with a groan, squinting at sunlight streaming through the plastic blinds on the single window over my bed.

Claire returned later than I expected with a tale of Fred Meyer's empty shelves of over-the-counter pain relievers and no Coca-Cola, only Pepsi, which apparently Ethan doesn't care for. Personally, I can't tell the difference, but I hardly ever drink it. Gran won't buy it because it's expensive and rots your teeth. Walmart, apparently, was also busy, although she did manage to snag six chili cheese hot dogs from their deli. Since we hadn't had any real dinner, I ate my share, which I'm paying for now with stomach cramps. I usually avoid junk food.

A gentle knock sounds at my bedroom door, and Claire peeks her head in. She's dressed and brushing her beautiful blond hair.

I pat the empty sheet beside me. "I didn't hear you get up."

"That's because you were sound asleep. I've been up for hours." She slips in beside me, careful not to put her shoes on the bed.

"Liar."

"How did you know?" She chuckles, giving me a buttery, warm, kiss. "I got up about ten minutes ago. Ethan's also up. He says he's ready to go to the police station and wants us to go with him."

"Both of us?"

"No, just me." She pokes me in the side. "Yes, both of us. You're his sister. He says you had a great talk last night. You even showed him your tattoo."

"I did?" I must have, although I don't remember doing it. It's a yin-yang on my hip matching Amber's. Gran would have a fit if she saw it. I wish I hadn't gotten it.

My phone pings. Claire hands it to me from the bedside table making a face. "Jesus. It's Amber again. Fourteen texts. Will she never give up? Call her back."

"I'd rather not."

"Up to you, but she isn't going to stop. Listen, are you hungry? I thought I'd make pancakes, but I can't find a mix."

"Gran makes them from scratch."

"Then forget it." She claps her hands and snorts.

I fall back against the pillow. We're both a little out of sorts. Who wouldn't be after what happened last night? "Omelets are my specialty. Can I talk you into helping me locate my shoes and socks if I make you one?" I don't really need help, which she undoubtedly knows. My room is neat. I always keep it that way.

"Sure."

"Holy shit!" Ethan roars from the other room. At the same time, my phone rings.

"This better be good," I punch the button and answer.

"Trust me, it is," says Amber. "Turn on your TV, channel thirteen. You're going to want to see this."

"You guys, come quick," Ethan yells.

Claire takes off for the living room. I trot along behind her in my boxer shorts, self-consciously pulling my skimpy nightshirt over my hips.

The local news is on, featuring a special report. Ethan, wearing nothing but a pair of black briefs with the tag facing out, sits on the edge of the couch, his knobby spine protruding down his back, his eyes fixed on our tiny convex television screen.

"Breaking news," says a female reporter in a smart blue windbreaker bearing the station logo. "A parking lot behind a midtown coffeehouse was the scene of a possible homicide last night. The body of a woman, now identified as forty-two-year-old Alice St. James of Juneau, was found beside a dumpster earlier this morning. An exact cause of death is unknown at this time. Witnesses say she was seen arguing with three unidentified individuals at approximately ten p.m. last night. If you have any information that might help, you are asked to contact APD. The police have released this photo taken from a surveillance camera at the coffeeshop's rear entrance." A grainy picture appears. Three figures.

"Are you seeing this?" says Amber. "St. James, like in *Ethan* St. James? Claire's friend? Tell me that isn't you, Ethan, and Claire. There's a picture of the body on 4chan. So gross. It looks like half her face has been smashed in. I'm sending it to you now."

"Don't," I say. I'm too late. It's pops up on my screen. "I've gotta go, Amber."

"Are you home? Do you want me to come over?"

"No, thanks. I'll call you later." I end the call.

Thankfully, our faces in the photo are unrecognizable due to the camera angle. I can make out the top of Claire's blond head, nothing else.

Ethan throws back his head and lets out a long, loud, and very wrong kind of laugh that makes me cringe. I didn't think it was possible for the day to start out even worse than yesterday.

CHAPTER TWENTY-EIGHT

Claire

"Ethan, get a grip." I push Gran's crumpled crocheted blanket aside and drop to the couch beside him as Nora heads for the kitchen. Ethan instantly clamps his jaw.

"Sorry, Claire Bear. That was weird, right?"

Very. Awkwardly, because he doesn't have a shirt on, I put an arm around his muscular shoulders and pat his back. I can't believe it. Now he's lost three people: the parents he never knew and the woman he's grown up believing was his mother. He didn't take the first part well, hiding tears from Nora and pretending like he didn't care, but I know better. Ethan's deeper than he lets on.

He goes rigid under my embrace, not pushing me away exactly, but not yielding to my comfort either. I'd forgotten that he doesn't like to be hugged unless he initiates it. A massive bruise like a shadow from a beard has materialized on his jaw. His knee is red and puffy, though less swollen than last night. The mark on his ribs has taken on the shape of a face, like one of those potato chip photos people post on Instagram, saying they've found Jesus or Abraham Lincoln.

"She's dead," he mutters. "Christ, I'm not sure if I'm supposed to celebrate or cry. She wasn't my mother. I hated her, and she made it pretty clear last night she didn't like me either. All that crap about some Oliver lady…she called me a crack baby loser, an ungrateful piece of shit.."

And you both said you were dead to each other.

The reporter has moved on to a story about another rainstorm coming in from the coast, this one milder than the one last night. My eyes remain on the screen, still sifting through the reporter's words. Alice St. James is dead beside the dumpster where we left her.

I force myself out of my stupor. Ethan needs me just as I needed him when my cat died. "You know, it's okay to feel something, even if it's anger. Do you want to talk about it?"

"Which part? How she stole me from my parents, or how people will assume I killed her?"

"I know you didn't. Nora knows it too."

He shakes his head. "They have us on camera. The reporter mentioned witnesses. It's only a matter of time before the cops decide to arrest me."

"We won't let that happen."

"How are you going to stop it?"

I have no answer for that. My mind returns to the parking lot, to Alice on her butt, propped next to a dumpster. Could she get up? I have no idea, except I do know she was very much alive when we left her, which means someone came along after us. A mugger thinking to roll her for easy cash? The man in the car who drove off? Is it possible he returned?

Nora steps back into the living room, sucking in a breath as if to let us know she's there. "Coffee should be ready in about five minutes. Who wants breakfast?"

"Me," says Ethan.

"Sure. If you don't mind," I say. I feel like I should be comforting her, but that's ridiculous. Nora didn't know Alice. She'd never met her before last night.

"Give me ten or fifteen minutes. I'll let you know when it's time." She goes back to the kitchen. The sound of pots and pans clanging on the counter accompany her low voice a second later. She's on the phone, probably with Amber who texted her fourteen—count 'em—fourteen friggin' times last night. The way she won't let go of Nora irritates the hell out of me. Nora plays her part in it too.

I push that aside and turn my attention back to Ethan, who puts a hand on my knee and gently wiggles out from under my arm, saying he's uncomfortable with me sitting so close. I shift to Gran's chair in the corner to give him space. Five years ago when he first moved into my neighborhood, we talked about everything because he was the kind of kid who, when a thought entered his head, he had to express it. He talked about how much he hated school yet idolized his art teacher. How he loved Grape Nuts because they didn't get soggy in milk. How he wanted to be a deejay or a roadie for a band after high school. How he could barely get out of bed when it rained.

The day his stepfather ran over my cat, Ethan shouted at him for driving too fast, then kicked a back tire so hard I just knew he'd broken a toe. He offered to take Sampson to the vet. Later, he stole an LOL Surprise Queen Bee doll from the Imagination Station so she could watch over Sampson's grave.

I'd never had a best friend who was a boy before. We tried the couple's thing until I finally admitted I didn't like kissing guys. Even then, he took it pretty well. We stayed friends. Recently, he's started hiding behind silly jokes. And now he's shutting me out completely. He's growing up. I miss the old Ethan.

I fold my hands in my lap, not knowing what to do next. Obviously, we need to go to the police even if he doesn't want to. It'll look better for all of us if we're proactive. We ought to call Riley and let him know what's happened too. Who's going to make Alice's funeral arrangements? This is the kind of thing I used to talk over with my father. Never again. I shut out what happened after I left to get Ethan's ibuprofen. I can't think about that now. My stomach roils. I'm already regretting it.

Presently, a talk show comes on television with a celebrity speaking of the health benefits of Botox. She says it can prevent migraines. I press my fingertips to my temples, thinking I might have one coming on. That reminds me we have bigger problems.

"So, listen. We'll go to the police right after breakfast. There's no sense in waiting until they come looking for you," I say.

Ethan pops to his feet. "Don't be stupid, Claire. Use your head. There's no way I'm talking to them now. I told you they're going to think I killed her!"

"We'll—"

"Unh unh. Nope. Not happening. Call them if you want. But if you do, I'll leave right now and you'll never see me again." He pauses as an apparently new thought occurs to him. "If you do decide to call them, are you also going to tell them how you stood by and watched me hit her?"

If I didn't know him better, I could almost believe Ethan's threatening me. He wouldn't do that. Not my friend, not this guy I know and love. "At least let us take you to get your knee looked at."

"Forget it." He plops back down on the couch. "I'm not going anywhere."

I give up. Hopefully, he'll come to his senses if we give him some time to think about it.

The coffee's still bubbling in the old-fashioned electric percolator by the stove when I join Nora in the kitchen. I wrap my arms around her waist from behind, inhaling her slightly stale scent.

Startled, she gestures to the phone cradled in her neck.

"Amber?" I mouth, backing up to the little table against the wall to give her some room. Why does Nora always have to answer when she calls?

"Gran," Nora mouths back, and then continues: "We're fine. Just making breakfast now. I'm teaching Claire to make omelets…Fluffy, yes. I know that. Did you get your test results? Oh, thank goodness. I'm so glad to hear it. Where are you and Melanie off to today?" She shifts the phone to the other ear, cracks an egg with one hand and tosses the shell in the sink.

Her grandmother must say something about the DNA test because Nora gives a light laugh and says, "It was hilarious." Then it appears they're talking about Nick's abduction because the merriment leaves her voice. "And no one ever came forward? Why wasn't I told? You went along with it? Then who's buried in the grave? Oh, I see."

See what? I'm hearing only Nora's end because her grandmother's replies are inaudible. It's a long conversation with Nick mentioned several times. Nora releases a fake laugh, nearly drops the phone and regains it as she pours her egg mixture across the bottom of the skillet, adding cheese and salt and pepper a moment later, then expertly scooping and flipping the concoction like a pancake before folding it in two.

She lifts her chin at the toaster, which I take to mean I'm supposed to drop in a couple of slices of bread. I do, then slather them with margarine from an open tub by the ancient microwave. She dumps the first omelet on a plate, sticks it in the oven and starts a second. This goes on for several minutes while I watch.

I'm an outsider, caught between my friend who doesn't want my help and my girlfriend having a one-sided conversation with her grandmother who vaguely disapproves of me but is too polite to come right out and say it. "Promise me you won't hurt each other when you break up," she said long ago at dinner.

For the first time, I wonder if coming to Anchorage with my father was a good idea. He's been too busy with a lot of stuff, and not just business. *Claire's father and his slutty girlfriends staying out all night.* I shudder. Should I have stayed in Juneau with my mother and her new family? Maybe, except I wasn't wanted there either. Her husband's oldest daughter made that very clear. So, I'm stuck with a growing thought that I made the wrong choice.

Nora hangs up and sets her phone upside down on the counter, probably so I can't see the recent text exchange between her and Amber. I force those thoughts aside and assume my usual cheerful face. "Anything I can do to help?"

"You can set the table." She's missed my meaning completely.

"I'd be happy to." I pull out three white china plates with pink flowers along the border from a cabinet and set them at a table built for two.

"Who's buried in the grave?" I venture, stacking toast on a saucer and moving a bowl of wax fruit from the table to a windowsill.

"What?" She sets the omelet plates onto overlapping plastic placemats. Steam rises from the last and freshest omelet. The scent makes me hungry. Still, I'm thinking, Don't you *What?* me. You know exactly what I'm talking about.

"Nick's grave. You asked your grandmother about it." Feeling my smile slip, I hastily push my lips back in place.

"Oh." She shrugs. "No one. It's empty. Ethan, breakfast's ready," she calls, then turns back to me. "Coffee? Forks and napkins?"

Get them yourself. "Right." I grab flatware from a flimsy drawer and pour black coffee into three mismatched mugs, taking the chipped one advertising an auto body shop for myself and remembering at the last second to grab a carton of milk from the refrigerator because I know if Nora's having unflavored coffee she prefers it with a splash. When I look up, Ethan's standing in the doorway, watching us. *For Pete sakes, dude, put a shirt on.*

"Do you have ketchup? And can I have another Pepsi?" he says. Then he strolls to the placemat with the steaming omelet and plops into a chair. He spears it with a fork without waiting for either of us to join him.

CHAPTER TWENTY-NINE

Nora

Yeah, I'm a wreck. I'm not going to deny it. I don't understand Claire's hesitance to call the police or the odd look on her face last night before she left for the store. It feels like back in Juneau when we kept misinterpreting each other's signals. Worse, Gran was like a bloodhound on the phone, sniffing out my secrets. She kept returning to the DNA reports I stupidly mentioned yesterday. My claim that I'd misread them only partially allayed her curiosity, and she's mad at herself for not telling me about Nick's abduction sooner. Somehow, her anxiety about all this has morphed into her believing most of this is Claire's fault.

"Maybe it's time for Claire to go back to her own house," she said more than once.

I definitely don't want that. I love Claire, even if she's acting strange. "That's hilarious," I replied, hoping Claire wouldn't guess what she was saying.

The whole conversation felt like a balancing act. I kept wishing Claire would go back into the living room and let me handle Gran in private.

I didn't dare tell Gran that Ethan's staying with us too. *Or* that he might be implicated in a homicide. I have to keep reminding myself that Alice was alive when we left her. Still, their fight was the worst I've ever seen. And I don't buy his whole *my knee hurts too much to get my lazy butt off the sofa* after seeing him walk into the kitchen a minute ago without so much as a limp.

He makes an annoying humming sound with his tongue between his teeth as he cuts into an omelet oozing with melted cheese. He says that I, Nora the Explorer, must be the best cook in the world. Please. I can fry an egg and slow-cook a roast. The guy keeps trying too hard to make me like him. And it pisses me off that Claire gave him the best omelet when I meant her to have it.

I bite into a slice of damp, overly-buttered toast and start thinking that maybe I should call the cops myself. Will Ethan try to stop me? Will Claire? The TV is still on in the living room. Voices punctuated with laughter from a talk show distract me from my thoughts.

Gran doesn't like TV on in the daytime. "Only after dinner, and only if you've done your homework," she says. It's a good philosophy because before I came to live with her I wasn't a straight-A student. I was satisfied with B's and an occasional C. I used to imagine my parents' pride if they could see me.

If I could see them, I'd want to know why they let me believe a lie for so many years.

Plainly, my emotions are all over the place.

When Claire finishes her breakfast, she gets up, drops her napkin on the webbed lawn chair she insisted on taking since we have only two kitchen chairs, and starts clearing dishes off the table.

"You'd make a good domestic," Ethan teases.

She squints. "What does that mean?"

At the same time, I say, "Why don't you shut up?"

"My bad, Nora Lee. I was making a joke to lighten the mood. Clarice knows that."

"Do I?" she replies, her tone harsh. Her back is to us as she turns on the kitchen faucet and sets the dirty skillets in the sink.

Before I can decide how I feel about all this, I hear a chime from the television indicating the news is starting up again. Usually, it's a weather report, but this time the same reporter who came on earlier is standing outside yellow crime tape sealing off Caseo's rear parking lot.

Amber texts: "*Shit, girl. Are you seeing this?*"

The reporter holds a microphone in one hand as she reads off her phone. "Mimi Rodriguez here at the scene of last night's midtown homicide. Police now tell us that the victim, forty-two-year-old Alice St. James of Juneau, died from blunt force trauma to her face and abdomen. It appears she was beaten to death with a heavy metal object between the hours of ten p.m. and midnight."

Wait. The rod Ethan ripped from her hands?

"A Caseo's employee has identified the young man seen with her shortly before ten o'clock as the victim's son, Ethan St. James, also of Juneau. Two other persons of interest are as yet unknown. If you have any information that might help, police ask that you contact the Crime Stoppers number at the bottom of your screen."

"Karen," Ethan sputters. "What a train wreck."

Does he mean Karen's the train wreck since she's likely the one who identified him, or the utter fiasco of last night? *Beaten with a heavy metal object.* Cringing inwardly, I replay their nasty argument in my head.

"Can they just say my name like that on TV when I'm still a juvenile?" Ethan asks, pacing back and forth.

"No," says Claire.

"Yes," I reply.

"Probably," we agree.

"They may not know it and you've only been named as a person of interest." I shrug. A better question might be how do they know Ethan's from Juneau and that he's Alice's son? "Did you tell Karen you used to live in Juneau?" I ask him.

"Maybe. I don't remember."

Seems to me there's quite a bit of information missing from his story, things he isn't saying or doesn't remember. Is it possible he took my car after I went to bed and went back to kill his mother?

The three of us have moved into the living room to better see the television. The sound of water splashing in the kitchen sink penetrates my consciousness. I step back to shut it off. On my return, my eyes take in a cell phone lying unattended on Ethan's placemat. A white banner in the center indicates a message with the name Riley in bold letters at the top.

"*Hey prick. Saw the news. So you finally did it. You won't get away with it. Flying in this morning.*"

Riley, as in Riley Crew, Ethan's stepfather? How has he already heard of this? The situation keeps getting worse. Ethan stretches his long body on the couch, propping an elbow under his head. I drop the phone in his lap.

"You have a text. I think you're going to want to see it."

He glances down, then leaps to his feet and heads to the bathroom. The door lock clicks behind him while the news reporter goes on about a recent rise in criminal activity in midtown, citing three incidents of busted-out car windows on Northern Lights, a shooting that put a man in the hospital, and some poor guy who got rolled for change a couple of blocks away.

"What was that all about?" asks Claire.

"Nothing much. A message from Riley calling Ethan a prick and saying he's on his way to Anchorage."

"Oh. That's not good. I may have mentioned they don't get along."

"Really? I never would have guessed."

She sticks out her jaw, obviously upset. "Damn it, Nora. You act like this is my fault. Alice was bad news. Believe it or not, Riley's probably worse. Most of the time they didn't get along with one another either."

What's this, her fault? We're still on different pages and I don't understand it. "I never said it was your fault, Claire. In fact, yesterday I specifically said I didn't blame you."

"Same difference. I'm sorry about the DNA test. I wish I'd never bought the damn thing." She looks like she's about to cry.

I take her hand and gently rub her arm. "Don't be upset. I'm not mad, just confused. Tell me more about Ethan's shitty, fake parents."

She sniffs and wipes her eyes. "Once, when Ethan and I were in the backyard Alice and Riley were screaming so loudly at each other Ethan told me to go home."

"Did you?"

"No. Not at first, because they were yelling about my father. Riley wanted to hit him up for a loan; they never had enough money. Alice didn't think it was a good idea. When Ethan and I first met, they lived up the street in a rental house."

"I think you mentioned that."

"Yeah. Anyway, a couple of months into their lease, they snuck out in the middle of the night, stiffing Mr. Gilson on the rent. He was a sweet old guy. He didn't deserve it."

Does anyone deserve it? "So that's what the argument was about, asking your dad to pay their rent?"

"Not exactly. Before the dumpster diving business took off, Riley did odd jobs around the neighborhood. Mowing lawns, cleaning gutters, fixing broken windows, that kind of thing. Apparently, one of our neighbors accused him of stealing money from her house. Alice said to forget the loan because now they'd to have to move anyway. She said they couldn't take that kind of scrutiny so close to home. One thing led to another. Riley bashed her head into the wall."

"Oh, my gosh!" I can feel my eyes widen.

"I know, right? It was like that all the time with them. Alice had a mild concussion. But she gave as good as she got. Riley needed stitches after Alice stabbed him with a knife."

"Holy shit!"

"Yeah. Holy shit. Bad parents. The thing is, they're adults. But Ethan, imagine how hard it was on him. Some nights he didn't go home. He didn't want to. He slept under trees or in the doorways of shops. When he finally let me know how bad it was, I invited him to stay with me. On the floor, of course. But at least he had a roof and a pillow and a blanket."

"Did your parents know?"

"Not that he was staying in my room, not then. Dad definitely knew Riley wanted money from him. It probably seemed like we had a lot, but they had no idea how hard Dad worked…"

There's something in the way she says it that puts me on alert. How hard her father worked?

"Dad said no to the loan. And no surprise, Riley resented it. He made that very clear."

"And?"

"That's it."

"Okay…So Alice was a shit. Riley's a shit. You're saying Ethan isn't?"

"That's precisely what I'm saying, Nora. Look, I know I shouldn't have bought the DNA tests without asking, but aren't you a little glad to know you have a brother?"

"Yeah. I guess. Okay, I'm very glad," I say, when she rolls her eyes. "But we're so different. Maybe if we'd grown up together he wouldn't be such a mess."

Claire purses her lips. "Do you think he killed Alice?"

"I don't." *Not exactly.*

"Good. I don't either."

She goes back into the kitchen, where she fills the sink with soapy water. After a minute, I turn off the TV and follow her, wondering if I imagined the catch in her voice, or the slight hesitation when she spoke of Alice, Riley, and her dad. Am I making a thing of something that doesn't exist? Why am I so suspicious all the time?

I think about how Claire sat in the lawn chair leaving the kitchen chairs for us. How she kept the chipped mug for herself instead of giving it to Ethan. How she sticks up for me with Amber at school. I grab a towel and dry the dishes, trying to think of something that will make this all feel better.

"So. Letting Ethan stay with you in Juneau and now here…" I make my tone soft. "It's generous. You must be his superhero."

I mean it to sound like a compliment, but she rears back with a furious expression.

"There are plenty of people I can't stand."

I blink, startled. "I don't…Okay. Like who?"

"Well, obviously Alice for everything she did to Ethan. But Nora, why do you let Amber get inside your head? Why do you talk to her at all?" Claire shouts. "She texts and calls. You act like it bothers you, but you always pick up. I need to know the truth. Are you still in love with her?"

The idea is so absurd I almost laugh. I stop when I see Claire's expression. "Claire, I'm done with Amber. I promise."

"So you say." Her unexpected flare of anger's gone, but she isn't convinced. She unplugs the coffeepot and places the washed mugs in a cabinet.

I don't tell her they go in the cabinet next to it because I'm too busy thinking how lucky I am to have her. I love our conversations, the way her nose wrinkles when she laughs, the animated sparkle in her eyes. I love the sound of her voice and the exhilarating warmth of her body lying next to mine the last two nights.

So it's Amber she's upset about.

The toilet flushes. A second later the bathroom door creaks open.

Ethan. Damn it. We still have a major problem on our hands. "Is Riley going to make trouble for him?" I eye him from the kitchen as he heads for the couch.

Claire runs the towel across the counter and mutters something like, "We're back to that. Yes, Nora. In case I didn't make it clear, Ethan's stepfather, or whatever Riley is to him now, isn't the forgiving type. Alice is dead, and Ethan ran off with his money. What exactly did his text to Ethan say?"

I'd almost forgotten the money. "He accused him of killing Alice."

"Worse than I thought. Okay. We can handle this. Look, I know it's a lot to ask, but is there any chance you'd go back to Caseo's with me?"

"Why?"

"Because Ethan refuses to go to the police and I feel like we're missing something. I feel like if we don't check it out, something worse is going to happen. Remember the employees by the door and the girls in the alley? What if one of them saw something and didn't bother to report it?"

Somebody saw something. My brain itches with the thought. No matter how hard I try, I can't put my finger on it. "It's possible, I guess. How about we wait until the chaos there settles down."

"How long?"

"Not long. We'll go this afternoon. I've got to start my book report and I need a shower. Mmm." I run my tongue across my teeth. "Probably ought to brush my teeth as well. Here, smell my breath."

Claire sniffs and draws back quickly. "*Oof.* Not that bad," she says politely, which makes me want to giggle. "I should brush my teeth too."

I squeeze her hand. "Then we have a plan. You're okay with it?"

"Sure. Fine."

"Do you want to tell Ethan, or should I?"

She lightly smacks my butt. "I'll do it."

"Great." Relieved, I start for my bedroom, glad that it's only Amber she's upset about. We could go to Caseo's sooner, except I'm serious about the book report and I need time to process everything that's happened. That's just me being me.

CHAPTER THIRTY

Claire

Thank goodness Ethan's dressed by the time I finish the dishes. He wears his pressed, black jeans, checkered shirt and ridiculously expensive leather shoes. He's got his feet propped on the coffee table, watching TV again.

"Hey." He glances up.

You can do this, Claire. Neither of them knows what you did.

"Hey, yourself. Nora and I are going back to Caseo's to talk to Karen."

He sits up straight. "No, you're not. Claire, I swear to god, if you rat me out—"

"Relax. Karen may not be your biggest fan, but she isn't going to lie about you." *Hopefully.* "Naturally, she'd tell the cops she saw you, but what if she saw something else later, something she didn't understand herself?"

"Like what?"

"I have no idea. That's why I want to talk to her. Just think about it. What if she went out back for a break—"

"Why would she do that?"

"Because smoking isn't allowed inside. She vapes. You didn't know? You never noticed the cartridge in her rear pocket?" Ethan's smart, but he's not particularly observant. You ask him to describe a person or a place, he's clueless. He's better with music. He can tell the notes, the clef, the tempo, who wrote it and who was the last person to sing it. He's usually more aware of girls he likes. He can talk about hairstyles, shopping, and clothes like no other guy I know. Mom once called him a metrosexual.

"It's a compliment," she said. "He's like your father, meticulous about his appearance."

Her new husband is bald with a potbelly. His clothes are always wrinkled. But she's right about Dad. My father gets his hair cut every ten days, his teeth whitened twice a year. One of the first things he did when we arrived in Anchorage was arrange a mani-pedi, telling me his clients expect a certain look from him. *It's not all they expect.*

"Caseo's employees smoke and vape by the back door. There were two of them there last night. Probably others later."

"So?"

Are we doing this again? "So, we left Alice by the dumpster. Somebody came after us and killed her."

"Right." He nods. "Right. That makes sense. Probably robbed her to. She always carried cash, you know."

I didn't know. "Speaking of cash, how much did you take from Riley?"

He hesitates. "A couple of grand."

"Two thousand?"

"Maybe more. I haven't counted it." In other words, likely everything Riley had stashed. He's going to want it back.

"Do you have any of it left?"

"A little."

"Where is it now?"

"Hidden."

"Hidden where, here at Nora's house?"

"No."

"At my house?"

"Maybe."

"Shit, Ethan. You left stolen money in my house?"

"See, that's why I didn't want to tell you. Jesus, Claire. I wouldn't do anything to put you in danger." He's obviously insulted by the idea. He wouldn't put me in danger but he doesn't mind hiding money at my house. My house. I don't want to think about that right now.

"No one's going to find it, Claire Bear. Cross my heart." He nudges me with an elbow. "You don't think I should go with you to Caseo's, do you?"

"Lay low for now. Let us handle this."

I allow myself a grateful breath when he nods again and turns his attention back to the TV.

For the rest of the morning, Nora works on her book report while I pretend to study for a test. We hole up in her bedroom, leaving Ethan alone in the living room. I check my phone for messages. The longer I wait, the more nervous I get. Last night, I was pissed and reacted on a whim. Or maybe a fit of rage would be a better way to describe it. Now, I'm filled with regret. Maybe I should stay away from Caseo's. What if someone recognizes me? Can I take that chance?

Panic bubbles up inside me when I catch sight of something brownish under my thumbnail. Curling my hands into fists, I rise from Nora's bed. "Just need to wash my hands."

"Again?" Nora glances up from her battered laptop. "That's the sixth time. Everything okay?"

"Are you seriously going to ask me that?" My chuckle sounds halfhearted.

She grins at our inside joke. "Sorry. You're right." Thankfully, she can't see the self-loathing on my face.

When I return from the bathroom, Nora's combing her hair. She looks so innocent, trusting me when she shouldn't. "You ready?"

"As I'll ever be."

Ethan is in the kitchen, rummaging through cabinets. When he sees us, he glances guiltily at Nora and says, "I'm a growing boy."

"There are a couple of boxes of cereal on top of the refrigerator. Help yourself," she says.

"Thanks. I will."

* * *

There's still a lot of activity at Caseo's when we arrive shortly after two o'clock. People mill about on the sidewalk, others crowd the door inside. It's probably not unusual at a crime scene, given what I read in *Scientific American* about our nation's fascination with violent crime. The author called it the trigger to our most powerful emotion. Fear going hand in hand with our longing for survival. In other words, we need to believe that getting beaten to death can't happen to us.

The parking lot is taped off, with cars parked bumper to bumper on both sides of Northern Lights. Same thing with the side street. Nora slots her car between two driveways a few blocks over. We walk back past a couple of skeezy-looking guys drinking from bottles hidden in paper bags. "Hey, pretty girls. Wanna drink?" one calls after us. They openly leer as we hurry past them.

When we arrive at Caseo's, I'm startled to see clusters of pedestrians pausing to take pictures and idly chatting with one another outside the rear parking lot.

"The news says she wasn't from around here. She'd just flown in from Juneau."

"Jesus. From Juneau? That's sick. What was her name?"

A slightly hysterical cackle escapes my lips. Is that what most of us will be reduced to if our lives end suddenly, a footnote and a pic? And is coming from Juneau really sick?

Nora and I stand on the sidewalk beyond the crime tape. She pretends to take photos while we wait for another group to pass. "Oh." She glances up. "I nearly forgot. Oh, never mind. It's not important."

"What isn't?"

She drops her hands to her sides. "It's just that Amber found a picture of the body on 4chan. It's pretty awful, but I'll show you if you want."

I don't want. *Amber again.* I don't need to see a dead body. Imagining it is bad enough. "I'm good. As soon as the guy over there moves on, you keep a lookout and I'll slip over to the garbage bin and see if the cops missed something."

We wait as a man with a colorful sleeve of anime ink coughs, blows his nose and disappears around a corner.

"Now," Nora directs.

With my heart thumping painfully inside my chest, I duck under the tape and step behind the yellow dumpster. I force myself to look around. Nothing. When I emerge a minute later, Nora eyes my empty hands.

"No luck?"

"Just grease and dirt. A few spots that might be blood, more likely coffee stains." I swipe my palms across my butt. Nora frowns as I glance up. My heart skips a beat. "You remembered something?"

"Alice had a phone. I'm pretty sure she dropped it when Ethan shoved her. Ethan picked it up."

"Really." So, that's where it went. Crap. "We'll ask him about it when we get back to your house. Let's go see if Karen's working today."

Inside Caseo's, there's not an empty table to be had. We thread our way through the crowd to an orange laminated counter on the left side of the door.

I catch the eye of a barista and ask if Karen's there.

"She's in back. Do you want to see her?"

"Please. Tell her Claire and Nora would like to talk to her. We're friends of her boyfriend." I don't think Karen will remember either of our names, but mentioning Ethan might pique her interest enough to come out and speak to us.

"Okay. But if you want to order, you'd better do it now. The place is starting to get crowded again."

Again? I've never seen so many people at Caseo's, even on Wednesdays' open mic night.

"You heard about our murder last night?" the girl goes on, wiping down the counter with a dirty rag.

"Saw it on the news," says Nora. "Any arrests?"

"Not that I know of. They're looking at a guy who was in here last night." She gives Nora an extra long look. "Can I get you something to drink?"

We request our usual vanilla smoothies, and she says again that she'll let Karen know we're here.

"Do you know her?" I ask as the girl steps away to a refrigerator partially hidden by the kitchen door.

Nora shakes her head. We get our drinks and remain standing at the counter, hoping that a table will open up. The TV is on, the sound turned low. Subtitles play across the bottom of the screen.

Karen comes out a couple of minutes later.

"I thought it might be you," she says at once, thinning her lips. "Look, if you're here to give me shit about identifying Ethan, forget it. The guy's an ass. I don't owe him a damn thing. The cops showed us all that photo from the security cam. And yeah, I pointed him out. If I knew your names, I would have told them that too."

"We get it," I assure her hastily. "All we want to know is if you saw anything later, because Ethan didn't kill that woman."

"Says you. And how exactly would I have done that?"

"Well, you vape. I mean, right? You do, don't you?" She shrugs. "Which means you must take your breaks in the parking lot out back. We left before ten, all of us. By any chance did the victim leave and then return? Or did you see anyone else who might have looked like they didn't belong?"

Karen blows an irritated breath. "I didn't take a break, so I didn't see anything all. You want to know why? I requested the night before off to go bowling—you know, with Ethan, your buddy who stood me up? And now I'm working overtime to make up for staying home. Alone."

This girl is seriously upset. Still, I don't give up. "How about any of the other employees who worked last night?"

Karen slams her hands on the counter. "You don't get it, do you? You want to know, ask them yourself!"

A woman in a blue and white stripy shirt reaches for a bag of chips clipped to a moveable rack in front of me. She glances our way, puzzled, just as Nora tugs my sleeve and points at the TV screen.

The reporter from this morning is back in the studio behind a clear acrylic desk with the skyline of Anchorage behind it. "We can now confirm that one of the three persons of interest in last night's midtown homicide is Ethan St. James of Juneau, adopted son of alleged victim, Alice St. James," reads the crawl.

Adopted? Not really, but where would they have gotten that?

"Sources tell us St. James may be dangerous. If you see him or have information as to his whereabouts, please call the number at the bottom of the screen. Don't approach him. We repeat, don't approach him."

Karen widens her eyes at us. Pretty sure she didn't miss the dangerous part. What sources? I wonder. Obviously, not Karen. "What did you say your names were?" she asks softly.

My heart hits my chest wall with a thump. "We didn't." I grab Nora's hand. "Let's get out of here." And then I remember. *Yes, we did.*

CHAPTER THIRTY-ONE

Nora

Claire drags me out of Caseo's onto the sidewalk still damp from last night's rain. We don't stop until we get around the corner. My head's about to pop off at the news. She told me Ethan graffitied a school building, which to many (not me) might seem like a prank.

"Dangerous? Care to explain?" I keep my voice low, the words coming out in a hiss.

Claire stares off down the street. "It isn't as bad as it sounds. Ethan got in a fight in middle school. The other kid started it, but his arm was broken and the other parents decided to press charges."

So, in other words, it's not Ethan's fault. Where have I heard that before? "He was arrested?"

"Not exactly. He served eight months in a youth center. I should let him tell you about it. I didn't know him then."

A text comes through my phone from Amber. "*Please tell me you're not involved in this. Ethan's dangerous? I'm coming over.*"

"*Don't,*" I text back. "*I'm not home.*"

"Then meet me somewhere. How about Caseo's?"

There's no way I'm doing that after Claire just got through asking me if I was still in love with her. I slide my phone into a pocket, attempting to break the loop about my brother's history of violence that's cycling through my brain.

Ethan's still lying on the couch with the TV blaring when we get back to the house. There's a spilled box of Wheaties on the coffee table beside him and a steaming bowl of something else resting on his belly, staining his shirt. Gran's chicken tetrazzini, I realize when I take a seat across from him. It's one of the dishes she keeps in the freezer for emergencies.

"Hey, Nora the Explorer." Ethan cranes his neck to see around me. "Do you mind? You're blocking my view. I meant to ask earlier, do you have a PS6? Your TV's pretty old, but I think I can get it to work. I looked around, but I couldn't find any gaming systems, and I didn't want to go through your grandmother's stuff in her bedroom. Our grandmother," he amends, offering up a goofy grin. There's a piece of chicken caught between his teeth.

My nostrils flare in revulsion, but I manage to keep my voice reasonably steady when I say, "The police are calling you dangerous."

"Yeah. I saw." He sets the bowl on the coffee table amidst scattered cereal crumbs.

"Are you?"

"Of course not. I admit that I've been in a couple of fights. Who hasn't? Besides, you know I didn't kill Alice. She died after we left."

I consider that again. Do I really know it? I pause a beat for maximum impact and say, "Where's Alice's phone?"

Ethan's face falls. His lips turn down at the corners. His eyes narrow. He glances at Claire, but she won't meet his gaze. "I don't have it," he says at last.

His expression says something else. "Really? Because I saw you pick it up."

"No way. When would I have done that?"

I sigh and wait. It's like arguing with a two-year-old. Claire has shifted to the window, running her fingers down the sheers as if contemplating her escape. "Are you getting in on this?" I ask her when she doesn't weigh in.

Her turn to sigh. "Ethan. We both know you have it. Hand it over."

He stands, sits, stands again. Then reaches between the cushions of the couch. "Good luck unlocking it. I've tried every passcode I could think of."

"I don't need to unlock it. I'm turning it over to the police."

"Crap. Seriously? You can't do that. How are we going to figure out who killed her?"

"We're not. We'll let the police figure it out." But even as I say it, I have my doubts. I have a stake in this. Claire does too. How long will it be before Karen puts two and two together and gives our names to the police? I'm not sure what to do.

Claire reaches over and punches the knob on the right side of the TV, turning it off as Ethan drops back to the couch. "Please," he begs. "You don't have to do it right now."

Don't I? Am I committing a crime by withholding it? I'm so fed up with Ethan's lies that I want to call the police just to get him out of here.

I take a couple of deep breaths and start to go for a Xanax in my bag, then tell myself I don't need it. Gran's been after me to stop taking it. She says there are better ways to cope with stress than pills, like my deep breathing exercises and finding my safe spot.

Claire follows me into the kitchen. I set the phone on the table, eyeing the casserole dish Ethan left out and the empty soft drink cans that are leaving rings on the kitchen table.

"What do you want to do?" she says quietly.

"I want to drive my car into a tree. I want to cut my arm off and beat Ethan over the head with it. Claire, we don't have to be a part of this."

I stop just short of asking her why, last night, it took more than an hour to pick up Ethan's pain pills because she's giving me a doe-eyed look, soft and vulnerable, like when she asked if she could kiss me in Juneau. I don't want to be suspicious. I don't enjoy my doubting nature. I want to have friends. I don't want to be the weird one. The kiss we shared last spring was perfect. Our conversations this summer were even better. Claire is kind, thoughtful, generous. All the things I'm not. It's why she puts up with Ethan's antics, because she genuinely cares about other people.

"I vote no on wrecking cars and sawing off limbs." Her tone is gentle.

"You still think he's innocent?"

"Of course. Also, he's your brother."

Good point. I turn back to the counter to re-cover what remains of Gran's tetrazzini with one of her funny plastic "hats" that remind me of shower caps. Claire takes the dish from my hands and sticks it in the refrigerator, while I rinse out soft drink cans and carry them out to the recycle box.

When I get back, she's scrubbing away at the hopeless marks they've left on the table. She glances up. "I'll pay to have your table refinished."

"Why? You didn't do it, and he's my brother not yours."

"I know, but he's my family too."

I'm not sure I understand that. But she's so beautiful. Especially so, when she says, "You can kiss me if you want."

"I want."

We're alone in the kitchen. We press our bodies together, inhaling each other's scent. Her fingers trace my pant line. I feel a delightful tingle between my legs.

"Sunshine," she whispers into my mouth.

"Rain," I whisper back.

"Red."

"Blue."

"Summer."

"Winter at its darkest."

"Your omelets were delicious."

"You're delicious. You were supposed to have the fresh one," I breathe into her ear.

"You should have told me."

"I'm telling you now."

She draws back, her arched eyebrows furrowing though I don't know why. "Nora, there's something I need to tell you…"

Before she can finish, Ethan shouts from the living room, "You guys. Come quick. Nora's picture's on the news."

CHAPTER THIRTY-TWO

Claire

It's a headshot, likely taken from North's school yearbook. *Nora Thomas, co-president of North Anchorage High School's LGBTQ+ Alliance Club*, reads the crawl at the bottom of the television.

"A witness has come forward identifying seventeen-year-old Nora Thomas as one of two young women seen with person of interest Ethan St. James in last night's homicide that left the victim, Alice St. James of Juneau, dead from blunt force trauma. If you have any information on the whereabouts—"

Nora grabs the remote and shuts off the TV. "This is bad. This is really bad." She yanks off her glasses and clenches them in her fist. "I need to call Gran before she sees this."

I follow her down the hall to her bedroom, wondering if she'll let me inside. I didn't get a chance to tell her what I'd done. It's weighing on me. I'm a criminal.

Nora holds the door open, then slams it shut behind us. She collapses on the bed and powers up her phone. A whole new string of texts from Amber appears. She swipes them away and speaks. "Gran, it's me. Call me back when you get this."

The phone rings less than thirty seconds later, and once again, I'm only tracking Nora's end of the conversation, leaving me to guess what her grandmother is saying. I pace her excessively neat room, trying to figure it out.

"Wait until tomorrow when Rosh Hashanah is over, Gran. You know you shouldn't travel. You probably can't get a flight until then anyway…I'm fine. I promise." There's a very long pause while Nora's silent.

Then she says, "I don't. How could I? Are you sure? Yes, I think it's possible. Fifty percent. I know. Because I didn't know how else to explain it."

She must be talking about the DNA match again. Looking at me, she goes on, "They're back at Claire's house. Gran, I told you I'm fine."

There's a lot more said, but most of it flies by me as fear ramps inside my chest. Is she going to send me home? Oh, hell, I still haven't told her what I did.

She punches off her phone and for a second I'm afraid she knows.

I can explain—" I'm not sure if I say it out loud because when she starts talking again, her words make little sense.

"People said there was a boy with her. Mom was occupied, talking to somebody she knew from work. Apparently, I'd wandered over to the Once in a Blue Moose gift shop to look at the stuffed polar bears in the display window. I don't remember much of it. The little boy called me by my name, a security guard told me later. And when I went to find out what he wanted, the lady grabbed me by the hand and said…and said…"

"Said what, Nora?" Nora's having a full-blown panic attack. I drop to the bed beside her and rub her back in tight, soothing circles. "Can I get you your pills? Water?"

"No pills. I'm okay. The lady said Mom had been hurt and I had to come with her. I didn't understand because my mother had been right beside me. But then the little boy started crying. I'd forgotten that. I'd forgotten he was there. She kept tugging me toward a car in the parking garage, telling me Mom was hurt…They're so dark inside with so many levels and echoes.

Voices you can hear but you don't know where they're coming from. Cars honking. Brakes screeching. The smells. God, I hate those places. That's when Mom and the mall guards caught up. But the lady got away. And the boy—he had dark hair like me—and he was crying. I'd forgotten that." She lays her head on my shoulder and shivers. Her fingers grip her knees, knuckles white.

"This happened when you were four at the mall downtown?" She's told me the story before, but not the details, not like this.

"It was the spring before I went to kindergarten. Claire, Gran thinks the woman who tried to take me was Alice."

Oh. My stomach does a flip-flop like a belly dive off a high board. It's the kind that can really take the wind out of you. I don't want to say it, but I have to. "And you think the boy might have been Ethan?"

"It has to be. That's got to be why he's here. Alice sent him to get me. First Nick, then me, because I wasn't in my bassinette when she slipped into the nursery to abduct us. She was only able to kidnap him. So then later, he tried to lure me away from Mom so Alice could have me too."

I don't believe it, but I still can't catch my breath. "Nora, even if it's true, Ethan was just a child himself. He wouldn't have known what he was doing. You said yourself he was crying. He was a victim just like you. And now, well, it was a long time ago. He left Juneau to get away from her, not to take you back to her."

She doesn't seem to hear me. I go on massaging her back. However this plays out, this is my fault because I brought them together. I feel worse than before. Alice is dead, and Ethan may very well have killed her. And me...I've been lost in my own little world since last night. My mind replays the scene in Caseo's parking lot with Ethan and Alice yelling at one another. I was as shocked as Nora when Alice punched him in the face. Even more when Ethan shoved her into the garbage bin. But before that, I'm trying to recall...did Alice look at Nora with a shred of recognition? Did she speak to Nora? Everybody was so upset. I was furious and lost.

Nora pushes herself off the bed and stomps into the living room where Ethan has turned the TV on again. She rips the cord from the wall and shouts into the instant silence, "Stand up!"

"What?" He glances at me, confused.

"Stand up, jerk. On your feet. Don't bother faking a limp because I know you're pretending. Just admit that you went back to Caseo's and killed Alice. You took my car after I went to bed. You grabbed that metal rod and hit her over and over again until she died. I've seen the picture of her. But hell, I don't blame you. I wish I'd done it myself."

Her chest heaves so that she has to stop. She bends and curl her fingers on her knees. When she starts up again, her tone's a shade calmer. "I don't blame you, Ethan. I swear I don't. But you have to get out of the house. Leave now. You're eating all our food. You're watching my grandmother's television. You're leaving your shit everywhere for me to clean up. Gran doesn't know you. She doesn't want to know you, and I don't either. She's my gran, not yours."

Poor Ethan. I recoil in sympathy for him. He throws his phone on the floor and kicks over the coffee table.

"Guess what, Nora," he shouts back. "I don't want to know you either. I wish I'd never met you. I wish I'd died at birth just like they told you." His chin trembles. "I wish I'd never been born."

And suddenly I realize it's up to me to make this right. "Let's try to be rational, all of us."

"You tried to kidnap me," Nora cuts in, her fury building again like a geyser threatening to erupt.

"What are you talking about?" Ethan's eyes flit to the spilled cereal and his empty plate on the floor.

"Thirteen years ago at the Fifth Avenue Mall. You and Alice. You were with her. You talked to me. You told me I needed to listen to your mom. And then, she grabbed my arm and tried to steal me away from my real mother. But I got away."

Ethan's anger fizzles out. "No, I didn't. You remember that? Because I don't."

Nora looks a shade less certain. "Everybody said it. The guards, the witnesses, my gran."

"Your grandmother was there too?"

This is my opening. I splay my fingers across the back of the sofa. "Come on, you guys, we're all upset, saying things we don't mean."

"Was she there?" Ethan yells again.

"You know she wasn't."

"No, I don't, because I wasn't either. Or if I was, I don't remember. But look, if you want me to leave your house, I will. If you want me to turn myself in, I'll do it. Man, for a sister, you're a piece of work."

"Stop it. Listen to me, both of you," I try again. "We don't have all the facts. We need to talk to the woman Alice was staying with." They turn and look at me as if just now realizing I'm here. "Della Rhodes? Your old neighbor, Ethan? Alice said she lives on Camelot."

Nora nods slowly. Her breath comes more evenly. "Camelot and Boniface. I know where it is, on the east side of the city by Fairview."

Ethan scratches the back of his neck. "Mrs. Rhodes was our next-door neighbor when I was a kid. But how's she going to help?"

"Well, for one thing, she can tell us more about the Alice she knew, the one who ran a home daycare business. She and Alice must have stayed close for Alice to call her when she got in yesterday." Neither Nora nor Ethan look convinced. "Isn't it worth a shot?" I say. "Or do we want to end this and have your brother turn himself in to the cops. Is that what you want, Ethan?"

"Obviously not," he mumbles, gazing at the overturned table.

"What about you?" I say to Nora.

She doesn't answer right away, but I figure she's on board when she lets loose a sigh and starts scooping up the cereal spilled all over the floor.

CHAPTER THIRTY-THREE

Nora

That damn Ethan. Okay, maybe he is my brother and I shouldn't be so hard on him. The thing is he's also a pain in the ass. He's hungry and insists on stopping at the City Diner before we go to see Della Rhodes. Like we have time? The cops have my name. It won't be long before they show up at my house. They may be there already.

Ethan glances at a menu on his phone and sends Claire inside, telling her to get us each a tuna melt with fries. He doesn't ask what we want. He pays for it with a handful of crumpled bills. Probably some of the money he stole from his stepfather.

When Claire returns, he puts his big brown shoes on my dashboard, muttering for the millionth time that this is a wild goose chase while stuffing french fries in his mouth.

"You've got a better idea?" Claire asks, reaching between the seat and the door and squeezing my arm. She knows I'd rather have her in the front seat next to me. Our peacemaker is trying to make everyone happy as usual. It's clearly an impossible task.

What I want to say to Ethan is, *If you think we're wasting time, why don't we simply head down to the police station? I'd be happy to drop you off and let you work this out on your own.*

I'm doing this for Claire because he has no clue how worried he's made Gran, and I doubt he cares. Gran was beside herself with guilt for not telling me about his abduction or discussing my attempted kidnapping with me.

We were given a temporary reprieve when she agreed to wait until tomorrow to fly back to Anchorage. However, with the mess Ethan's made at her house, there's no way she won't figure out he's been staying there. Just something else to worry about.

The burnt orange sun slips in the sky as Ethan noisily slurps the last of his Coke. He wads his sandwich wrapper into a ball and starts to toss it over his shoulder into the back seat next to Claire. He catches my annoyed expression, and says, "You know your car is really old, right?"

"Meaning it's okay to make it your personal trash can? Next time let's take your car." That shuts him down, but only for a minute. He climbs out and walks our trash to a can beside the building.

When he comes back, he says, "She won't recognize me." He must mean Della Rhodes.

"Maybe not," says Claire. "But you'll know your old house, won't you?"

"Probably, I guess."

"And Alice said she lives next door. Ergo, it won't matter if she doesn't recognize you. You'll be able to direct us to her house, and she can tell us about Alice and whoever might have killed her."

"Ergo," Ethan scoffs as I start the car and head north again on Minnesota. "What, are you like, a college professor?"

"Don't be an idiot. You can wait in the car if you want. Nora and I are going to introduce ourselves and find out what she knows."

I feel like I'm chauffeuring children. Still, I wonder if Ethan may be right. If it's been more than a decade since Alice and

Della last saw each other, are we wasting our time? Not if the police have reached my house.

I slow and skirt around a moose that ignored the fencing designed to keep it off the road. From there, I head east until we find ourselves in a rundown neighborhood of small apartment buildings and split-levels with box fans in the windows, chain-link fences surrounding weedy front yards, and double wide driveways dotted with oil stains.

Ethan takes his feet off the dashboard and points to a small yellow house with a for lease sign by the driveway and a dead tree in the yard. "We lived in that one. Story of my life…ugly, huh?"

And you had the nerve to make fun of Gran's house? There's a fourplex on one side and an olive-green ranch with a newish-looking roof on the other. I park and turn off the engine. It's almost five o'clock. Cars whizz by us. A semi spewing black smoke nearly runs over a squirrel. It barely manages to scoot under a car without tires parked halfway up the block. Country music from the nineties echoes from one of the lower units in the fourplex.

Claire and I get out. "You've got this?" I say.

"Sure. But feel free to jump in with questions of your own anytime you want. Last chance, Ethan. Are you coming?"

"No way. That woman gave me the creeps. Ask her what she was doing last night between ten p.m. and midnight."

Claire hesitates as if she thinks he'll change his mind, and then we open the gate and walk up to the front porch of the green house. The windows are masked with heavy drapes. A terra-cotta pot of dead chrysanthemum stands guard on a dusty glass table by the door.

Clair pushes the doorbell a few times. No one answers. She raps her knuckles on the splintered slab, eyeing a daddy long-leg crawling out from what looks like fur under the mat. I guess I'm lucky insects don't scare me.

I lift my gaze in time to see a curtain shift. Claire knocks again.

"Whatever you're selling, I don't want it," a middle-aged female voice calls from inside.

"We'd like to talk to you about Alice St. James," Claire calls back.

"Just a minute." A chain audibly slides back, and the door creaks open a crack. "Wait here."

Naturally, I peek inside as a woman in her forties wearing a calf-length terry bathrobe with wrinkled beige pajamas underneath steps through a small living room and shuts a door down the hall. When she comes back, flopping her fuzzy mules across a brown shag carpet, I understand what Ethan meant about creepy. Granted, I can be a little judgy about people who don't get dressed first thing in the morning, but even if you work from home, where's your sense of pride in your appearance? It's Gran's voice speaking in my head.

Not relevant, I tell myself.

"Are you Mrs. Rhodes?" Claire asks.

"Who wants to know?" the woman responds in a guttural voice. She wears her mousy brown hair in a twist like mine. Hopefully, mine looks better. Her cheeks are pale like she doesn't get outside much. "Are you cops?"

"We're not," Claire replies crisply, gesturing to the car where Ethan sits slouched in the front seat. "We're friends of Ethan St. James, Alice's son. I'm Claire, and this is Nora. We talked to Alice last night. She indicated that she planned to stay with you while in Anchorage."

"Did she now. Well, that's interesting. What did you say your names were again?"

I start to open my mouth, then shut it. It's too late to give fake names.

"Claire and Nora. And that's Ethan in the car. You knew him when he was a little boy. He's seventeen now, almost eighteen."

"Is he shy?"

"A little. He doesn't think you'll remember him."

"Of course I do. He was an unusual child, quieter than most. Alice ran a daycare center next door. The woman loved having kiddies around the house. She even liked the babies, which some won't take. I saw on the news this morning that she'd passed. I should probably call the authorities, but honestly, I don't know what I'd tell them. She called me yesterday and said she was coming for a visit. Asked if I could put her up for the night. We chatted for a moment when she dropped her stuff off, and then she left again. Said she was meeting up with Ethan and that he'd run away. I guess I could pass that along to the police."

"Yeah," I mumble. "Why don't you do that?"

Somehow, we've worked our way inside the tiny house. I scan the walls for pictures of Ethan or Alice, anything that might help. There are a couple of family-type photos above a big screen TV. A younger, more vibrant version of Della Rhodes, with a clean-shaven balding man in navy coveralls, likely a husband or brother. Another with two older people who are probably her parents. There's a jute dream catcher on the wall (spider catcher, in my opinion), some pretty decent leather furniture that's too large for the room, and a stack of cardboard boxes in a corner. A crumpled mess of tissue paper rests on top. The house is laid out a little like Gran's but better furnished. I hate to say it, but Della Rhodes may have better taste. No kitschy Hummel figurines on the pony wall between the living room and kitchen for her.

"I'm pretty sure the police already know about Ethan," Claire continues smoothly. "In fact, we're on our way to see them now. Ethan didn't kill her, by the way. We're hoping you could help us understand who might have wanted to hurt her. It's possible"—Claire leans in as if confiding a secret—"Ethan isn't her son. We have reason to believe she kidnapped him from the hospital shortly after he was born."

This doesn't come off as the bombshell it should. Claire's eyes slide over to meet mine as Mrs. Rhodes touches a cleft in her chin thoughtfully. "I always wondered. It was, how should I put this? Alice ran a somewhat dubious operation. The daycare thing, I mean. I don't think she had a license, and you know that woman absolutely adored babies. Loved the way they smelled and their sweet little feet. Didn't even mind changing diapers. She worked at a hospital when she first moved in next door. Then one day, she up and quit and started babysitting. Just one child at first. That might have been Ethan, I suppose, because one minute he wasn't there and the next he was. And then five or six others who rotated in and out. Come to think of it, there was a little girl who disappeared from her care. It turned out, I think, to be a custodial abduction. You know, a parent?"

I'm bobbing my head like crazy at her because it's all I can manage. Della Rhodes knew or at least suspected Ethan wasn't Alice's son and never said a word? And a little girl might have vanished from her care? "Did she"—I don't know how to say it—"was the little girl ever found?"

"Oh, I think so. I'm sure the cops can tell you. You know"— she takes a closer look at me—"she would have liked you. She liked the dark ones. I don't mean dark skin really. Dark eyes and hair. Not the fair ones. Alice St. James had a type."

This creeps me out more than anything. Alice had a type. Kids with dark eyes and hair like Ethan and me. Normally, it's loud noises, unfamiliar smells, and strangers invading my personal space that trigger my anxiety. But I feel dangerously close to losing it right here. My vision swims. My stomach gets tight.

Claire must see it in my face because she traces the inside of my elbow subtly with a finger, bringing me to my senses and guiding me back to the front door.

"Do you have any idea who might have wanted to hurt Alice? Anyone with a grudge against her?" she asks.

"You mean besides her boy, Ethan?" Rhodes shakes her head. "She was just saying yesterday how he'd become quite a handful."

Claire blinks, but manages to maintain her composure. "Thank you for talking to us. You've been most helpful."

"Well, certainly, if you say so. Happy to be of service." Rhodes makes a noise in the back of her throat. "Guess I'd better go call the cops. No sense waiting for them to contact me. Goodness, Alice offed last night. Who'd have thought? Bye now. Tell little Ethan hello for me, will you?"

"We will," says Claire. "We will."

CHAPTER THIRTY-FOUR

Claire

Nora says she's glad to get out of Della Rhodes's house. I am too. Talk about unproductive. I wish I hadn't suggested the visit as all it seemed to have accomplished was to ramp up Nora's stress. A moving van roars by, filling the air with the scent of diesel and vibrating her car as we climb inside and lock the doors.

Ethan glances up from a game on his phone. "Creepy. Am I right?"

"Not wrong," Nora says quietly. She starts the car and waits as more vehicles go by, then pulls around the block to the parking lot of a cannabis dispensary. She puts the car in park and shuts off the engine.

Ethan sits up with a grin. "Okay. I like where this is going. Do you have your fake ID with you, Claire?"

"Shut up."

"I'm only saying…"

"Don't." I'm in the back seat again and can see Nora's anxious eyes in the rearview mirror. I don't know this area of town, but I seriously doubt she stopped here for weed. A group of middle-schoolers mill about on the walk in front. An older guy with clip-on suspenders and a Santa Claus-type beard says something to them that I can't hear and heads inside.

"Obviously we can't go back to Caseo's, but maybe if we found a coffee kiosk where we can sit for a bit and think," I start.

"No more coffee. If I have another cup, I think my head will explode." Nora keeps both hands on the steering wheel.

"Me, too," Ethan agrees. "How about ice cream?"

"No thanks," we say.

"Then how about heading back to Clarice's house?" He glances over his shoulder to where I'm crammed behind Nora with my legs folded like a letter in an envelope. "Maybe your dad has bought more beer? I think we could all do with a six-pack."

Nora frowns, and I say more nastily than I intend, "Seriously, Ethan. You've got to stop being such a freeloader. You know you're never going to pay him back for what you've already taken."

He gazes over his shoulder at me with a gloomy expression. "Jeez, Claire. Why don't you just say what you're really thinking." He reaches into his back pocket and tosses a twenty from his wallet in my lap. "Here. This ought to cover most of it."

Now, I really feel awful, but I don't know how to back out of it. "This isn't necessary."

"Please," he says archly. "I insist."

"Dad has company," I mumble, then again wish I'd kept my mouth shut. This is the problem with dishonesty. The deeper you dig yourself in, the harder it is to get yourself out.

Nora starts the car and drives a few more blocks to a funky little trailer park with ceramic pots of colorful flowers flanking a gravel entrance. Ethan rolls down the window and sticks his head out to look around. "I don't get it."

"There's nothing to get. I need to think." She takes out her phone.

I'm as lost as Ethan, but I'm accustomed to her moods.

After a couple of minutes, he climbs out and gently shuts the door. He makes his way to a baby-blue vintage trailer with its hitch resting on a cinder block. He circles it, eyeing it curiously, then cups a hand to one of the windows as if not considering that there might be people inside. And Nora's right. He doesn't limp at all.

I wait a second and crawl awkwardly over the stick shift into the passenger seat, banging both my knees in the process. "I don't want you to think I'm making excuses for him…"

"Hang on." She studies an open browser on her phone. "I think this is the right story, a little girl taken from a local daycare center fifteen years ago. Mother dropped her off, warned the provider that only she was allowed to pick her up. Provider couldn't find the girl at first…Looks like it worked out okay though—" Nora nearly leaps out of her seat as Ethan bangs an open hand against the side of her car.

"Hey, sis. Any chance you could show me where I'm buried?"

He peers through the front windshield at us, looking like a werewolf with his shaggy bangs hanging in his face. "I mean, I know it's a crazy thing to ask because I'm dead. Only not dead. I show up out of the blue and we don't exactly hit it off. It doesn't take a genius to figure out that I'm not what you're expecting, and I gotta be honest, you're pretty unusual too. The only thing we have in common is we both know Claire. So, anyway, I'm just trying to understand it. Does that make any sense? What do you say? Show me where I'm buried, if it's not too much to ask?"

Nora's expression barely changes. "I guess it's not. You want to go right now?"

"Sure, if that's okay." He eyes me sitting in the passenger seat and when I don't move he says reluctantly that he'll get in back.

Nora takes Northern Lights, but we don't pass Caseo's. We turn before it, heading south through a nicer, more genteel neighborhood to a small graveyard squeezed between two houses. Anchorage is like this. Odd places like abandoned car lots, trailer parks, homeless camps, and little graveyards tucked behind strip malls and interspersed with tidy suburban homes.

We get out. Nora leads the way to a row at the very back. There are several stones embedded in the ground. All children, I realize, looking at the dates. Some babies, some a few years old. An entire graveyard just for children makes me very sad.

"Here's Nick's." Nora squats, scooping away damp, decaying leaves from a monument in a corner beneath an old cherry tree. "Well, not here, of course. It's where I thought he was." Her words trail off.

When Ethan kneels beside her, she stands and moves away abruptly.

"It's really empty then? There's no one there at all?" he asks.

"That's what Gran says. Mom and Dad were determined not to forget you. They bought the stone and everything. Used to visit regularly. Gran told me they never got over losing you."

Ethan doesn't say anything to that. He wipes a sleeve across his eyes and stays where he is for several minutes hardly moving. At last, he rises and heads back for the car. We let him get ahead of us.

"I do feel sorry for him. I really do," Nora whispers. "Growing up with Alice and everything you've told me would've been a nightmare. I just don't know if I believe much else of what he says. He lied about the student exchange program. He lied about attending North. He lied about his host family—a pretty elaborate story, you have to admit—and he clearly hated Alice. I'm going to drop you guys off, and then go back to Mrs. Rhodes's house and talk to her again."

I open my mouth.

"Claire. Please don't try to talk me out of it."

I'm not happy about it, but what am I supposed to do? We stop short of the grave of an infant who lived a single day. "Okay." I swallow. "I'll go with you."

"No." She shakes her head. "But not because I don't want you there. You aren't objective. Face it, Claire. You love Ethan. There's nothing wrong with that, but you don't see his faults. You said you don't want to make excuses for him, but that's exactly what you do. And anyway"—she pauses as her gaze drifts back to her brother's marker—"Amber's going. I knew you wouldn't want me there alone, so I texted her the address. She's meeting me."

She might as well have punched me in the gut. I'm barely listening when she says she won't be gone long. Thirty minutes, forty tops.

"Do you want me to drop you off at your house?"

My heart quickens. "I'd rather stay with you at your house."

She lifts her chin. "All right then. Gran's place. I'll be back before dinner."

CHAPTER THIRTY-FIVE

Nora

Amber steps out of her car on Boniface and hurries over to embrace me. "Hey, you! You don't know how happy I am that you've finally come to your senses. Let's get this over with, and then we'll go out. A movie, the post-game bonfire at East, anything you want. Who knew Claire would be such a mess? She seemed pretty normal back in Juneau, which just shows you how people can be really good at hiding who they are."

So true, I think. I lock my car, catching a glimpse of a tiny flake of adhesive on her nose, probably from the charcoal strips she uses every night to reduce her pores. Her scent is so familiar. Not unpleasant, but it never meshed with mine.

I had to fill her in on recent events to get her to meet me here, but the fact that I've been identified as one of the persons of interest seen with Alice last night came as no surprise to her. Amber follows the local news.

"This is Della Rhodes's house. That's where Ethan and Alice lived." I point as we cross the street and enter Della's front yard.

"Ah," she murmurs, for once keeping her opinions to herself.

Della opens the door right away when I knock. "Oh, dear, you're back. I don't know what else I can tell you. But come on in if you want."

I stay put. "That's okay. This won't take long. I had another question about Alice."

"I'm listening."

"You seemed to indicate earlier that you hadn't kept in touch with her since she left."

"That's right. I'm not much on phone calls. We exchanged a couple of emails, and I used to pick up her mail. Lots of collection notices and catalogues."

"Did she have any family around? Brothers, sisters, parents?"

"Mmm. Nothing like that. But I have no way of knowing, really. We weren't that close."

"No friends stopping by then?"

"Like I said, we weren't close, so I wouldn't have noticed."

Amber starts to do a little dance beside me that I pretend not to see. "What about her husband, do you know him? His name is Riley Crew."

"Never heard of him." Della's placid expression is beginning to give way to something else. She looks irritated, as if I'm keeping her from another engagement. Perhaps a cocktail, or a bath. Maybe she gets dressed up in the evenings for a night out on the town. I try to picture her sitting on a stool at a club, chatting up out-of-town businessmen while sipping a dry martini.

"May I use your bathroom?" Amber asks. "Sorry, I'm on a liquid diet."

"First door on the left down the hall." Della turns back to me as Amber scoots by to get inside. "Listen. I don't know how I can make this any clearer. Alice wasn't social. I'm not social. She ran a daycare business. That's pretty much all I can tell you."

"So, a dozen or so years pass without any sort of communication, and then out of the blue she called and asked if she could stay with you?" I'm trying to sound casual, but the new me is tired of feeling anxious, sick of feeling that events are beyond my control.

"Yes. No. A dozen?"

"Thirteen years. Ethan says they moved to Juneau before he went to kindergarten."

"That isn't right." She frowns and glances at a phone that appears from a fold in her bathrobe amid a wad of tissues.

Amber comes back out, wiping her palms down the front of her crisp, linen sundress and adjusting her designer frame sunglasses on the top of her head. "Thanks," she says to Della. "Nora, are you done?"

"In a sec." I stifle my own irritation because hurrying me along wasn't part of the plan. "I'm sorry to keep bugging you, Mrs. Rhodes. The thing is, I just don't feel like I've got a good read on the situation. Ethan's my brother, but I don't know him. And Alice may have tried to kidnap me before she left for Juneau. Now she's been murdered, and Ethan will probably be blamed. You're the only person here who seems to know much of anything, so if you can think of something else…"

"But I didn't know her. I've said that." Della pulls her bathrobe around her shoulders, like a cloak. The phone vanishes back inside her pocket. "Alice and I were neighbors. Neighbors chat. That's all. Listen, I can only tell you this. Alice and Ethan left, came back five years ago, and then left again. All this business about abductions—that's for the cops to figure out, don't you think? I'm not saying Alice had a heart of gold because she didn't, but we got along. Tell you what, leave me your number. If I think of anything else, I'll give you a ring."

Amber hands me a pen and a slip of paper from her handbag. I write my name and number on it. "Thanks," I say, probably not sounding very grateful. The door closes behind us, and we head back to our cars.

"Neighbors only, so that's the end of that." Amber stops beside her car.

"What did you see inside?"

"Not much. The house is clean. Empty boxes in the living room like you said and a locked door down the hall. No illegal drugs in the medicine cabinet. I didn't check the toilet tank because I didn't think it was that type of operation."

I smile in spite of myself. Amber can be funny when she tries, and she's smart. I called her because I needed a fresh perspective. Also, because I need her once and for all to understand that I'm never getting back together with her. I owe it to Claire.

"Now what?" She leans against her car trunk. The light at the corner changes and a fresh wave of cars rushes by in a deafening roar. The color of the sky changes to a bruised blue as the fading sun dips behind a cloud.

I tap a foot in thought. "One, Rhodes said Alice and Ethan went to Juneau and came back. Ethan never mentioned that. And two, how does Riley Crew fit into this?"

"The stepdad? Maybe he doesn't. Were he and Alice married when they lived here?"

"No idea."

"Ethan can tell you."

"Right." I make a mental note to ask him. "Three, she didn't blink when I mentioned Ethan was my brother."

"Well, again, maybe she doesn't care."

"Or she already knew."

"Possible." Amber shrugs. "Okay. Four, she never asked who I was."

"An appalling lack of curiosity?" I'm only half-kidding.

"Or distracted. What about the house next door. You said Alice and Ethan lived there?"

I eye the for-lease sign in the yard. "It's owned by a real estate corporation. I checked. Corporations apparently buy up older houses on a down market, fix them up, and resell them when the economy improves."

Amber stares across the street. "Huh. Still waiting on the fix-up part, I guess."

I nod. The house where my brother once lived is a mere two-point-seven miles from where I grew up in a home that's more like Claire's. To think that Ethan and I might have passed on the street when we were younger. That we might have played in the same playgrounds and parks. Or stood in the same cotton candy line at the state fair in Palmer next to one another, never knowing, never recognizing one another as brother and sister.

He also might have willingly participated in the plot to kidnap me. *"Bitch. You're the one that's dead,"* he'd said.

I blink, attempting to break the loop of images running through my mind that starts with Ethan tiptoeing into my bedroom for my car keys, then quietly easing the car out of the driveway and driving back to Caseo's to crush Alice's ribs with a piece of metal pipe.

Back at the cemetery, I felt an almost irresistible urge to get down on my hands and knees and claw through the dirt below Nick's gravestone. I managed to stop myself. But I might still do it.

"What are you going to do?" Amber's voice brings me back to a cool afternoon ripe with mosquitoes and the scent of diesel from a trash truck rumbling by. Instinctively, I count the rubber cans assembled in the bed. Seven. Two rows of three neatly strapped in. One rolling loose behind the others. I've never liked odd numbers; they're so untidy.

"I don't know," I say.

"Well, I have an idea. Let's go grab a bite to eat and head over to the bonfire." She pats her pockets.

"Looking for something?"

"My phone. Never mind. I must have left it at home. We'll get cozy under a blanket. I've got a bottle of whiskey in my trunk that's guaranteed to make you forget your troubles."

"Amber," I say earnestly. "This has got to stop. No more texts or phone calls."

"None?" Her curious gaze settles on my face, as if she's trying to decide if I'm joking.

"Only if it's absolutely necessary. Life or death."

She lifts her chin. "Oh, come on. You don't really mean it. We belong together. If it weren't for you, I might have died in Juneau."

So, that explains it. "I did what anyone else would do."

"Claire didn't."

"That's because she was driving. She got out to help as soon as she could. Amber, we weren't good together. It took me a while to see it, but I think you must have known it early on."

"Oh, dear God, not that again," she scoffs. "I've apologized a hundred times for breaking up with you. It was a mistake, I admit it. Do you ever think you might be too sensitive?"

It's exactly the wrong thing to say. Resentment floods my veins. I want to yell at her for all the times she trivialized the things I've said and done. "That's not it! You don't care about me. I know you think you do, but what you really want to do is change me."

"That's not true."

"Really? Tell me you don't wish I wore contact lenses."

"You'd look better in them."

"Maybe so, but I can't put my finger in my eye. I just can't. Same reason I won't wear earbuds. Amber, you know how I am. I file my emails under labels so that at the end of every day my inbox is empty. I delete my text streams when I'm done with them. I color-code the clothes in my closet. I line up my shoes, heels facing out. I do my homework the day it's assigned and can't think about much else until it's finished. I sweat over whether or not to use an Oxford comma on school reports. If my gas tank falls below the halfway mark, I have to fill it right away. Sometimes—"

"Okay! Okay, I get it." She lifts her hands in surrender. "You tend to be obsessive. At least you see it and can change if you want."

"That's just it. I like who I am. It's you who wants to change me. You should find someone who's more like you. But it doesn't mean we can't be friends."

She makes a face. "God, I hate it when people say that. It's so dismissive, like, I'm the one with the problem, not you. If it weren't for Claire getting between us—"

"Don't," I say. "Claire's got nothing to do with this. You and I broke up weeks before we went to Juneau."

Amber gazes off down the street, her perfect skin glowing in the early twilight. She sighs, draws her sunglasses off her forehead and over her eyes and leans in unexpectedly to kiss my cheek. I give a start, which causes her to draw back with a chuckle. "What's that song you play on the piano? 'Don't Go Changing?'"

"'Just the Way You Are,' by Billy Joel."

"Yeah, that's it. Isn't it funny how there's a song for every situation, for every mood you feel? Anyway, don't go changing, Nora Thomas. You're weird, but okay."

There it is. I'm still weird. "Thanks, I guess?"

That makes her laugh even harder. "You need any more help with this Ethan stuff, just let me know. I'm here for you. And"—she pauses—"I really am sorry for giving you such grief about him before. I totally get it now. He's your brother. Just be careful, will you?"

My brother. "Yes, of course."

"Good. Talk at you later, then. Take care."

She gets in her car and drives off.

I watch her go, then do the same. For the first time in a long time, I believe she understands me. Too bad it didn't happen before. Then again, if it had I wouldn't have gotten to know Claire. Speaking of which, that little itch in my brain has returned, the one that tells me something with Claire is off, and it has nothing to do with Amber, despite what she said this morning. I'm not even sure it has anything to do with Ethan. I wish I could put my finger on it because I don't like feeling suspicious. It's just the way I am.

Claire and Ethan are waiting in the living room when I get home. Ethan practically pounces on me the second I step inside the door. "Well? What did she say?"

He follows me around the couch, nearly tripping on my heels.

"She says you've moved back and forth between Anchorage and Juneau a few times. That you lived here as recently as five years ago."

He steps back, eyeing me in surprise, then lifts himself onto the back of the couch to sit, banging his heels and no doubt leaving marks that I'll have to clean up later. "Bullshit. That's a lie."

"Why would she lie?"

"How should I know? Because she's creepy?"

"Anything else?" Claire asks.

"How long have Alice and Riley been married, Ethan?"

"I don't know, exactly. Five years? Happened when I was in juvie. They'd known each other a while."

"Did they know each other when you were little, like before you entered kindergarten?"

"You mean when we tried to kidnap you?" He sticks out his tongue.

"Yeah," I say. "It's exactly what I mean." Ethan and Claire have done a pretty decent job of straightening up the house. Or more likely, Claire has. She understands how I hate a mess and cares enough to try to make things better for me. To that end, the coffee table has been righted, the TV muted, and there's no more cereal on the floor. In the kitchen, all the dishes have been put away. I see no sign of moisture rings from Ethan's cans on the table.

We stare at each other for a couple of seconds. Ethan backs down first. "Probably." He shrugs.

"How many times have you lived in Anchorage?"

"Once. Twice, if you count now. Nora, I swear it's the truth, and I can prove it. I spent eight months at JYC for the broken arm thing when I was twelve. I met Claire a month after my release. She'd know if I left since then. Tell her Clairy Toons, tell her I've been in Juneau ever since."

"It's true," says Claire. "We met freshman year."

A scene on TV catches my attention, the reporter Mimi Rodriguez sitting behind her desk.

"As we mentioned earlier today, forty-two-year-old Alice St. James, victim of last night's homicide in the parking lot of a midtown coffeehouse, has now been linked with two persons of interest, Ethan St. James of Juneau and North Anchorage High School senior Nora Thomas. Authorities now have reason to believe that Ethan is Baby Boy Thomas, Nora Thomas's twin, an infant kidnapped mere hours after his birth from AC eighteen years ago.

"The sensational story captivated the city for weeks when a woman walked into the unattended maternity ward and stole the newborn from his crib. Nora, who was with her parents at the

time, was unharmed. Though the entire area was on alert, Baby
Boy Thomas was never found. Unconfirmed reports suggest
that Ethan, incorrectly identified as adopted earlier, may have
recently learned that last night's homicide victim was not his
biological mother and that he is indeed Baby Boy Thomas. Stay
tuned as we follow this rapidly unfolding story."

Ethan eyes the screen dully. "Oh, goodie. Now I have a
motive."

CHAPTER THIRTY-SIX

Claire

For half a second, Nora looks like she's about to collapse. She straightens her shoulders and heads for the kitchen, dragging the kitchen chairs into the living room.

"Have a seat." She motions me to take the one on the right, lowering herself into the other. She looks almost as prim and proper as her gran. "Has anyone been here since I left?"

Ethan, still on the back of the couch, shakes his head. We both stay quiet, neither of us mentioning the loud, insistent knocking on the door a short time ago. I haven't answered my father's texts either, which are coming more frequently, along with an angry voicemail, saying I need to get my ass back home.

"Let's take a moment then to think this through. Someone told the reporter we're siblings. Somebody also told her that you, Ethan, are Baby Boy Thomas and that Alice abducted you."

"Could it have been Nurse Berg, or even Della Rhodes?" I say.

Ethan groans. "It's got to be Riley. I took his money, every cent he had."

"You're saying this is the type of thing he'd do?"

"Oh, yeah. He's doing it to get back at me. It was a lot of money. He'll kill me if he finds me."

I can feel my eyeballs bulge. *Was it Riley at the door then?* I'd just assumed it was the police.

Nora purses her lips, looking thoughtful. "If that's true, it means we have another problem. Where's the money?"

"I've got it," Ethan replies cagily.

"Here in my house?"

"At Claire's."

"Awesome. So, you're keeping stolen money at the house of a friend who took you in. Have you given any thought to how that might have put her and her dad in jeopardy? Or us, if Riley thinks to look for you here?"

Ethan bounces a knee nervously. I can tell the idea hasn't occurred to him. "He doesn't know where I am."

Nora sighs. "You really believe that? Ethan, you just got through telling us he must have told the reporter we were twins. And she just said I go to North High School. How hard would it be for him to find my address?" Ethan doesn't reply.

I pipe in with, "She's right, Ethan. We can't do this on our own any longer. You can't run away. It's time to go to the police."

"Man, I hate this. I really hate it. You guys saw what happened. Alice hit me first. I was trying to protect myself."

A shadow passes over Nora's face. I can't tell if she's feeling sympathetic. Ethan's eyes fill, but he picks up his jacket and we head for the front door.

We don't get far. Outside stands a uniformed cop. A female officer, with her arms folded, is behind him. At the curb, I see my father getting out of the big black Tesla he bought three weeks ago, his phone as always in his hand. Our eyes meet. A small piece of me dies inside. This is what cop shows call a reckoning. It's over for me now.

The first officer speaks. "Ethan St. James? My name is Sergeant Miller and this is Officer Deidra Wolluk. We'd like you to come with us and answer a few questions regarding an assault that occurred last night."

"Am I under arrest?"

"Not at this time. For now, we just have some questions, a few items we need you to clear up. It's no good attempting to avoid this, son," Miller says as Ethan skirts behind me. "First, though, we've been given a bit of misinformation. As I understand it now, you're a minor without a proper parent?"

"I'm seventeen."

"I see. Then Officer Wolluk here will act as your advocate until someone from social services is available. Let me see your hands, please. Do you possess any weapons on your person? Anything that might be used to hurt me, Wolluk, or yourself?"

Ethan assures him that he doesn't. Nora surprises me by asking if we can go with him.

Miller turns his attention to her. "Ah, you must be the sister. We're going to want to talk to you at some point too. I know your grandmother very well, a fine lady. You owe her a phone call. I trust you'll take care of it and not go anywhere tonight?"

Nora gulps. "I'll call her right away."

"Good. She'll appreciate that. As for you"—he turns to me—"You, young lady, are wanted elsewhere."

"Claire, get over here," Dad shouts.

Nora's neighbors are assembling on their lawns, their faces illuminated by the squad car's flashing lights. Miller leads Ethan away. I head over to my father's car, not daring to look at Nora. Will she ever forgive me? I hate myself. My stomach hurts. My throat's dry. I can't seem to get enough saliva in my mouth to swallow. I want to start the day over. I want to make pancakes from scratch. I want to mow a yard, or walk a dog. I want to be anywhere but here. My chance to explain myself to Nora has come and gone.

A woman in an orange raincoat passes me on the way to Nora's front porch. I reach the car. Dad gives me a disappointed look. "My God, Claire. How could you?"

CHAPTER THIRTY-SEVEN

Nora

How is it I'm feeling sorry for Ethan after all his lies? And what the hell is going on with Claire? I'm at a loss for words, but I'd better find some quick. I've got to call Gran.

Mrs. Miller—no relation to Officer Miller, I assume, since they didn't speak to one another—is Gran's long-time friend and neighbor. She's well into her eighties but as sharp as a tack. A former math teacher who tutors middle school students from all over the district, she's kind and strict and talks too much. She used to drive me crazy with math riddles when she'd see me after school.

She makes a tut-tut noise with her tongue—which might be just her dentures clicking—and maneuvers me back inside the house. "You heard him. Call your grandmother."

She slips off her rain jacket as I punch in Gran's number.

"I'm fine," I assure her. "You don't need to come home."

"I would if I could," Gran predictably frets. "I can't get a flight out until tomorrow."

I have to explain about Ethan, of course, as well as fill her in on everything that happened last night, including Alice's death,

Riley Crew's existence, the money Ethan stole and the fact that it's hidden at Claire's house. When I finish, her silence speaks volumes. I bet it takes every ounce of her strength not to fuss. Gran never yells, but the quieter she gets the madder she is.

"Nora, do me a favor," she says at last. "Lock the doors and windows and stay inside until I get back. Tell Edna I want her to stay with you."

"Yes, Gran."

"And please. Don't do anything reckless. Promise me? I have to say I'm glad that Claire's gone home. The two of you seem to have a knack for finding trouble. Ethan, my lord. I have a grandson."

"You do." She's taking it better than I expected.

"Will I like him?"

Good question. "I think so. He's weird like me, but in a different way."

She has a dozen more questions about him and ends by saying she's going to get an attorney for him. I can tell by the sound of her voice she's eager to meet him, looking forward to it. I wish I felt so sure of his intentions.

When I hang up, I slide my phone onto the table by the door, steeling myself for the horrible lie I'm about to tell. Fabrications don't come naturally to me. Up until now, I've made my life about being honest. But still, isn't a bit of dishonesty worth it for my brother and my girlfriend?

I turn to Edna Miller. "So, it's been an anxious couple of days, but everything's cleared up now. Gran said to tell you thanks for coming over. She should be home later tonight."

I hold my breath. Will Mrs. Miller buy it? What kind of person have I become? Am I a girl with a knack for finding trouble?

Mrs. Miller doesn't expect me to lie any more than Gran does. "Are you sure, dear? I don't mind waiting with you. I've got a couple of frozen pot pies in the freezer I could bring over."

"That's sweet of you, but I've eaten. You don't need to stay. I'm a big girl."

"That you are, practically grown up. Say, have I told you the fraction joke? Who's the inventor of fractions?"

"I give up."

"Henry the Eighth."

I chuckle. "That's a good one. I don't usually make jokes about fractions, but I will if I halve to."

She gets it right away. "Be safe, dear."

"I will."

For a good solid minute after she leaves, I remain where I'm standing, contemplating my options. Should I lock the doors and hide? Clean the kitchen? Dust and vacuum?

What happened between Claire and her father? Is Ethan okay?

Ethan, *my brother*. Yes, he's weird. I'm weird. Do I owe him the benefit of the doubt? Probably. Likely. Yes. I need to see this through. All at once, I remember Alice's phone. I should have turned it over to Sergeant Miller. I could still do it.

Instead, I head for my room to change into my running clothes. Back in the kitchen, I slip the phone in the tight pocket on the thigh of my leggings and tuck my glasses into the one at my waist. The thought of what I'm about to do is exhilarating.

Freshman year I begged my parents to let me try out for cross country. Dad, and later Gran, believed I wouldn't be safe. Now I know why. Mom suggested track, racing along a confined course where somebody would always be there to prevent a stranger from abducting me. I don't need that anymore.

Locking the front door behind me, I start out at a slow pace through another light rain shower. Reaching the end of the block, I go faster, kicking up my heels. Blood surges through my veins. Adrenaline powers me forward. I pump my feet faster. *Promise me you won't do anything reckless.* This isn't reckless. It's possibly foolish, but for once, I'm taking control over my life.

Claire's house is six-point-four miles away. Cars roar by me. Invisible dogs in backyards bark. Music sounds from inside homes I've never noticed when I drove by them in my car. This is life. This is living. This is becoming myself.

With a euphoric feeling I've never before experienced, I reach the wooded park at the end of Claire's block. Beside me is the home of the mythical Sinclairs, Ethan's host family. Slowing to a walk, I see Claire's house ahead.

LIAR reads the ugly word painted across the front. The neatly trimmed bushes lining the foundation are trampled into broken sticks. The vertical glass panel alongside the door is shattered. Reflective shards like diamonds lie scattered on the ground below it.

I stare, then spurt forward with a burst of energy. Riley must have gotten here before me. If he's hurt Claire I'll kill him. I'll find him wherever he is and tear his guts out. I'll burn his body to ashes. All at once, my feet slip out from under me, and I collapse onto the lawn.

CHAPTER THIRTY-EIGHT

Claire

"I didn't faint. I swear I didn't. Promise me you believe me," Nora pants, sitting beside me in the wet grass. Tiny raindrops swirls through the air like snowflakes before a winter storm. Solar lights pointing to the house illuminate my handiwork. Nora motions to it. "What happened? Did Riley do this?"

"I believe you, about the fainting, I mean," I say because I know it's important to her. "And no. I did."

It pains me to admit it. Our brains' interpretations of what we see can lead to false perceptions. Even expert naturalists can misidentify animals in photos, leading them to believe they've seen unlikely creatures like Bigfoot or the Loch Ness monster. That's not what's happening here, as much as I wish it were so.

"Riley hasn't been here as far as I know."

Nora puts her hand to her forehead. "I don't understand."

Of course she doesn't. Who would? I'm supposed to be the sweet one. Thoughtful and courteous, not the one with a temper. The truth is I'm mean, vindictive, and vicious. How do I explain that I'm not the person she thinks I am?

"Claire?"

"Last night," I say slowly, "when we were at Caseo's, Alice made a comment about my father's slutty girlfriends."

"I remember."

"Well, all at once it hit me. Dad's girlfriends, the late-night phone calls...Mom didn't ask for a divorce because he worked too much. He was cheating on her. And I took his side. I took his side, Nora! I hated Mom. I yelled at her for not being fair to him. I said such awful things to her. And Dad, all the times he claimed he was working, he must have been out screwing one of his skank clients. I don't know how Alice knew, but she was right."

Nora takes this in with no expression. "So...what? You came home and confronted him?"

"I had to talk to him. I wanted to believe it wasn't true."

"Even though it was?" She folds her knees to her chest, likely to get as far away from me as possible.

Yeah, totally true. It wasn't a client. Dina, from the candy shops—it was her mother. "When I got here, I looked through the window and saw him with a woman. They were both naked. She, my dad's assistant from Juneau, rode him like a bucking rodeo horse. I lost it then. Something inside me snapped. I know I'm supposed to be the calm, clearheaded one, but I couldn't stand it. All Dad's stupid lessons about how important it is to make friends. To be nice to people. I smashed the window and jumped all over the bushes. I found an open can of paint in our neighbor's driveway and I painted liar across the front of the house. And then...I ran away."

"Oh!" Nora doesn't know what to say. I get it.

"Go on and say it. I deserve it. You hate me."

"Claire." She drops her hand to the grass. "I don't hate you. I'm just confused. I thought you were mad about me texting Amber."

"I was. I am! Don't you see? This is the real me. I'm jealous. You have every right to break up with me." Tears sting my eyes. I furiously wipe them away. I have no right to feel sorry for myself. I did this. I brought this on myself.

Nora runs her tongue across her teeth, glancing back at the house. Her shirt's wet from the fall. Yes, I did think she keeled over from another panic attack. What have I done to her? When I rise to help her up and get her inside the house, she pulls me down beside her, grasping my fingers.

"Listen to me, Claire. What I see is another flawed individual like Ethan and me. Yeah, you've got a temper. I'll give you that. But it's not the worst thing in the world. Remember what you told me in Juneau? Don't sell yourself short. You're also kind and giving. This morning, at breakfast, you took the outdoor chair. You gave Ethan the best omelet and you kept the chipped coffee mug for yourself. You even got me milk for my coffee because you know I like it. But can I ask…your idea to go back to Caseo's…was it really because you wanted to talk to Karen?"

"Partially," I admit. "I saw Alice drop her phone. I didn't see Ethan pick it up. I thought if I could find it, there might be a picture of my dad and one of his slutty girlfriends."

"Huh."

I take a quick breath and then I have to ask. "Are you breaking up with me?"

Her face goes slack. "No. How about you? I'm a mess too."

"A perfect mess."

"Well, okay then. Is your dad home?"

"What do you think?" Naturally, he's not. He dropped me off, said he was disappointed in me, and took off again. *Well, guess what, Dad. I'm disappointed in you.*

I push him out of my thoughts. Something has passed between Nora and me. Not to get all sciency again, but there's a hormone called oxytocin produced in the hypothalamus and released by the pituitary gland into the bloodstream. It facilitates childbirth, sure. But it's also called the love drug because it promotes positive feelings, like trust and overall psychological stability. Music and exercise can increase oxytocin levels. So can the immediate release of stress, which is what I'm feeling now. Nora still loves me.

We help one another up and head inside the house. Nora says she wouldn't mind a beer. Neither would I. She tells me about the heady feeling she got running here in the dark.

"It's oxytocin," I explain.

"Really? You should study science."

"Maybe I will." *Maybe I will.*

Together, we search Ethan's bedroom for Riley's money. Nora finds a wad of cash between his mattress and box springs. I discover more bills in a pocket of a pair of pants he's left on the floor. We look everywhere we can think of. We even check the freezer, recalling movies where criminals hide money in empty ice cream cartons. At last we give up and count what little we've found on the kitchen counter. It's almost six hundred bucks. Good, but not anywhere close to the two thousand Ethan mentioned.

Nora eyes it gloomily. "He must've spent the rest. Why don't you hold on to it for now? We'll turn it over to Sergeant Miller in the morning."

"Yeah. Okay." No sense worrying when there's nothing we can do. I slip the money in my messenger bag, and then allow my fingers to creep over to Nora's. I've tossed our empty beer bottles in the recycle. There's nothing left to do here. "I'm still feeling, you know…"

"An oxytocin boost?" She gives me a heavy-lidded smile.

"The simple act of touch or an exchange of saliva can enhance amorous feelings," I say, then have to add, "God, I'm such a geek."

"You are. We both are." Nora chuckles. "Mm. Do you need to stay here, or would you rather head back to Gran's with me?"

"Need you ask?"

She presses her lips to mine and breathes, "I really like the exchange of saliva part."

CHAPTER THIRTY-NINE

Nora

Claire's propped against the headboard beside me studying Alice's phone when I awake the next morning. She left her father a note on the kitchen counter, saying she'd be back to clean up the mess she made later.

After we arrived, we locked the doors and checked to make sure all windows were securely shut, then climbed in bed and spent another hour guessing Alice's passcodes. Our efforts came to nothing, so we moved on to other things. Gran would undoubtedly consider my behavior the last few days reckless. I'd argue that I'm doing what I want. I'm being my own person.

"What combinations have you tried this morning?" I lay my hand on Claire's thigh, feeling delightfully spent after another night between the sheets with her. Gotta love that oxytocin.

"A little more of that and I won't want to talk about phones." She glances at my hand and grins. "Ethan's birthday. Alice's birthday. His name. Her name. Several random combinations. I looked up common digit combinations online a few minutes ago. Tried those and got nothing. Then I found a story about a

YouTuber who unlocked an iPhone by asking Siri what time it was."

"Did it work?"

"I wish."

"Doesn't matter. We'll give it to the police today. Whatever's on it may help Ethan. Have you heard from him?"

"No. You?"

"I don't think so." I check my phone. Thank goodness there's nothing from Amber. She's leaving me alone as I asked. Nothing from Ethan, either.

"Let me try one more thing," says Claire. She taps the screen while I scooch beside her and resettle my pillow behind my back. The bed's narrow, a twin they call it. I have a twin, one who needs my help.

Claire lets out a huff, dropping the phone in the sheets between us. "I give up."

"Have you tried—"

"Hold on. The case!" She snatches it up again. "Alice was pretty forgetful. Ethan said she liked to write things down. Fingers crossed." I dutifully cross my fingers as she slides a fingernail between the side of the phone and the dirty rhinestone-covered skin.

The phone pops out. And there it is, a yellow Post-it filled with two columns of letters and numbers. Claire examines the Post-it and tries a six-digit combination. It doesn't work. She tries another. Same thing. On her third attempt, the phone unlocks and a picture of a hundred-dollar bill appears. "Well, damn."

"Good work," I say.

It takes us more time to go through all the emails in Alice's inbox. There are hundreds of them, mostly spams and bill reminders. I'm not surprised to see she was completely unorganized, never deleting anything or using labels. Next, we scan her messages. Same thing. Claire punches a stream from Riley, and for a minute we read in silent shock.

"I'm coming for you bitch."

Then, *"You're not gonna cut me out."*

And, *"You oughta know better than to mess with us."*

"Oh!" Claire gulps. "Us? Who's us?"

"No idea." The last few are time-stamped Friday morning.

Claire scrolls up the screen and we try to make sense of a shorthand involving shipments, merchandise, customers who haven't paid, stock that's apparently gone missing. Stuff about trucks, duplicate orders, personal bills that each expects the other to pay.

This is a dumpster diving business? It sure seems like a lot. I have to admit that most of it is over my head, except for the more personal parts where they call one another names and say how much they hate each other. Alice keeps referring to items she's supposed to take care of. The "she" seems to indicate someone else. Riley responds by telling Alice it's her responsibility. *"Your job,"* he writes. *"Quit fucking around."*

Claire passes the phone to me. "Who's *she?*"

"Another partner?" A new idea wiggles like an earthworm in my brain. "What time did Alice tell Ethan she was coming to Anchorage?"

"Friday afternoon."

"Specifically?"

"I'll look." Claire takes the phone. I read over her shoulder through another stream dating back a couple of weeks ago that's mostly Alice directing Ethan to run errands. He doesn't respond until Friday morning when he tells her he's in Anchorage and the hospital can't find his birth certificate. He asks her where it is. She replies that she has it, and then says he needs to get his ass back to Juneau.

There are several more texts between them, notably one in which he mentions the DNA test. An hour passes before she tells him she'll come to him in Anchorage and explain. That's when he tells her to meet him at Caseo's.

Claire sets the phone on my knees and says she's going to make coffee.

"It's a percolator," I call after her. "Do you know how to use it?"

"I'll figure it out."

I give up on the phone, stop off at the bathroom and brush my teeth. I find Claire in the kitchen with the mixing bowl and a bag of all-purpose flour puffing dust from the top. "What are you doing?"

"I thought I'd surprise you and make pancakes from scratch." Unexpectedly, her eyes fill. "Oh, Nora. Look what I've done."

"Misplaced the percolator?" I glance along the counter, startled.

"It's next to the stove." She chuckles through her tears. "I've come into your neat, orderly life and messed it up. I brought you a brother you didn't want along with all my own horrible, personal baggage. I wanted to make things better for you, not confuse you. Not make a mess of your house."

I fold my arms around her, gesturing with an elbow to the otherwise clean countertop. "A mess you've already cleaned up, I'd say. And I hope you're kidding about the rest of it. Claire, you have to know you're the best thing that's ever happened to me."

She leans into me, sniffling.

"My life before you was small," I continue. "Did you know that before last night I'd never run after dark? It blew my mind. I loved it. I don't regret a single minute—you and all your horrible baggage. Honestly, I didn't want a brother because I didn't know I had one. I had an ex-girlfriend who belittled me every chance she got and a grandmother who, I'm just going to say it, is a bit controlling. Come on, what's this really about? Are you still thinking about your dad?"

"I guess I'm feeling overwhelmed right now. I vandalized my own house! What the hell was I thinking?"

"That the father you worshipped lied to you."

"And I lied to you. I wanted to tell you what I'd done. I couldn't bring myself to admit it."

I hide a smile. "I'm still upset about that."

"You are?" She knits a worried brow.

"Don't be silly. It made me realize I shouldn't have been so judgmental about Ethan and that story about his fight in middle school."

"He isn't violent."

"No, I get that now. Just goofy and weird."

"Like both of us."

"Like both of us," I repeat.

She playfully slaps my shoulder, swiping the back of a hand across her eyes. "Ethan ate the casserole I bet your gran was saving."

"That's definitely a crime. But I think we'll have to let Gran handle his punishment. Right now, she's desperately trying to get back to Anchorage and save me from—Oh my god!"

"What? Save you from what?" Claire calls as I race to the bedroom for Alice's phone.

"Can you unlock it again?" I return and hand it over.

"What are you looking for?"

"Riley sent Alice a text Friday. Here it is. *I'm coming for you bitch.*' No comma by the way. Do you have any idea how much that bugs me?" Claire gives me a somber nod. "His message to Ethan said he was flying in this morning—flying in *yesterday morning.* Saturday. You used to work at the airport. Is there any way you can find out when he got here?"

Claire leans back against the sink to think. "Maybe. I have a friend who works for Alaska Airlines. Let me try. You make coffee. I'll give him a call."

"Do you want pancakes?" I ask as she heads into the living room with her own phone.

"Only if you do. Truthfully, I'd rather have an omelet."

"Coming right up."

She stops in the doorway. "Sunshine or rain?"

Our quiz. She's so adorable. "Sunshine?"

"You're saying it like a question."

"Okay then, sunny." And as the word leaves my mouth, I realize I'm getting there.

CHAPTER FORTY

Claire

"You know I'm not supposed to do this. If you weren't so nice, I'd tell you no," my friend at Juneau International Airport says, the one who used to bring me coffee every time I gave a tour. I hear the click-clicking of buttons from his keyboard, the sound of voices in the background. "Here we go. Alice St. James first. Why does that name sound familiar?"

"She was murdered two days ago."

"Goodness. Sorry I asked. Anyway, it appears Ms. St. James left for Anchorage Friday afternoon on the two o'clock, Flight 478."

"Good." I pace the room. Now we're getting somewhere. "And Riley Crew?"

"How do you spell the last name?"

"C-R-E-W."

"Friday, as well. An hour and a half later. One stop in Sitka. The plane was late. It got in shortly after six."

Aha. Still time for Riley to find his way to Caseo's to kill his wife. I pace faster.

"Anything else I can do you for?" says my friend.

"How about a lottery ticket? You've been unbelievably helpful, Ryan. If you ever come to Anchorage, please give me a call. I owe you a steak dinner, an eighty-dollar bottle of champagne. Whatever you want."

"I may just take you up on that," he replies with a smile in his voice. "My husband mentioned a weekend getaway the other night. I suppose I owe him. This information is just between us, right? I could get in a wee bit of trouble for sharing it."

"No problem. Great to talk to you, Ryan."

"You too, doll."

We hang up. I can't wait to tell Nora. She doesn't count in the "non-sharing part," I hope.

I toss my phone on the back of the couch. Nora's just taking the sizzling skillet off the stove. The aroma of eggs and cheese fills the tiny kitchen. She cuts the omelet in half, sliding each onto her gran's white plates, the ones with the tiny roses. "Well?"

"Looks delicious."

"I meant what did your friend say?"

"I think we have a winner. Riley came in Friday night."

"I knew it. I just knew it. Wait. In time to get to Caseo's?"

"Plenty of time. The only issue is"—I hate to say it and spoil our happy mood—"how would Riley know Alice would be there?" Because that's our next problem. Given the heated text exchange between them, there's no way Alice would keep him up-to-date on her whereabouts. I imagine she had two reasons for leaving Juneau. Talking to Ethan and escaping Riley and his temper.

Five years ago, the man ran over my cat. He wasn't sorry. The look on his face was downright gleeful. If it hadn't been for Ethan, I might have punched Riley in the belly. And where would that have gotten me? With my own face beaten in. The asshole was never above hitting his wife and her kid.

Nora sits, sticks a corner of the omelet in her mouth. Her face assumes a dour expression. "It's the business," she says, around a mouthful of cheese.

"What is?"

"Dumpster diving. Invoices. Trucking receipts. Customers who don't pay on time…Something's not right. Is it possible Alice was skimming off the top?"

"I wouldn't put it past her." Alice was every bit as bad as Riley—a total cheat. A different kind from my father though. I know I need to let that go.

I inhale a forkful of gooey cheese and egg, and then return to the living room for my phone. "They called their business 'Seconds.' Ethan said they sold on eBay and Facebook Marketplace. I'm looking it up."

It's hard to eat and browse my phone at the same time, but I manage. I'm not letting Nora's culinary masterpiece get cold. "Here we are," I say a minute later. "Shoes. Designer clothing. Household goods. Computers. Video games. Jewelry." I show Nora one of the websites with pictures.

"It doesn't look like old merch."

"It's not. Remember? It's the stuff customers return and stores throw out. I've read about it. People post about the treasures they find behind Amazon warehouses all the time."

She gazes thoughtfully at my phone. "That's not what I mean. I read about it too. A lot of places mark what they throw out to keep people from finding and reselling it. Some lock their dumpsters. They claim it's to prevent vandalism and keep scavengers from getting hurt. In reality, it's lost revenue for the stores. What I mean is, this looks new. Retrieved merchandise would at least be dirty and scuffed."

"I'm sure Alice and Riley clean it all up before they sell it," I reply. Still, Nora has a point. I finish off my omelet, thinking if Nora doesn't go into politics, she could have a career as a chef. I tell her that, then sit back and consider the implications. Finally, I say, "You're right. And that can only mean one thing. It didn't come out of the trash."

"It fell off the back of a truck?"

I can't help smiling. We both like old movies and TV shows like *The Sopranos* and *The Wire* in which gangsters offer stolen merchandise to their gangster buddies, spouting lines like, "It fell off the back of a truck."

"We're not yet there," says Nora.

"I know. We're missing the piece that's gonna save Ethan from the slammer," I imitate a gangster and she laughs.

The phone rings. It's my Eminem ringtone. My heart sinks. I put the phone on speaker. "Where are you?"

"Still here at the station. Claire, I need help. Can you get your dad to call a lawyer for me?"

"Gran's taking care of it." Nora leans in to the phone.

"Nora? Is that you? I swear I didn't go back and kill Alice."

"I believe you, Ethan. Gran does too. She's sending an attorney to talk to you. What did you say to Sergeant Miller?"

"Only that Alice and I argued and that she hit me with a pipe. They have my fingerprints on it."

When Ethan took it away to keep her from hitting him again. It's probably the murder weapon, conveniently left beside her.

Nora gazes at my phone, her expression tight. "What else?" Like me, she knows there's got to be more because we both know Ethan.

"They asked why didn't I call them when I found out the whole Baby Boy Thomas story."

Damn it, we should have called. "Sit tight," I say, "until your attorney gets there. Don't say anything more."

"Except that they need to know that Riley came to Anchorage on Friday. They should be looking at him for Alice's murder too," Nora adds. "Claire checked his flight. He arrived in Anchorage Friday night and got here in plenty of time to meet Alice at Caseo's. Be strong, brother."

I press my lips together to stop myself from asking Ethan if he told the cops about Riley's money. He would have mentioned it if he had, and I don't know who else might be listening to our conversation.

He sighs. "Okay. I gotta go. Thanks, you guys. I mean, really, really, thank you. I just want to say I don't know what I'd do without you." There's a moment of static, and I think he's hung up.

"Ethan, are you still there?" I ask as Nora carries our dirty plates to the sink.

"Yeah. But I gotta go. Nora, can you tell your Gran…Just tell her I'm not bad. I wouldn't hurt anybody."

"I'll tell her."

The line goes dead. Nora and I look at one another. The gut-wrenching anguish I feel is reflected in her expression. "We're going to get through this, Claire."

I nod. "I sincerely hope so."

CHAPTER FORTY-ONE

Nora

All at once Gran's tiny house feels stuffy. I need to get outside. I tell Claire that I'm going to run Alice's phone to the cops; we have no reason to keep it any longer and it may help Ethan's case if they can see the texts. "I'll be right back," I say.

She's sitting on the front step when I return, petting one of the black and white chickens that lives across the street. Four of them circle her feet, having one of their weird little clucking conversations.

"Did you get to see Ethan?" She looks up.

"Sergeant Miller didn't think it was a good idea. But his lawyer's with him now. Miller wanted to know why we hadn't turned over the phone last night."

"And you said?"

"What could I say? Because we didn't think of it. We're not detectives. I gave him the Post-it with the combination and pointed out Riley's texts. I started to tell him about Seconds and the ideas we had. He said he'd take it from here."

"Dandy." Claire stands, likely feeling depressed like I am. "Assuming these aren't your chickens, where do they belong?"

"Over there."

We herd them back across the road. Half a second later, they're following us again. "Honestly, you'd think people who keep livestock could build a better gate," I say loudly. I march up through the yard and ring the doorbell. A small child answers, so I fuss at her about the dangers of cars and dogs. The three of us get them back into their coop, and the little girl goes inside her house. She comes back out with her mother, who offers me a store-brand double fudgesicle.

"Here, Nora. You look like you could use this. What was all that commotion about at your house last night? Is your grandma feeling poorly?"

"She's fine. It was just a little mix-up. The police were looking for a guy who's been stealing chickens. You might want to keep yours in the coop." Claire covers the smile forming on her face.

"Yes. Yes. Good idea."

After checking to ensure the fudgesicle's wrapper is intact because I'm going to throw it away if it isn't, I split it apart, giving half to Claire. She regards me anxiously. "I'm just remembering that Dad knows a criminal attorney who's supposed to be the best in the business. Do you think I should I call and get his name?"

"Do you want to?"

"Not really."

"Then don't." We start walking down the street. "Did you and your father talk about what he did?"

"I tried. He basically told me it was none of my business."

Harsh. "Are you okay with that?"

"Not really, no. But what choice do I have? He called while you were out, wanted to know when I'd be back to clean up. He's expecting me."

"Then I'll go with you."

"You don't mind?"

"Of course not."

We reach the end of the block and turn around in the Holiday Convenience store parking lot. I look around for a trashcan in which to deposit the popsicle stick. Claire says she'll take it and drops it into her messenger bag. When we get back to the house, she checks her phone again, holding it out for me to see the news alert she's set. I can feel my eyes widening by degrees.

"Police continue to investigate a homicide that occurred Friday evening between ten p.m. and midnight behind a popular midtown coffeeshop that left forty-two-year-old Alice St. James of Juneau dead from blunt force trauma. The victim's body was found by the shop's owners shortly after opening at six a.m. Saturday morning. Authorities now seek to question the victim's husband, Samuel Regan Crew, forty-five, who goes by the name Riley. Crew, a military veteran, who served three years in prison for the criminal assault of his first wife in 2015, originally provided information about Ms. St. James. He's now being viewed as a person of interest in her murder, thanks to a new lead. At this time, Mr. Crew's whereabouts are unknown. If you have any information that might help, please contact Anchorage Crime Stoppers."

A criminal assault on previous wife? More and more I'm convinced Riley's our man. Below the article is a photo of a guy in military dress uniform. "That's him?" I ask.

Claire eyes the picture. "He's heavier now, more muscly and nearly bald. I probably wouldn't recognize him if it weren't for the cleft in his chin. But this is good news, right? Sergeant Miller must have taken our lead seriously."

"Right."

The chickens are out in the middle of the road again. I corral them back into their own yard and prop a stick against the gate that won't properly latch. When I return to the stoop, I voice a random thought.

"I used to be afraid of everything. Spiders. Clowns. Enclosed places. Loud noises. Certain smells. The dark. Strangers who got too close."

"Xenophobia, fear of strangers," says Claire, my beautiful science geek.

"Yeah. But what I'm getting at is that my fears made Amber the wrong fit for me because she isn't afraid of anything. It also means she doesn't have patience for that kind of thing."

"I would have said she's shallow and narcissistic."

"That, too." I lace my fingers with hers. "Have you noticed who *hasn't* called or texted since yesterday?"

Claire grins. "Amber."

I tap my nose. "I'm done with her. I told her so yesterday. Claire, what are you afraid of?"

"Let me think. Spiders. Clowns. Losing the affection of someone I've really come to care about."

"Your dad?"

"Ha-ha. I mean you."

My heart soars. "Are you okay with nicknames?"

"Not really. You?"

"Me, either. But, I guess, if you care about someone you may be willing to tolerate a little quirkiness." Me. Claire. Ethan.

"I agree. Like when one of you likes horror movies and the other doesn't."

I lean sideways and purse my lips "Do we fit?"

Claire meets them with her own, then offers me a crooked smile. "I think we do."

CHAPTER FORTY-TWO

Claire

Feeling more confident about the cops closing in on Riley and Ethan now having an attorney, Nora and I go back to my house to deal with a more immediate problem.

"Start with the glass," Dad instructs. "You'll find a sheet of cardboard in the garage. Tape it to the window. Trim the bushes back so they don't look broken. Then grab a rag and a bucket of soapy water and wipe down the siding." I don't speak. "And go over and apologize to the neighbor for stealing his paint," he calls as I head out front where Nora waits.

"Fuck you," I mumble under my breath. With our garage still full of unpacked boxes, I finally give up on finding hedge trimmers. I borrow them from the neighbor after telling him I'm sorry. I'm still mad. Mad at myself for idolizing my father. Mad at him for cheating on my mom. Mad at her for not telling me.

Nora and I work for several hours. It's hot, and I build up a pretty good sweat under my pits. Nora undoes her hair, shakes it out and twists it on top of her head. Short hairs curl around the sheen on her neck.

We talk about school. What Ethan was like when I first met him. I tell her the story about my cat getting run over by Riley's truck. She tells me about her parents, her piano lessons, how she first met Amber. Talking about her ex doesn't bother me as much, especially since Amber's leaving her alone now. And somehow, as the hours go by and the more I sweat, I find my rage dwindling. I don't notice at first, then I realize I'm starting to feel better about everything. Ethan will be okay. Dad's got his own life, which I don't have to be responsible for. I don't have to be an architect because I like science better anyway.

Cleaning is cathartic. I get why it's Nora's go-to remedy for anxiety.

The sun sits high in the sky when I sneak through the back door to the kitchen to grab a couple water bottles from the fridge.

"Phone your mother. She's expecting your call," Dad yells from the living room over the noise of a football game on TV.

He must have filled Mom in on the events here Friday night. I call from the kitchen phone.

"Why didn't you tell me?" I say sharply when she picks up. I mean it to sound confrontational, but my voice merely comes out sounding weary. Hers, too.

"Is that what you would have wanted, Claire? To know that we had problems? I was trying to protect you because I knew how much you admired your dad. Ever since you were a little girl. Have you finished straightening everything up?"

"Nearly. How long did you know he was cheating before you asked for the divorce?"

"Not long." She sighs. "I'd suspected for several weeks, but there were other times I wondered…late nights when he came home smelling of wine and perfume. I knew he had female clients, of course. So I told myself I was imagining it. Then one night, a woman called and asked for him. Something didn't feel right, maybe it was her voice. After that, I started watching, and he started slipping up. When I finally questioned him, he admitted it. But Claire, you have to know you were never part of the equation."

Resentment, watered down by fatigue, flushes through me. "That's supposed to make me feel better, Mom? I wasn't part of the equation? You didn't want me to live with you."

"Don't be silly, sweetheart. You're always welcome here. What I meant was, the problem was between your dad and me. Somewhere along the way we both stopped trying. Initially, he didn't want the divorce because he was afraid of losing you."

I'd really like to believe that. My father's always been there for me. He cared little for school himself but encouraged me to do my best. He came to my science fairs, my volleyball matches, every teacher conference. I probably wasn't much help when I used to hang around his office and pretend to answer his phone, but he never sent me away. We say our goodbyes and I end the call.

When I get back to the yard, the word I painted on the siding glows faintly pink but at least you can't read it. Nora catches the water bottle I throw her in one hand. We sit cross-legged in the driveway, a row of tiny ants making their way toward her shoe.

"Are you afraid of ants?" I ask.

"No. Not spiders either, really. I actually like bugs in general. Did you and your dad work things out?"

"Not yet. We probably will eventually. I talked to Mom. She told me not to blame him."

"Good advice, I imagine."

"I suppose. Thanks for helping me with this." I gesture to the house.

"What else did I have to do today? I was looking at pictures of Ethan on your phone while you were inside. I hope you don't mind. I've got to say he was a cute little boy."

"Adorable?"

"Exactly. Same as me." She grins. "There's a photo of him at some sort of school assembly. Looks like middle school. He's on the stage. Did he win an award?"

"I don't remember. Let me see." She passes me the phone. "Oh, yeah, that. He used to send me pictures all the time. That's the end of his eighth-grade year. He'd made the dean's list by the skin of his teeth. He joked about it all summer long, saying he'd fooled his teachers into thinking he was smart."

"He is smart," Nora says softly.

"True that." I scroll through more pics. "Here he is hamming it up doing chin ups on a playground where we often met. And here's one with Alice and Riley. Look at all the boxes. It must be Christmas."

Nora draws a breath. "That's Riley?"

"Yep."

"I've seen him."

"I know. The article we looked at at your house."

Nora realigns her glasses on her nose and squints. "Not that. It was old. He was wearing a military uniform with his cap pulled over his eyes. Another photo."

"Where?"

"Della Rhodes's house. Della and Riley. Claire, the picture hangs over her TV."

CHAPTER FORTY-THREE

Nora

The significance of Riley's photo in Della Rhodes's living room strikes us at the same time. My heart leaps inside my chest.

Claire takes a stuttering breath. "They know each other. Is it possible Della's his first wife, the one he went to prison for assaulting?"

"Doesn't seem likely," I say. "Why keep a photo reminding you of bad times? Seems to me, she's probably a girlfriend or a sister."

"Yeah. That makes sense. Oh! The cleft."

"The clef?" I'm thinking music. Claire has something else in mind.

"The dimple in her chin. Riley has one too. They're siblings, Nora! And the boxes...Holy shit. Remember all the boxes at her house? What if she's the business partner, the one from Alice's and Riley's text stream? '*She's supposed to do it.*'"

She's quoting Alice's text. "My god, you're right. Alice said that. He replied, '*It's your job.*'"

I feel an energy building inside me. A match to a firecracker. It starts in my belly and races up my spine. It's exactly like last night when I took off running in the dark. Exciting. Thrilling. I forgot all about my weird phobias. For once, the control I'd lost as a child in a parking garage, was back. I've been without it too long.

My phone pings, signaling a text. I automatically take it from my pocket. Amber. Crap. She'd promised to leave me alone. I put my phone away.

"Who was that?"

"You don't want to know."

"Don't I? That must mean Amber. What did she want?"

"I didn't look."

"Go ahead."

"I broke up with her, Claire. Yesterday, once and for all. I told her not to text or call me unless it was an emergency."

"Maybe that's what it is."

I can't read the expression on Claire's face. She gazes at me. I feel a tiny throb behind my eye. *Only in an emergency. Life or death*, I'd said.

"Go ahead," Claire repeats. "I trust you, Nora. I admit I have little faith in her, but I know you feel the need to look, so go ahead."

I draw my phone out of my pocket with some reluctance. *"Important. Meet me at Rhodes house."* I show the text to Claire.

She runs her tongue across her teeth. I can almost see the wheels spinning in her head. "Answer it."

"Why?" I type.

"Important!" comes her reply a second later.

Claire gulps her water bottle. I draw my knees up to my chest. I hate this. I know what I ought to do: call Sergeant Miller and tell him about the boxes in Della Rhodes's living room and the picture of her and Riley. Explain to him what Claire and I have figured out. On the other hand, what if Amber's in trouble? Because, somewhere deep inside, I'm sensing a trap. Why is Amber there? Have they abducted her? Are they holding her hostage? Is Riley there too, destroying evidence of his crime? Their crime, his and his sister? God, I don't know what to think.

"We could—" I start and stop.

Claire draws a breath. "I'm listening."

"You're not going to like it." I mouth, "Sorry," to her and tap Amber's number. It goes immediately to voicemail. Of course. What else was I expecting? I hold the phone out so Claire can hear it too. "Speak," says the voice I know. "If I'm not picking up, it's because I'm busy, or I don't want to talk to you."

Claire chews her lower lip in thought. "Lovely. You don't need to say it, Nora. We've got to check this out. But first, call Sergeant Miller and let him know what's going on. Second, if there's anything in the least bit hinky, we stay in the car. No, never mind, we stay in the car regardless until he gets there. Deal?"

We? "I should go alone."

Her single note laugh sounds false. "You're kidding, right?"

"Listen to me, Claire. If this goes sideways, I can't be responsible for you getting hurt. I couldn't live with myself. You get that, don't you? I love you. I don't want anything to happen to you."

"Ditto." She stands and holds out a hand. "Come on. What are we waiting for?"

In the inner recess of my warped brain, I'd already been considering making a run at Rhodes, even knowing it was reckless, the complete opposite of Gran's advice. I'm tired of being careful. Tired of being afraid of my own shadow. Tired of hiding behind potted plants at music recitals. When was the last time I felt confident entering an enclosed parking garage? I despise my panic attacks. I want nothing more than to march up to Rhodes's door and say, 'Hey, lady. Hey you in your ugly bathrobe. Excuse me. Where were you at ten o'clock Friday night?'

I even know what she'd say. 'None of your friggin' business, kid. Get the hell out of my house.' I'd snap a photo of the boxes in her living room and one of the picture of her with Riley on the wall. I'd take it to Sergeant Miller. Ethan would be freed. I would be his superhero sister. We could be one happy family the way we should have been the last seventeen years.

Claire's shadow blocks the sun. Her arm's extended. "We wait for Sergeant Miller in the car. Got it?"

"Got it." She helps me to my feet. I phone the police and explain to the woman who answers that I need a cop, any cop, to meet us when she says Sergeant Miller is away from his desk. "Sergeant Miller or anybody. ASAP," I repeat, giving her the address at Boniface and Camelot.

"Ready?" I say to Claire.

She draws me close and whispers, "YOLO."

I agree. You only live once, but I'd like to keep on doing it for a while.

CHAPTER FORTY-FOUR

Claire

Dad comes out of the house and waves as if to flag us down, but I pretend I don't see him. "Where do you think you're going?" he shouts.

Nora shoots a quick glance at me.

"This is more important." I glance away with a shrug.

As she drives by the park, we pass the house where Ethan once told me he was staying. I don't know why I believed him. When I think of it now, I realize that most of what he said wasn't true. I never saw him go inside the Sinclair's house. He smelled like the outdoors, like he wasn't bathing. And the guitar he kept in the woods, why not store it in a bedroom? He didn't have to play it inside. He explained that the Sinclairs couldn't tolerate noise, but watched TV with the volume high because they were both half-deaf. Ethan never went to his locker. He had no schoolbooks. Of course, he pretended he had the other lunch period. He had no lunch hour because he wasn't enrolled at North. Even the ruse about his supposedly "effed" up schedule was for my benefit. He probably said hello Mr. Henderson and asked him where the bathroom was. I can't believe I was that naïve. Several times Nora tried to tell me something wasn't right, but I refused to listen.

Still, Ethan St. James has always been my friend. Despite all his lies and lame jokes, I trust him. I should have done more for him when I knew Alice and Riley were abusing him. And now I have to think about Amber and worry if she's in danger. I'll help her if I can.

Nora informs me that it's four-point-one miles to Della Rhodes's house. Her precision is endearing. Adorable. Presently, we cross the intersection of Boniface and Camelot and find a parallel parking spot across the street from Della's house. A car occupies the gravel driveway of Ethan's old house. Probably new renters.

Nora cuts the engine as Della, in her bathrobe, steps out her front door and beckons to us. "There you are. Come on in."

I roll down the window. "Where's Amber?" A car zooms by. Her lips move as she says something I can't hear. "Amber. Is she here?" I say again. A tingle of dread crawls up my spine.

Della beckons again. "Inside. Hurry."

No way. This is wrong, just as we were afraid of. There's no sign of Amber's car or the cops, although the neighborhood looks peaceful enough. Several houses away, a guy saunters to his mailbox. A small dog trots along beside him. Strains of country music sound from a nearby apartment building.

Della hasn't left the doorway. "Are you coming?"

Nora leans over my seat and shouts, "No, thanks. We're waiting for the police. They're on the way. They'll be here any second."

Where are those damned police?

Della leans sideways into the house, her arm extended, her fingers grasping something dark that's mostly out of sight. I catch only a glimpse of it. "Suit yourself. I didn't want to hurt your friend, but you're leaving me no choice. I just want my money."

There's no use pretending we don't know what she's talking about. As they say on TV, the jig is up.

"I don't have to hurt any of you, if you'll only come inside so we can talk." Her voice is calm, like she's inviting us in for a cup of tea or a Coke.

"I have your money in my bag," I say a second before Nora's hand clamps down on my arm, undoubtedly to warn me to keep my mouth shut. Too late for that. "Send Amber out and I'll throw it in the yard." Della's fingers, I see now, are wound around a thick clump of Amber's hair. *Ugh.* Nora's ex must be scared to death. Is she hurt? Beaten? Alive? I have no idea what this woman is capable of.

"I'm sorry. That's not going to work. Come to the door and I'll send your little friend out. She's a sweet thing. Been telling me all about you two. Meeting in Juneau. Eating sushi and getting sick. In love with Ethan's twin. Now there's a story."

A high-pitched squeal hits my ears.

Nora unlatches her seat belt first. "Wait here," she tells me. "I'm going in."

"Not by yourself, you're not."

We race across the street to the door. However I might have imagined what would happen next, it's worse. Della jerks back. At the same time, a large, square hand shoots out from behind the door, grabs my elbow and drags me inside.

"You two are so easy. How can you not love a couple of gullible teenage girls?" Della chuckles, tossing a dark wig to the carpet.

I shift backward on my heels, attempting to push Nora outside to save her. I scream at her to run before calloused fingers smelling of cigarettes clamp hard over my lips. I'm hardly surprised when Nora doesn't run anyway. My brave, dumb, wonderful girlfriend remains in the doorway, probably thinking she's going to save me. "Where's Amber...Oh!" She spots the wig and blinks.

"There she is, right there." Della points and laughs.

"She left her phone," Nora says dully.

"Why, yes she did. In the bathroom, and I found it. That's exactly what happened. Lucky for us, not so much for you. Took a few hours, but my resourceful brother broke it open. Sushi.

Hospitals. Juneau. Such useful teenager info at my fingertips. It's all right here." She pulls Amber's phone from a pocket in her bathrobe and drops it on the floor by the wig.

"Come on inside. Don't be shy now. You certainly weren't yesterday with all your questions. Sending your friend in to spy on me. You're clever, I'll give you that. I still don't know how you worked it out, but I will say, Nora Thomas, Alice was right about you. You look so much like her boy. Same dark hair and eyes. Especially the eyes. Step on in and meet my brother. We're not twins, like you and the boy, just business partners. Close enough. Huh, I guess Claire already knows him. Nora say hello to Riley, Alice's husband."

Nora grunts.

Riley pretends to be more friendly. "Hey, Nora. Delighted to finally meet you. I've heard so much about you from my dearly departed wife." He yanks me off my feet and tosses me to the couch. I land sideways, bang my shin, and have to bite my lip to keep from crying out. I won't give him the satisfaction of knowing he's hurt me.

Nora starts over to help me up. Riley holds out a hand to stop her. She backs away from him as fast as she can. Della shuts the front door and clicks the deadbolt in place.

"Now then, enough of the pleasantries. Time is short, as we all know. Give us our money and we'll be on our way. There's a good girl." She smiles as I reach inside my messenger bag and drop the money we found on the table."

My eyes take in the stack of cardboard boxes in the corner as she counts. I see a dozen shoeboxes on the kitchen table. The box on top is open, displaying a shoe wedged on its side. Brown, with off-white soles. It does me no good to recognize them as identical to Ethan's Derbies.

"Where's the rest? This isn't all of it." Della snaps. She tosses the wad of cash to Riley who looks even less happy than his sister. "Well?"

I swallow. "That's all there was."

"But we can get you the rest," Nora says quickly. "It's at Claire's house. Give us a sec and we'll call her dad. He can bring it over."

"Yeah. Like that's going to happen." Gone are their pleasant demeanors. Stepping around the coffee table, Riley wraps his thick fingers around my jaw and squeezes. "Where's my money? Where's the rest? Don't make me do something you won't like."

Aren't we past that? Tears come to my eyes as he pinches my cheeks.

I bite my tongue, recognizing the coppery taste of blood. "Let go of me," I gurgle. "I—we can get it. It's back at the house."

"Bullshit. With the cops on our tail? Isn't that what you said? Too fuckin' bad for you."

He shoves a flat hand against my chest. Nora springs forward. He backhands her with a fist, then grabs us, one in his right, the other in his left, like a couple of dolls and starts dragging us into the hall.

"Is this wise, Brother?"

"Do we have a choice?"

Della demurs and steps aside. "Do it quietly."

"I will. You finish loading the car. I'll"—he glances around—"I'll tie them up. A fire should do the trick. I got a can of gas in back."

Thinking to slow him down, I say frantically, "Just one more question. You knew, both of you, you knew Alice kidnapped Ethan. Why didn't anyone stop her?"

"Would have if I could," he answers.

"Me, too. She always had a soft spot for the kiddies. First, Ethan. Then this one." Della motions to Nora. "There was another child in her care she tried to keep, but the mother wouldn't give up. Questions. Threats. We'd all had enough of it. Alice passed off some tale about a custodial abduction. Not sure how she got away with that one. Anyway, it was a pleasure meeting you girls."

"And the reason you killed Alice?" Nora asks, also desperate.

"She did the books. Took more than her share. Should have done it along time ago. Now move." Riley shoves Nora with a fist in her back. She stumbles, then turns around and tries to hit him. Her hand glances off his shoulder. He knocks her easily to the floor. "Try that again and I'll make it much, much worse."

Worse than this? I can't imagine. We're about to be torched.

He unlocks a door down the hall and shoves us in. "Sit," he directs, wandering around, looking for something. What? A meat cleaver? The room is full of empty metal shelves, all their stolen merchandise already taken away.

Riley rubs his jaw, frustrated apparently, because he can't find what he wants. "Your fuckin' dad, Claire. That son of a bitch. Man, I hated him. One damn loan, I asked for. Prick wouldn't give it to me. None of this might have happened if he hadn't been so stingy."

Something snaps inside of me. My father's a lot of things. A liar. A cheat. A conman himself. Stingy though, he's not. And despite his flaws, I know Mom's right. He loves me. "You make me sick."

Riley spins around. "You wanna repeat that, bitch?"

Nora nudges me with a foot. She wants me to be quiet. What does it matter now? He's going to kill us anyway.

"You heard me. You disgust me. All three of you. You, your sister, and your wife. You let Ethan believe you were his parents. You steal. You cheat. You beat your own wife to death and you're perfectly happy to let your son take the blame for it."

Riley stomps down hard on my foot. "That pussy was never my son. I never liked him. As for you, let me tell you something. I ran over your cat on purpose. Needed an introduction to your dad. And what good did it do me? It didn't. Just the pleasure of seeing you hurt." He slaps me across the face.

A searing hot pain radiates from my ankle. My ears ring. Nora starts to get up to go after him. "Don't," I whisper hoarsely. "Please don't."

It won't do any good for her to get beaten too. We're both going to die. Riley will set fire to the house. He thinks it will look like an accident because he's just that stupid. He obviously doesn't know fire marshals can tell the difference between an accident and arson.

Where are the cops? I'm angry and scared, sorry that I ever got Nora involved in this. If I'd only stayed in Juneau with my mom. I miss her. I miss my old life. My love for Nora isn't going to make her any less dead.

Riley finds what he's looking for on the windowsill, plastic zip ties. He drags me to a rack, yanks my hands behind my back and secures them to a metal leg. Then he does the same with Nora. A sob escapes my lips, which makes him happy.

"There we go, girls. All tied up. Bye now. Don't cry. It will all be over soon." He pats each of us on the head, then heads out. The door clicks shut behind him.

CHAPTER FORTY-FIVE

Nora

Claire's crying. She doesn't want to let me know it, but I hear her quiet whimpers. We're on the floor in an empty room, zip-tied to a rack.

Where the hell are the police? I refuse to panic. If ever there was a time to be strong, it's now. With my elbow, I try to rub Claire's arm to let her know we need to act. This isn't the time to feel sorry for ourselves because I'm not letting that ape push me around. I wanted to kick Riley in the balls when he started beating on Claire. *Pick on someone your own size, dickwad.* Once we're free, it's the first thing I'll say to him—after I mash his testicles with my foot.

"Claire. We're going to get out of here, I promise. Have you got anything in your bag to cut these ties?"

The whimpering stops. "Nail clippers. Actually, I have a pair of sewing scissors, but I don't see how to get to them."

I rock the rack with my back. A couple of boxes on the top of it I didn't see hit me in the head. Ouch. When the foot of the rack comes up high enough, I slide to my elbows and drag my hands out from under it. Claire's hands come out too. She maneuvers around so she's lying on her back, then rubs her shoulder on the carpet to slide her messenger bag so it's lying beside her. Next, comes unclasping it. No easy feat when her hands are zip-tied behind her.

"Damn it," she grumbles more than once.

"Sun or clouds?" I say.

She glances up, giving me a weak smile through her tears. "Sun always. Here." She's managed to untangle a three-inch pair of scissors from the mess in her bag. She scoots upright, shifts around so our backs are to one another and hands them to me.

I pass them back. "You take them. I can't see the ties, and I can't hold the scissors at the right angle to cut them. You're going to have to do it."

"But—" She stops. "You want me to cut through the ties on your hands? Nora, I can't see them either. I could stab you. I could cut through the radial artery on your wrist. You might never be able to play piano again. You might even bleed out before I'm done. I won't do it." She fumbles, trying to make me take the scissors again.

I'm not going to do it either. "The same could happen to you. We're wasting time. Here. Take them. I love you, Claire. I really didn't faint on your lawn last night. I tripped." I need her to know I'm strong. We can do this.

"Shit. I love you too!" Her voice is hoarse. "Can you move your hands, maybe just a hair to the right? That's it. Now closer. Stretch them apart as much as you can."

I fold my lips over my teeth and hold my breath to bite back a cry as I feel a sharp point dig into the area just below the base of my thumb. I can't let her know she's cut me. She's got to keep going. I have one of my weird irrational thoughts that if I told her, she'd say something like, *That's called the scaphoid,* and then go on to explain how it rotates the joint as you move your wrist.

I focus on other thoughts instead, like the first time I saw her in the airport and how I assumed that she was a girl who had everything. She was beautiful, smart, sunny, and always knew just the right thing to say to people. Claire is all that and more.

A regular person with her own set of problems. I need to stop judging others when I meet them. From here on out, if there is a here on out, I'm going to make an effort to be sunny like her.

The ties drop off just as footsteps thump in the hall outside the door. "Turn around quick, Claire. I'll cut yours."

Her eyes pop and she gasps at the sight of the jagged, bloody skin at my wrist. Still, she does what I ask. Awkwardly, we clamber to our feet and make a dash for the window. Pushing aside another rack, Claire slips off her jacket, wraps it around her elbow and jabs the glass. The first punch doesn't break it. She hops on one foot and hits it again. It crackles in shards that drop outside. We kick aside the rest.

A split second later, Riley's in the room shouting at us.

CHAPTER FORTY-SIX

Claire

With a firm palm planted on my spine, Nora launches me
out the window where I land in the middle of a prickly bush on
the side of the house. I smash through it with my hands, knees,
and elbows, then struggle to regain my footing before spinning
around and grabbing her by her forearms to pull her out.

The back of my brain hears Riley and Della screaming
at each other not to let us get away. The odor of gasoline
permeates my consciousness. My ankle throbs like a heartbeat.
Riley throws himself out the window after us. Nora and I grab
for one another's hands. We stumble across the yard as a police
car comes roaring around the corner.

Neither of us checks for traffic as we tumble into the street.
A truck skids around us, honking. The car behind it slams into
Riley, catapulting him upon its hood with a tremendous thwack.
His body cracks the windshield and rolls off into the road.

Horrified, Nora and I pause and stare. I'm aware that I'm
still breathing. My heart pumps blood through my heart. In
movies, people get hit by cars all the time. They shake it off and
resume pursuit.

Riley doesn't move.

Cars coming from both directions stop. The drivers and passengers get out to see what's going on. They ask if they can help. Sergeant Miller steps over and asks if we're okay. Presently, an ambulance appears. A paramedic directs us to hop in back. Hopping for me involves one foot. He bandages Nora's hand, tells me to scoot back to elevate my ankle, then he pops open one of those bags of artificial ice. "Pulvoy," I read the label. "Reusable for injuries." Normally, I could probably tell you the chemical makeup. Right now I have no idea.

"He's dead," Nora says faintly.

She must mean Riley. He lies on his back in the street. I probably ought to care, but I don't. I tell her it was smart of her to think of the scissors in my bag. I carry all kinds of stuff. A sewing kit, a hairbrush, a tube of lipstick. Foundation. An extra pair of socks. Even a couple of popsicle sticks, although I can't remember where I got them.

We watch as Della makes a run for the car parked in Ethan's old driveway. The police intercept her. They drag her to another squad car. Miller meanders over to speak with her, like he has all the time in the world. I keep waiting for her house to burst into flames. It doesn't happen. My perceptions could be a little off. My ankle pulses. Presently, the ice bag gets too cold. I push it aside with my other foot.

"How's your wrist?" I ask Nora.

"Not bad. The medic says I don't need stitches."

When did he say that? The police cordon off the area where Riley's body lies. They direct traffic away from Boniface.

It feels like hours later that Sergeant Miller comes over. When he apologizes for missing Nora's call, it surprises me.

"You got it, and you came. That's what's important," Nora tells him. "Will Ethan be released now?"

Miller adjusts his belt with his gaze on the street. "It's not up to me. But I'd say, likely, yeah. Probably this afternoon. Talked to your grandmother, by the way. Her plane landed a short while ago. I think she's going to visit him first, then she wants to see you. Listen."

We wait, but he doesn't go on. "Was it stolen merchandise?" I ask, motioning with my head at the house. "Because Ethan really believed they were dumpster diving." I don't want Ethan taking any blame for these people who robbed him of his childhood.

Miller doesn't answer directly. Instead, he asks me if I know anything about Riley's cash. I'm not going to answer that either. I don't know how he knows about it. He won't even say how the media got Nora's name.

After a while, I climb gingerly off the back of the ambulance. Nora starts to come with me. "Gotta call my dad."

"I get that."

"But later?"

"Later." We each manage a nod.

EPILOGUE

One Month Later-Nora

Gran opens the front door with a smile I can see from the table. "Come on in, Claire. Nora and Ethan are in the kitchen. How was your trip?"

"Good. Just glad to be home."

Home, I like the sound of that. To me, a trip is a weekend away, a vacation to a semi-nice hotel in the Valley. Claire's been gone four weeks.

Like last summer, we've called and texted daily—often several times a day—but it's nothing like seeing her again in person. For a moment, I revel in simply observing her, appreciating her pretty smile, enjoying the way she smooths her hair behind her ear with a short index finger. I'm not upset she went away, but I missed her.

After everything that happened, Claire and her father sat down for a long, much-needed talk and decided they needed time apart. Not wanting to miss any more school than she had to, Claire re-enrolled at Bay Charter in Juneau and lived with her mother, while Ethan and I got to know one another as sister and brother.

He's still a slob, still makes not-so-funny jokes, still calls me Nora the Explorer, even though I've asked him not to. He means it affectionately; I understand that now. He's gotten to know Gran as well. She adores him.

The first week after he moved in, he had a series of nonstop questions about Mom and Dad, eating up every detail Gran could give him. I contributed some, but it was good hearing her stories too. She told us things I never knew, like how my parents had tried to have another child after Ethan disappeared. Mom had gotten pregnant, then lost the baby in her first trimester. Gran said it was stress. I also didn't know Mom left a higher paying job with the parks department to man one of the visitors desks. She wanted to devote more time to finding her son.

Tomorrow, Claire will be back at North. I'm hoping we can pick up where we left off.

Gran retreats into the living room as Ethan and I make our way to the little hall. There isn't room for all of us in the house. Gran's bought a new place so that Ethan can have his own bedroom. We move in a couple of weeks.

At the last second he slips around me to get to Claire first, saying, "God, I've missed you, Clarice. Next time don't stay away so long." Then he gestures to the square, white box in her hand. "Hello. You brought me a present?"

Claire's eyes never leave my face. "I brought the two of you a present. Here." She passes it to me. Inside is a cake. "It's for your birthdays. I know we celebrated before I left, but everything was so up in the air back then. So many false starts. I don't know…I just thought we could do it again, for real this time. The three of us. Nora…" Her voice gets a little unsteady then.

I hand the cake to my twin and fold her in my arms. "No more false starts. No more staying away." And then, to take a little dig at Ethan, but also because I mean it, I add, "I love you, Claire Bear. Now, shall we eat?"

Bella Books, Inc.
Women. Books. Even Better Together.
P.O. Box 10543
Tallahassee, FL 32302
Phone: (800) 729-4992
www.BellaBooks.com

More Titles from Bella Books

Hunter's Revenge – Gerri Hill
978-1-64247-447-3 | 276 pgs | paperback: $18.95 | eBook: $9.99
Tori Hunter is back! Don't miss this final chapter in the acclaimed Tori Hunter series.

Integrity – E. J. Noyes
978-1-64247-465-7 | 28 pgs | paperback: $19.95 | eBook: $9.99
It was supposed to be an ordinary workday...

The Order – TJ O'Shea
978-1-64247-378-0 | 396 pgs | paperback: $19.95 | eBook: $9.99
For two women the battle between new love and old loyalty may prove more dangerous than the war they're trying to survive.

Under the Stars with You – Jaime Clevenger
978-1-64247-439-8 | 302 pgs | paperback: $19.95 | eBook: $9.99
Sometimes believing in love is the first step. And sometimes it's all about trusting the stars.

The Missing Piece – Kat Jackson
978-1-64247-445-9 | 250 pgs | paperback: $18.95 | eBook: $9.99
Renee's world collides with possibility and the past, setting off a tidal wave of changes she could have never predicted.

An Acquired Taste – Cheri Ritz
978-1-64247-462-6 | 206 pgs | paperback: $17.95 | eBook: $9.99
Can Elle and Ashley stand the heat in the *Celebrity Cook Off* kitchen?

Printed in the USA
CPSIA information can be obtained
at www.ICGtesting.com
JSHW020738060524
62557JS00001B/2